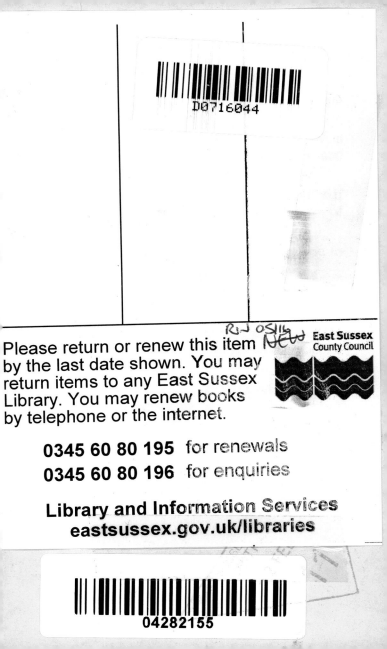

D0716044

Don't worry. I'll keep you safe.

"Yes, I know that." Sophia set aside the sketch and rubbed her hands together.

"Johnny, they are going to figure it out. And when they do, you are taking me out for dinner and dancing."

His gaze snapped to hers and his brow lifted as if he was checking to see if she was making fun of him. She wasn't.

"I'm serious. When you turn back, I want you to take me out."

He nodded slowly. A d-a-t-e. Then he lifted his brows.

"Yes. A date." She took his hand, happy to see the hope in his eyes and feel the warm reassurance of his strong grip.

They stared at each other. That was what this was about, really. Overcoming fear. He was afraid of waiting for a cure that would never come. She was afraid of screwing up again.

THE SHIFTER'S CHOICE

JENNA KERNAN

Published in Great Britain 2014
by Mills & Boon, an imprint of Harlequin (UK) Limited,
Eton House, 18-24 Paradise Road, Richmond, Surrey, TW9 1SR

© 2014 Jeannette H. Monaco

ISBN: 978-0-263-91415-3

89-1214

Harlequin (UK) Limited's policy is to use papers that are natural, renewable and recyclable products and made from wood grown in sustainable forests. The logging and manufacturing processes conform to the legal environmental regulations of the country of origin.

Printed and bound in Spain
by CPI, Barcelona

Jenna Kernan writes fast-paced romantic adventures that are set in out-of-the-way places and populated by larger-than-life characters.

Happily married to her college sweetheart, Jenna shares a love of the outdoors with her husband. The couple enjoys treasure hunting all over the country, searching for natural gold nuggets and precious and semiprecious stones.

Jenna has been nominated for two RITA® Awards for her Western romances and received the Book Buyers Best Award for paranormal romance in 2010. Visit Jenna at her internet home, www.jennakernan.com, or at twitter.com/jennakernan for up-to-the-minute news.

For Jim, always.

Chapter 1

Kamakou Preserve, Molokai, Hawaii

Private Sonia Touma's helicopter touched down on the landing pad at a marine base that didn't officially exist. Her orders read Oahu, which lay just past Maui, but instead she'd been rerouted here. The copilot slid the door open wide enough to heave her duffel and foot-locker to the tarmac then motioned with his thumb that she should get out. The pilot cut the engine. The rotors slowed as she hopped down.

She kept low and moved out of range of the blades, then straightened to glance about. Beyond the landing pad lay a dirt road. Parallel to the road stood a twenty-foot-tall security perimeter fence that stretched as far as she could see in both directions. *Keeping folks out or in?* she wondered. The cameras and other electronics topping the fence posts indicated in.

The hot, humid air rose from the tarmac and the yellow grass surrounding the landing pad. Sweat already beaded on her brow and she wiped it away with the sleeve of her uniform. October sure was different here than in Yonkers, New York.

Why was she here? It made no sense. She didn't have one single solitary skill that she could think of that would lift her above her fellow marines for a special assignment, unless you counted a criminal record, hitting people and a proclivity for telling people in authority to fuck off.

Her ears pricked up at the sound of an engine. She stared past the dry grass dotted with monstrous yucca plants until she sighted an approaching Jeep.

She eyed the driver, spotting the captain's stripes on his arm, and snapped to attention. The Jeep rolled to a stop beside her.

"Private Touma?"

She replied as expected, "Sir. Yes, sir."

Sonia waited until the captain's hand touched his forehead below the brim of his hat and then snapped her hand back to her side.

"I'm Captain MacConnelly. You'll be reporting to me." He looked her up and down, his brow etched with wrinkles. Whatever he'd been expecting, she had the feeling that she was not it.

He thumbed at the empty passenger seat. She lifted her duffel.

"Leave it."

Sonia dropped the heavy bag beside the footlocker and glanced back at the helo. The pilots peered past her to the captain who lifted a hand ordering them to wait.

Her skin prickled as she faced the captain. It looked like there was an entrance exam.

"Get in," he said.

She did. Sonia eyed her new superior officer from the passenger seat. The first thing she noticed was his left hand on the steering wheel and the shiny gold wedding band there, so bright and new it glowed. The second was the tight coil of muscle at his bunching jaw. The captain looked ready to grind nails between his teeth.

Her supervisor cut the engine, shifted in his seat and stared directly at her.

"I believe in getting right to it, Touma," he narrowed his eyes on her. "I've read your file."

His words sent a chill down her spine that cut through the tropical heat. She glanced at her belongings broiling on the tarmac and then back to the captain.

"Thick file." He showed her the width with his thumb and index finger. "Mostly just reports of you quitting. You a quitter, Private?"

His summary of her life hit her like a slap. "I finished basic and I'll finish my service, sir."

He snorted. "Like you had a choice. Back to the wall, right? Well, just so we understand each other, let me assure you that if you quit this time, you go back to prison."

And there it was. The reason she was a marine in the first place. Not by choice, but by picking the lesser of two evils, while this man probably enlisted in the Corps. That was obvious by his distaste of her. Right now she needed to get her gear in this Jeep and that meant being whatever he needed her to be.

The captain swept her with his cold blue eyes, his lip curling at what he saw. "Wearing the uniform doesn't make you a marine. You don't have the first idea of the code."

She was not going back to prison. "Duty, honor—"

"Oh, stow it."

She closed her mouth before saying country.

If he thought she was such a screwup, why was she here? It occurred to her that maybe it wasn't his choice. That he might be following orders he didn't like any better than she liked hers. That would make this just a show of strength. The thought gave her a glimmer of hope. But she had to be sure in order to know how to play this.

"Our security check didn't turn up one person who knew you well enough to complete a simple question-naire about you. You have any explanation for that?"

Let's see whose orders she was really following. "If I'm such a substandard marine, sir, why am I here?"

His brows shot up as if this was the first thing she'd said or done that surprised him.

"You aren't here yet, Private. And you don't get on base until we finish our chat. You're a contender for this assignment, that's all, and only because you have the necessary skill set and because my wife thinks you can do this despite all evidence to the contrary."

She didn't have any skills. This was a mistake. Wait…had he said his wife picked her? Was that who was calling the shots? She must be a general or some-thing. Well, that would explain why he looked so pissed. "But you don't, sir."

"I think you'll last about thirty seconds."

She pictured herself in an orange jumpsuit and set-tled into her seat. She'd make thirty seconds, all right, and she'd make it past this guy. Sonia stared at the captain. "I'll have to agree with your wife, sir."

"Your assignment is to teach an injured marine. He's depressed and occasionally suicidal and he is disinclined to learn sign language."

Warning bells rang in her head like church bells on Christmas Eve. An injured marine, likely deaf, angry, suicidal and possibly in denial. *This* was her assignment? Oh, she *was* fucked.

"I don't think I'm qualified to deal with someone with those kinds of emotional issues, sir."

"You don't?" The captain's cool eyes regarded her and he held her gaze a moment before flicking his attention out at the empty road. When he spoke his voice was sardonic. "Well, I'm sorry if I gave you the impression that I give a goddamn what you think, Private. You are a marine, at least that's a U.S. Marine's uniform. That means you follow orders. Maybe you didn't understand how that works."

What if her assignment was an emotionally shattered, unpredictable time bomb, like she was?

"Sergeant John Loc Lam had two teachers just this month. He chased them both off."

Did he say Lock? What kind of middle name was Lock?

"It's your job to make him want to learn how to sign."

Sign language? She'd never even considered she'd be asked to use that as one of her skills. She'd learned to sign right alongside her sister, Marianna, who was born deaf.

"My wife suggested I hire a woman this time."

Sonia wondered how many others had tried and failed at this shit job before they scraped the barrel and came up with her? Now she was frowning right back at the captain who hadn't missed a beat.

"I think you'll fall on your face or run, just like always. Might shit yourself first. But your assignment is to do everything and anything to get him on board."

She wondered how the hell was she supposed to do that. But she said, "Yes, sir."

MacConnelly made a sound that might have been a laugh.

"Despite his appearance, Lam needs sympathy and understanding. What he doesn't need is a woman who is going to hit and run. You understand?"

Appearance? Was he scarred?

"I do, sir." Of course she didn't understand.

"You run and he's won."

"I won't run, sir."

He made a sound deep in his throat. "That's what the others said, too. Both made it up the mountain to meet Lam." He reached to the seat behind him and retrieved a laptop. Sonia's stomach tied itself in progressively tighter knots while he booted up his computer. What was wrong with Lam that made the other's run? When the screen glowed a vivid blue he turned his attention back to her.

"Everyone here on base knows Sergeant Lam's situation. But every word I'm about to tell you is classified. Off base, you tell no one. This goes with you to your grave. Any violation will result in a court-martial and I will personally see that you go to prison for a lot longer than six years. Got it?" He lifted his brows so they disappeared above the rim of his hat.

Sonia's insides went icy as she nodded her understanding.

"I need to hear you say it out loud, Touma."

"I understand, sir."

He opened a presentation titled Sergeant John Loc Lam. He set the computer on the dashboard between them and adjusted the angle of the screen.

"Can you see this?"

"Yes, sir." She could also see her duffel on the tarmac. Somehow, she needed to get that bag into this Jeep.

The first slide was of a young, thin soldier grinning as he leaned on the hood of a Humvee. His helmet obscured most of his face. "This is what Lam looked like when he was in my command in Afghanistan."

So the captain had skin in the game. Sonia braced for what she expected next, the deformed face of a man struck by fire or lead or jagged bits of metal. Instead the next slide was the traditional graduation photo taken after boot camp. Lam was in full dress blues. She stared at the rich brown eyes, narrow brow, full lips and the short-cropped black hair, and her stomach did a little drop as if she'd looked down from somewhere very high and a little bit dangerous. The man was a knockout with film-star good looks, she decided. What had happened to that handsome face, she wondered as she braced for what was inevitable.

She pressed her lips together and waited but he didn't change the slide. She noticed suddenly that the captain was staring at her, instead of the screen.

"Problem?" he asked.

What could she say, that she was taken by his good looks? She glanced back at the image before she said the first thing she could think of to avoid admitting her physical reaction to Lam.

"He's Asian."

"He's American," said the captain, not hiding his annoyance at her observation. "His mother is naturalized from Hong Kong. His father is also of Chinese descent, but he is third generation, born in California. Mother is alive and father is deceased, heart attack. His dad ran a restaurant in San Francisco. He has a younger sister named Julia, legal name Joon. She's seventeen now."

Sonia wanted to ask what happened to Lam, but now she was afraid to find out. Had the other teachers quit because their student was unwilling or because of his current appearance? If it was his appearance, that was just wrong. He couldn't help what had happened or the results. But what *had* happened?

"Lam entered a building in Koppel at night under my order."

Here it comes, she realized, gripping the dashboard as if preparing for a crash.

"Two fire teams had already gone in and all died. Lam and I entered with the last team. We were the only two survivors. This is what attacked us." He pressed a button and there stood a huge gray animal standing on hind legs like an ape. But the body was elongated, wolfish, with a pronounced snout and back feet that more resembled paws. The hands seemed like a bear's with wicked curved black claws. She gaped for a moment and then laughed. The captain didn't even crack a smile.

She pointed at the image. "That's a joke, right? You're kidding me. Photoshopped it?"

Her captain shook his head. Her breath caught and she peered at the screen taking careful note of the creature's yellow eyes and the dangerous fangs.

"That's not a real animal," she said, trying to assure herself more than inform him.

"It is. I saw it when it attacked Lam and this is the result." The captain pressed a key and the image of a black-furred monster's face filled the screen. "This is John Lam today."

Sonia glanced at the screen and then the captain and then the screen again.

She didn't recall scrambling out the passenger side but found herself standing on the tarmac clinging to the doorframe. The heat rising from the tarmac baked right through her thick-soled shoes. She stared at the captain realizing he'd been right. Her stubborn side kept her anchored for a moment like a shipwreck survivor clinging to a piece of waterlogged debris. Then she pushed off.

"Hell, no." Sonia backed away from the Jeep.

"Touma!"

She kept walking toward the helo, running away from the captain, that monster and her very last chance.

When she reached the closed door of the helicopter her brain reengaged. The pilot and copilot stared at her through the thick glass. She stiffened, with one hand on the lever. What was she going to do, order them to fly her home to Yonkers?

Hit and run, that's what the captain said. But no one would blame her. That thing was a monster. She glanced back to see the captain now leaning against the fender staring at his watch.

"Thirty seconds. And you didn't even make it onto the base. Have fun in prison, Touma."

She turned and swayed on her feet. The captain lifted his radio making a call. Sonia walked to her gear and hoisted her duffel to her shoulder as if planning to hitchhike. She needed to go. Somehow she needed to get out of here.

A second Jeep arrived and two burly MPs climbed out. Sonia dropped her bag as the reality of her situation hit her like a punch. Her stomach pitched and she thought she might throw up.

The captain held up two fingers. "Two choices, Touma. Do the job or do the time."

Sonia stood with her chin raised in a stubborn attitude that had rarely brought her anything good. He couldn't make her. She'd appeal or something. But it was top secret. She couldn't tell anyone. Not even a military court.

"Fine," said the captain. "MPs! Take her to the brig."

Seeing the two marines approach, with jaws set in determination, knocked the stubborn right out of her. She pictured the cell. Felt the walls closing in around her and her mind slipped to that terrible place in her childhood, dark and smelling of plastic and urine, her urine. She recalled her cold, wet clothing chaffing her skin until she pulled it off, waiting in the dark like an animal.

"No!" She lifted her hands in surrender. "I'll do it. I'll meet him. I'll teach him."

Her captain pressed his lips together, hands on hips. Finally he pointed to his Jeep. "Get in."

Sonia lifted her duffel and placed it in the rear seat. The captain said nothing to this as he climbed back behind the wheel.

Once she was seated, he said, "If he doesn't like you or if you run off, you're back in the brig."

"But I can't keep him from chasing me off."

"You better."

She recalled the mention of the teachers before her and wondered what Lam had done to make them quit.

Sonia wiped the sweat from her upper lip. Whatever he did, it couldn't be as bad as prison.

"What if he hurts me?"

"He won't. I'd stake my life on it. But I can guarantee he'll try to scare the life out of you. So...you ready to meet your new pupil?"

"I'm not a teacher. I've never taught anyone anything."

"That's not quite true, Touma. You taught your sister, Marianna, her first signs and you took out that library book so you could both learn."

Man, somebody was scary good at research.

"Do we understand each other, Private?"

She saluted. "Yes, sir."

He returned it with a definite lack of enthusiasm. "Great. You meet him this afternoon at fourteen hundred. I'll take you to your quarters, but I wouldn't unpack just yet."

Sonia eyed her duffel bag wondering where it and she would be by nightfall. She'd made it to the barracks, but barely had time to wash her face before a young woman arrived to give her a tour. Her footlocker was delivered before they left their quarters. Her guide was chatty and asked too many damned personal questions. The private was a nurse, so once she reached the medical facility she felt the need to introduce Sonia to a lot of people she didn't have the first inclination to get to know. As a result, she brought Sonia back late. The captain was waiting outside their quarters, drumming his fingers on the steering wheel.

Sonia climbed in the Jeep and they were off on a road that led through the base and then scaled the mountain in increasingly harrowing switchbacks. Sonia clung to her seat like a monkey on her mama's back as the vehicle jostled on the unpaved road. The low dry scrub lining their way reminded her of West Texas where she'd first been stationed. As they continued upward, the yellow grasses gave way to tall, spindly pines rising eighty feet into the air. The Jeep trail cut through the giants, revealing the exposed red earth, dry as the dust cloud that rooster-tailed out behind them. Through the pine she could see the perimeter fence continuing parallel to their route. That was a lot of fence through a whole lot of nothing. Questions buzzed like flies in her mind.

She welcomed the shade but not the rush of air through the open window that played havoc with the neat knot of her hair. She kept one hand on the crown of her hat as they bounced through ruts and climbed into the tropical valley. The land folded back on itself like a ribbon. Ferns now clung to the red earth, growing in bunches, some so impossibly high they looked like trees. The landscape seemed a primordial forest and she could imagine prehistoric creatures roaming among the primitive plants. The pines had disappeared to be replaced by trees she couldn't name. Moss hugged each branch like a fuzzy green coat and the air hung thick and heavy all about her.

"Rain forest," said the captain. "On the top it's grass and rock, but in between the ocean and the mountain peak we have this. Outer perimeter is five square miles. UV cameras, motion detectors, electronic sensors throughout. Inner perimeter is higher with deterrents in addition to surveillance. Plus a lock-in facility down below."

Deterrents could be anything, landmines, machine-gun towers, gas, patrols.

Sonia wondered what they were protecting. Was this all for Sergeant John Loc Lam? She considered the possibilities as the captain continued on.

"Nothing gets in or out without us knowing." He eyed her for a moment and then returned his attention to the road.

Sonia nodded at his additional warning that running would not work. Her back was to the wall. She was going to teach John Lam or end up in jail.

"Where are we going, sir?"

They switched back again and again until she was looking out at the Pacific Ocean's deep blue water. She could no longer see anything but the narrow tracks of the Jeep trail and the encroachment of lush greenery.

The jungle grew in a green curtain right to the edge of the path. It seemed that if she took one step to the right or left she might vanish forever. Why did she want to take that step?

She tried to penetrate the foliage with her gaze and found one shadowy break. Something stared back with wide-set yellow eyes and a face surrounded with shiny black hair. She startled backward against the clutch and pointed but it was gone.

"What?" asked the captain.

"A-animal," she managed. "Big. Black." But not any animal she'd ever seen. It had a caninelike mouth complete with long saber-toothed tiger fangs. *Was that Lam?*

"Shit," said MacConnelly, and then, "We're nearly there."

She could see the foliage moving parallel to the Jeep. Whatever it was, it could run faster than they could drive. From the safety of the vehicle, her fear tipped toward fascination as she caught glimpses of its black hide in the forest. What else could John Lam do that a normal man could not? She supposed she was about to find out.

The captain slowed to pull into a drive that she had not even seen.

Without warning the path opened up and the sunshine they had left behind in the valley poured down on them. Sonia blinked in the brilliant light as she looked out the window. The house took her breath away. The exterior was painted a pale blue-green with white trim. A wide porch with white lattice work circled the second story. The roof had just the slightest pitch and peak. Of course, no snow here, so why have an angled roof, she thought. Still, this placed looked about as far away from Yonkers, New York, as one could get and that was exactly why she loved it on sight. It wasn't attached to other apartments, it had a yard, sort of, and privacy. She remembered the perimeter fence. It sure did have privacy. Her gaze shifted, searching for John Loc Lam.

"These are my quarters. My wife wanted a look at you."

Sonia's stomach dropped as she prepared herself for this next inspection.

His home resembled a two-story boathouse perched on stilts above a small stream that meandered past a brook that reflected the sky and trees. A small arched bridge allowed a visitor to cross from the path over the water to the house. She glanced at the bank of windows that covered the entire ground floor and saw a face. As quick as she could blink the face was gone. Had she seen it? She could have sworn there had been a woman there with long wavy hair as red as a new penny. That creepy feeling slithered down her back again.

"She won't come out," he said. "She has agoraphobia."

"Fear of spiders?" Sonia asked.

"Open spaces. She doesn't go out and you don't go in." He put the Jeep in park and exited the vehicle. "Wait here."

Sonia rolled down the window and stared out at the flower boxes spilling over with exotic pink blossoms. The porch had a swinging love seat, a metal fire pit and several comfortably padded chairs.

The deep sorrow that bubbled up inside her took her completely unawares. How could she miss something she'd never had? A pretty home of her own, with a swing and a garden. It had always been just a fantasy. But here, a man in uniform had it. The fantasy now seemed almost possible.

"If you stay out of jail," she muttered.

Something hit her door with enough force to tip the Jeep before the vehicle thudded back to earth. Sonia screamed as the tires bounced beneath her. She turned and there he was, filling the gap in the open window. Big and black and foaming from his snapping jaws. He lifted a clawed hand and reached for her and Sonia found herself on the driver's side with her back pressed up against the door.

He snapped his teeth. They locked with a horrible clicking sound as he went still and his strange yellow eyes went wide. He looked frozen while she had stopped breathing.

She released the latch and tumbled out onto the ground and took off for the house, running faster than she'd ever ran before. Behind her, she heard him coming after her, jaws snapping, the ripping sound of the grass as he tore it out by its roots. She scrambled up the steep stairs to reach the front door and bolted through it, throwing herself back against the solid wood frame. The thing pounded up the stairs and thumped on the door sending vibrations clear through her body. Sonia flipped the lock and stumbled back to land on the floor where she cowered for many long minutes.

Finally the pounding stopped and the silence descended around her, more terrifying than the beating of his fists against wood. Where was he?

He might have killed her. But he hadn't. Somehow she'd escaped. One thing was certain. She was not teaching that thing.

Her heart slammed in her chest, jackhammering against her ribs until they ached. Finally Sonia recovered enough to stand. Her mind began to tick again. She recalled seeing John Lam running beside the Jeep at twenty miles an hour, at the very least. Yet he had not been able to catch her as she fled. And he had reached for her, but not succeeded in grabbing her when she was trapped in the Jeep even though he had taken her unawares. He'd nearly tipped the thing over. Could have, she was certain. But didn't. If he'd wanted to grab her that would have been a good time to do it.

But he hadn't. The truth filtered through the fear. He hadn't caught her because he wasn't *trying* to catch her. He was trying to scare her.

What had the captain said, she might shit herself? Well, she nearly had.

Was this some hazing? Did the captain know this would happen?

Sonia's anger rose within her like lava, clouding her judgment with great plumes of black smoke. *That asshole!*

"Damn them both!"

She unfastened the lock and threw open the door. John was gone. Why hang around when he was sure that she would run back to the captain and quit. Well that is exactly what she would have done if she could. But she couldn't because despite how frightening John Loc Lam was, prison scared her more.

Sonia tugged her hat down low over her eyes and marched back outside. She was not going to let that overgrown wolf pup scare her into a jail cell. Not now. Not ever.

Chapter 2

Johnny heard the Jeep pull out. Why the hell hadn't Mac told him that this teacher was a woman?

He might have given her a heart attack. She'd had her head turned to look at the house when he charged the Jeep and he already had his arm in the window when she turned around. He'd never forget the look on her face for as long as he lived. There, reflected in her big brown eyes were all the things he knew he'd become. She'd been terrified, of course, and she'd run. He'd run, too, at first out of instinct. The flight of prey triggered something deep inside him now. Then he'd slowed to let her escape. He was ashamed. Even as he pounded on the door he wanted to beg her forgiveness for what he'd done and for what he'd become.

But he couldn't go back. He'd chased her away and that was best for them both. Maybe now Mac would give up this stupid idea and let him train for a combat mission. Johnny knew he could be effective in the field if they'd just give him a chance.

He headed up the trail that led from Mac's home to his quarters wondering what it would be like to have that woman as his teacher. Like she'd ever come back after the way he'd welcomed her. She'd have to be crazy.

Mac would give him hell and Johnny would let him because this time he deserved it.

When he reached his quarters, Johnny was surprised to hear the Jeep engine. He didn't understand. Mac hadn't had time to take the woman back to base. The first prickle of unease lifted the hairs on his neck. He loped the remaining distance to his yard. There he found his captain disembarking with the woman. Mac's mouth was set in a grim line but he did not look pissed, certainly not as monumentally pissed as Johnny expected after the stunt he'd pulled. Johnny's gaze flashed to the woman, surprised to see that it was she who looked pissed. Her pretty face was flushed pink and her pointed chin was raised like a dagger. She stared directly at him in an obvious challenge. Now this was unexpected. Johnny took a step in their direction, anticipating she would retreat or move closer to Mac. Instead she scowled as if she'd figured it all out. He didn't know if he should run at her again or beg her forgiveness.

The involuntary growl started in his throat. She was upwind so he lifted his nose and breathed deep. He did not scent fear. More like fury. He'd watched her run. So why had she come back and why the hell hadn't she told Mac what he'd done?

He could tell by Mac's hopeful expression that his captain was clueless about his trying to scare her away.

This was so weird. Johnny felt unbalanced, as if *she* was hunting him. He felt a rush of blood and a tingle of excitement.

This woman interested him.

But learning to sign did not.

Maybe he'd take the seat out of her trousers. He crossed to them both on his hind legs, clenching and un-clenching his fists as he came. She didn't retreat which showed a distinctive lack of self-preservation.

Instead, she snapped a salute and Johnny frowned.

Mac pointed at the woman's hand. "I think that one is for you, Sergeant."

Johnny straightened and returned a sloppy salute, now ill at ease. She was messing with him. He was certain now. He didn't like playing the fool so he bared his teeth.

"Sergeant Lam, this is Private Sonia Touma. I've briefed her on your condition and she's anxious to teach you the communication skills you lack. She is fluent in sign language."

Johnny tried to imagine what Mac had over her to make her agree to this. She'd been right the first time. Better to run and take the consequences. He didn't want a teacher, especially one who smelled like rose petals.

Sonia Touma stood at attention like a good little soldier. Johnny eyed her. She was short, curvy, from what he could see beyond her uniform. Slender wrists showed she was on the thin side. He studied her heart-shaped face finding her eyes angled and set wide be-yond a nose that was slightly hooked, bringing an ethnic flare to her features. When he'd chased her, her hair had come loose from its moorings, but now it was all tucked up beneath her cap again. Certainly she had a lovely mouth, full and pink. As he stared, her mouth quirked and Johnny's pulse kicked like a jackrabbit. Oh, hell, this little female was trouble. Their eyes met and she held his stare, issuing an unspoken challenge. That glimmer of determination and the flaring of her nostrils intrigued the hell out of him.

Brave, stupid or suicidal? he wondered. But, of course, he couldn't ask.

"I've got supplies in the truck. I'll set them up on the porch," said Mac, just plowing forward like always.

Mac was so sure that this was what he needed. If she tried to teach him one thing he'd chase her down the mountain because he was not learning to sign. But still Mac kept pushing.

Johnny glared as his captain returned.

"I'll just put the easel up." Mac walked around the house and paused at the fire pit to take in the number of discarded and crushed beer cans. They both knew that alcohol didn't affect him. Mac must have realized that drinking beer on the mountain was a nice perk for his new buddies. Only they weren't buddies. You didn't have to assign buddies or pay them. But that's what Mac had done and then he couldn't figure why Johnny wouldn't hang with them. The only one he even liked was Zeno because he could tell a story complete with punch line. He made everything seem funny. Only sometimes they weren't.

The easel creaked as Mac placed it in the shade on the right side of the porch. He pulled two markers from his pocket. One red and one black. The eraser came from the opposite pocket. Then he dragged a single chair before the large, blank dry-erase board and dusted off his hands. Did he have a pointer for his new teacher?

Johnny folded his arms and lifted a brow at Mac who ignored him. The woman had already stayed longer than the last two combined and Mac obviously took that as some kind of encouragement.

"I'm leaving the Jeep and walking down to see Bri. I'll be back in an hour." Mac pointed at his Jeep and then shook his finger at him issuing a silent warning to Johnny not to mess with his ride.

Johnny still considered rolling his Jeep again.

Mac handed over a phone to the woman. "Private Touma, if you need help just press dial. It calls the MPs directly. Otherwise, I'll see you in sixty."

The MPs? Johnny stared from one to the other as questions rose in his mind. Was this some trick, some setup to get him so curious he wrote on that damned whiteboard?

He glanced at Touma and decided that no one was that good an actor. Something was going on because the woman was shaking now, shaking like she was scared and not of him. What did Mac have over her that made her willing to stay?

Johnny could only wonder because he'd be damned if he'd lift one of those stinky dry-erase markers.

Mac gave Touma a hard look and headed for the trail on the opposite side of the yard. It led down past the waterfall and grotto to the captain's house, half a mile away.

A new scent came to him and he turned toward the woman. Now Johnny smelled fear. He glanced at Touma noting the strain on her face as she watched the captain depart. Was she dismayed at being alone with the big bad wolf?

She should be.

Mac disappeared down the trail and Touma blew out a breath. The smell of fear ebbed. Then Johnny realized something odd. She wasn't afraid of him. She was afraid of Mac. But that made no sense at all.

Had she thought that Mac's glare had something to do with her? He wanted to ask her and then was instantly annoyed at himself. He didn't need to ask anything. What he needed was to get rid of her before this got any worse.

The woman cleared her throat. Johnny emitted a low growl. Her eyes flicked to the hated easel and then back to him.

He wondered if she was stupid enough to pick up that red marker. She turned to the board and dropped the cell phone into the tray. She wasn't calling for rescue. Strange. But he found himself impressed with her bravery.

She met him with a direct look. "You want to show me around?"

Johnny stared at her for a long moment. She stared back with dark soulful eyes that seemed a little sad to him. He wanted to ask her what she'd done to get this shit job, but he didn't know sign language. If he learned he could speak to her. But that would be giving up. Sometimes he thought that all he had left was the daily fight to hold on to his hope. Learning sign would kill it.

"Listen," she tried again and this time, when she spoke she accompanied each word with a sign. "I'm stuck here for an hour and I'd like it very much if you didn't eat me while I wait."

Johnny exhaled in a short blast that was his laugh.

"So, do you want to show me your home or do you want me to go sit over there for the hour?" She finished signing and pointed at a bench facing the treetops and beyond that, the blue waters of the Pacific. Johnny spent a lot of time looking at those waters...imagining.

"Sit or tour?" she asked, making the signs for both.

He continued to stare, refusing to imitate her signs.

She smiled. "Great. My choice, then."

She walked to the bench and folded stiffly into the far corner. He remained where he was. She sat gazing out at the vista, a slight smile on her face. When fifteen minutes passed it became obvious that she was quite happy to sit there and wait him out. He worried about her. Why had she stayed?

It was one thing for him to give her the heave-ho but another for her to ignore him. He wasn't used to being ignored and didn't like it.

Johnny grabbed the dry-erase board and broke it into a manageable size, then retrieved the black marker and then returned to her.

He wrote one word. *Quit*.

She glanced at the board and crossed her arms, glancing back at the water. "Fat chance, furball."

He blinked at her. Had she just called him furball? He could snap her in two like a twig. He could throw her fifty yards like a football. He could...

He pointed at the word. She uncrossed her arms, lifted the broken piece of board from his hand and then threw it like a Frisbee over the edge of the embankment. Was she demented?

She started signing as she spoke. "Listen, I can't leave. You got it? I'm stuck here for—" she glanced at her watch "—thirty-one more minutes. So run along if you want to but quit bothering me."

Johnny growled and leaned in so that his nose nearly

touched hers. She turned her back on him. Johnny stomped around in front of her and gave her the finger before jumping over the embankment.

Her voice followed him, a shout and a challenge filled with fury and dripping with a mocking sarcasm that twisted him into an angry knot. "Oh, so you already know how to sign!"

Johnny tore through the undergrowth using his claws as his own personal machete against anything unlucky enough to get in his way. He could slice through metal as easily as he used to tear through paper so the foliage stood no chance.

What the hell was that? Furball? Run along? The woman must be suicidal or crazy. Maybe both. Where did Mac find these people?

Johnny slowed as he thought there might not be a waiting list of people willing to tutor a surly werewolf. He swung at a tall fern and greenery fell about him in tiny bits.

Beside him the dense, wet jungle clung to a cliff so steep that even he had trouble holding on. On more than one occasion he'd imagined just letting go.

"Johnny!"

He recognized the voice. It was Mac heading up the hill to collect his tutor. He sounded pissed.

Johnny took another step in the direction he had been going.

"I can hear you, damn it! Turn around or, so help me, I will take a chunk out of that tough hide."

Johnny knew Mac could do it, because his captain was also a werewolf. Bitten the same night as Johnny and in the same fight. Neither of them had known what they were up against, but their commander had.

Johnny turned back toward his captain. He turned for the same reason his friend hadn't given up on him—duty. Duty to each other, duty to the Corps, duty to himself, duty to his departed father, his struggling mother and the little sister he swore would go to college. He was so damned tired of doing his duty—but still he held on.

Nobody but Mac could keep up with him when he climbed this volcanic rock. Was it Johnny's fault that his new set of playmates couldn't keep up? Not that it was their fault. They were good guys. But they were still human and slow as shit.

Johnny crawled from the undergrowth a moment later. Mac met him, wearing a frown. You'd think being a newlywed living on a lovely tropical island would make his former squad leader happy. Johnny knew, if not for him, Mac would be.

Mac exhaled heavily as he rummaged in his pack withdrawing a black slate. Johnny snarled and Mac met his eyes and then scowled. Johnny didn't like writing because he couldn't really control the pen. It made him feel stupid, so he revealed his three-inch canines to no visible effect. Mac was one of the very few who could meet his gaze without turning away. That was saying something because Johnny knew what he looked like. In his werewolf form, he was nine feet of hideousness that could easily step into any number of horror flicks or out of every child's nightmare.

So Johnny avoided looking at himself. His long snout and black wolfish nose disturbed him nearly as much as the deadly claws and the thick canine pads on his feet. His eyes were no longer soft brown. Now they were as yellow as the rising moon. He still had black hair, but it covered his entire body, right up to his pointed ears and the knuckles of his distended fingers. Once upon a time in that old life, he'd kept his nails trimmed short. But he'd given up on that along with other things. So many other things.

Mac had gray fur when in werewolf form and his eyes were blue. Johnny wished Mac would run with him instead of sending his substitutions. His captain withdrew a broken nub of chalk from the depths of his pack. The bag and its contents had been his new wife's idea. Brianna knew that her husband transformed naked from wolf to man and that he and Johnny had an ongoing communication problem. So she'd modified a bag so it would fit around his wolfish neck. Then when he reached his destination he could transform and get dressed which explained why his clothes were often wrinkled.

Bri said she would make Johnny the same pack one day. But so far he didn't need it. They'd been here six months. A year and four months since the attack and still Johnny had to use shampoo on his entire body and had no need for clothing since his fur was so thick it covered his junk. Johnny picked the twigs and bits of moss from his furry shoulder and smoothed his glossy coat.

Mac held out the slate to Johnny. He took it and briefly considered throwing the thing as far as he could.

"You ditched her?" asked Mac.

That answer seemed obvious.

"Why not give her a chance?"

Johnny growled.

"Why do you keep ditching them?" asked Mac. "The guys, too. How can I help you if you keep running off?"

He meant the wounded warriors. Johnny's own private trial-by-fire team. One member was even a double amputee, as if having the name Dugan Kiang wasn't handicap enough. Dugan could really run on those kangaroo legs, as he called them, but none of them had experiences that quite matched Johnny's. They could all visit their mothers, for example, and go on leave and walk into a bar without people screaming. And they could talk to each other and they'd all had women since returning Stateside. All but him.

He shrugged.

"Are they bad company?"

Not bad. They were good guys and good marines. Better than Johnny. At least they still followed orders. While Johnny had been second-guessing orders since they'd entered that building in Afghanistan.

His new comrades talked about what most men talked about. Sports, getting laid, work, drinking, getting laid. But alcohol no longer affected Johnny and as for women, the only ones who had seen him since the accident were the medical professionals with top-secret clearances. None of them touched him unless absolutely necessary and he could smell their fear as clearly as he could scent the wild pig that had tracked past here last night.

There was one woman who didn't avoid him but she was taken. Mac's wife, Brianna, had some very special circumstances of her own and that gave her an understanding of Johnny. At least her friendship did not stem from duty or pity or guilt—like Mac's.

"Johnny?" Mac extended the chalk.

He didn't like having friends assigned to him like the most unpopular kid in class and he didn't want a teacher that ignored him. He accepted the chalk, holding it in his large hands with difficulty. It twisted in his fingers, breaking the unsteady white line he scrawled but he managed to write "They're young" on the slate.

"Twenties. Same age as you," replied Mac before Johnny had finished writing. "Touma is only twenty. On her second assignment."

Johnny released the chalk and dusted off his fingers on his hairy thigh. The fine motor control required for moving the chalk was a real pain in his ass. His handwriting had once been a source of pride. Now his words looked as if they had been penned by a preschooler. Johnny scowled at the slate.

"They're all learning sign language. They want you to start talking to them. But you have to learn first."

He shook his head. It didn't make any sense. By not learning he could only listen to the guys' conversation. By not learning he was keeping himself apart. But he still couldn't do it even though he knew that his refusal hurt and confused his captain.

"Aren't you sick of answering questions with a yes or no?"

Johnny answered no.

"Now you're just being a pain in my ass."

He was. And if not for Johnny, Mac could spend more time with his wife and less with his guilt. But Mac couldn't walk away—not ever, because Mac had been the second werewolf that had attacked Johnny.

The scientists said it was Mac's bite, that second attack, that now made it impossible for Johnny to change back into human form.

Johnny wiped his words from the slate and tried three times to pick up the chalk before succeeding. Then he wrote "Combat duty?"

Mac shook his head. "They said no. Christ, Johnny, you don't follow orders. You come and go as you please. And you want them to trust you in a combat zone? Not gonna happen. Stay inside the perimeter, follow orders, stop acting crazy and maybe you'll get an assignment."

Johnny threw the slate.

Mac watched it disappear into the foliage. "Damn it," he muttered. Mac's gaze flicked back to Johnny, hands on hips. His captain looked like his mother when he did that. "Give her a chance. Learn to sign and maybe then you can have a field assignment."

Johnny raised his lips, showing his teeth. Mac blew out a breath.

"I have to go get Touma. She better not be crying. I hate crying women." He stepped past Johnny and then paused turning back. "Bri wants you at dinner tonight."

Johnny shook his head. He hadn't been to Mac's place since reassignment from the mainland, even though his quarters were only a half mile away. A new couple needed privacy. While he missed his friend, Johnny was happy for him; though, adjusting to life without his captain as a bunk mate had been hard. Nobody understood him like Mac.

"Yeah. She said you'd say no and said to tell you that if you don't come she's coming to your place and cooking supper there." Mac waited.

Johnny glanced toward the rain forest feeling the urge to run again. That pig was upwind.

"She thinks you're mad at her for taking me away. I told her that's bullshit."

Johnny met his gaze and held Mac's stare. The pain and regret was back in his friend's eyes.

"Is it bullshit?"

Johnny picked up a stick and scratched his answer in the dirt. "What time?"

Chapter 3

The following day, Sonia's escort to Sergeant Lam's quarters was Corporal Del Tabron who was missing his left arm from the elbow. He said he was part of the squad that worked out with John, though she'd come to think of him as Johnny since everyone referred to him that way, every morning and sometimes hung with him at night. Each of the five members was missing something. Sonia asked what Johnny was missing and was met with a blank stare.

"He's a werewolf," said Tabron, his brow knitting as if just now considering that she might not know this.

Yes, she'd been made aware of that she assured him, but it seemed that these men were all dealing with loss, while Johnny was dealing with change. The two seemed very different to Sonia and assigning these men to Johnny seemed comparable to giving a gorilla a kitten. The gorilla might love the kitten but the kitten didn't really get the gorilla.

Del didn't know why Johnny didn't want to learn sign but they all agreed that nobody except the captain could ever get Johnny to do anything he didn't want to do. But lately, he admitted, the captain had struck out a few times, too.

Sonia said nothing to this as she was already familiar with the captain's charming powers of persuasion.

Del gripped the wheel with a claw that looked like a bent pair of kitchen tongs. Despite her apprehension, he was a competent driver and he delivered her all too soon.

Sonia stared across the open ground to his quarters. She really looked at the building closely for the first time. Nothing about it said military. She wondered if the home was here before the base because the lovely bungalow was set on stilts and surrounded by banana palms and ringed with greenery covered with tiny orange blossoms.

How much rain did they get up here that they needed to put all the buildings on stilts? The angle of the hillside put the second floor at ground level in the back, but from her seat she could not see the rear. The house was all stained wood with a wide porch facing the ocean. There were several chairs on the porch. The roof was tin and painted red. A stream snaked along beside Johnny's yard and then dropped down the hillside and out of sight. *The same stream that threads past the captain's?* she wondered. She must have jumped it yesterday, though she didn't even remember. Or had she used one of the large gray rocks set as stepping stones across the gap?

She lifted her attention to the small house. It looked like an adorable honeymoon cottage instead of quarters for a surly werewolf. She recalled his chasing her yesterday. He was all huff and puff, she decided. She had to believe that or she wasn't getting out of this Jeep.

Del called for Johnny who did not appear. "Sometimes he does that."

"What?"

"Ignores us. Takes off."

Good, she thought. *Stay away.*

"He might not be home," said Del. "But my orders are to leave you here either way." He gave her an expectant look and she wondered what he would do if she refused to get out of the Jeep. They stared at one another.

"Fine," she said and threw open the door, sliding to her feet. She slammed the door and stared at Del through the open window. He handed over the bag that included another set of smaller dry-erase boards and markers, paper, pens and a book of sign language. Del scratched his chin with his hook and put the Jeep in Reverse, but kept his foot on the brake and his eyes on her.

"He might come back."

Sonia didn't care if he stayed away for hours. She'd sit on that porch and stare at the Pacific, breathe the warm, tropical air and pretend she was here on vacation with a husband who adored her.

"Oh, and the captain said that he is picking you up and that he wants to see some progress."

"Progress?"

He shrugged.

"From the invisible man?"

"He's probably around."

Sonia stepped back as Del turned the Jeep around and vanished down the road.

Her heart rate increased at his leaving, but not from fear of the werewolf. The captain wanted progress. Johnny was screwing with her freedom. That made Lam's disappearance a problem.

Sonia's search of the grounds yielded nothing. His quarters were locked. She had one lesson to teach an oppositional werewolf some signs and she hadn't even seen Lam.

"Maybe I shouldn't have called him furball," she muttered.

Sonia was shaking now with a dangerous cocktail of adrenalin and fury. This monster marine was not going to be the cause of her going to a military prison. She'd rather die right here on this mountain than end up in a cage.

"So you want to play hide and seek? I'm good with that." Sonia dropped her bag of supplies on Lam's porch, squared her shoulders and crossed the stepping stones over the rushing water, aiming for the place she had last seen him yesterday. She knew she couldn't follow his trail. She could barely read a bus map and had completely blown orienteering in basic. Three steps into the deep cover of the tropical canopy and the temperature dropped, the air turned damp and the smell of rot mingled with the fragrance of jasmine. She paused to look about. The birdsong was everywhere, but she could not see a single bird.

"Johnny?" she whispered. He didn't answer of course. Though her surroundings were inviting they were also unfamiliar, so she turned around and walked back to the clearing. But after six steps she didn't find it. A little jolt of panic popped inside her, but she held it down. She'd only taken a few steps. *Think, Sonia.*

The water. She listened and could hear the sound of the running stream. She blew out a breath and then headed toward the sound. It was farther than she expected and on the way it began to rain, a soft patter on the leaves above that didn't reach her. She crept under vines and between wide palm leaves that were stiff and sharp as razor blades. The rain fell harder, dripping off the greenery and plopping down on her hat with giant droplets. The patter turned to a drenching. Her teeth began to chatter. She glanced up at the sky and spotted a lovely white orchid growing from the notch of a tree, bobbing in the falling rain as if it was laughing at her.

"That's why they call it a rain forest," she muttered and eased over a mossy log.

One moment she was standing and the next she was falling. Her hands went up as her butt struck the ground with a jolt that rattled her teeth. She landed on a dangerous angle and slid on her backside as the world blurred into a sea of green. Vines and leaves slashed across her face and she lifted her hands to protect herself from this new assault. She stopped abruptly by striking something solid and folded over a log losing all the air in her lungs. At least she wasn't still moving, but she was dizzy. Had she struck her head? Sonia opened her eyes to see she was lying with her legs on one side of a slippery, moss covered log and her torso dangling over the other side with nothing underneath her but treetops and hot tropical air. She stared at the cliff's edge where the steep incline fell away. The tree trunk, that had saved her life, grew perpendicular from the cliff.

Sonia tried to scream, but the fall had knocked the

wind out of her and breathing took all her energy. The dizziness increased and she knew if she passed out she'd fall and if she fell, she'd die.

Below her, silvery sheets of rain fell from the black clouds sweeping up the mountain.

Instinct took over and she grabbed her knees, holding herself about the mossy trunk like a ring on a finger. How long could she hold on?

Something grabbed her by the back of her jacket collar. She gripped the log tighter but was torn loose. A moment later she was thrown over a broad shoulder. Her hands braced on the man's back only to discover it was covered with soft thick fur. Sergeant Lam! He'd rescued her.

She groaned and relaxed, falling limp against the sable-soft hair that covered him. He gripped her legs and easily swung her before him, carrying her like a bride over the threshold.

Sonia trembled as rain streaked down her face. She was scared, but not of Lam. She'd almost fallen to her death. If not for him, she would have. She threw her arms about his neck and clung to Lam as the relief shuttered through her. Sonia nestled her face into his chest and tried not to let him see that she was crying as he climbed the incline that had nearly killed her. He moved with slow steady steps as if in no hurry to be rid of her. She was grateful because she needed a moment to pull herself together and here in his arms she was warm and safe.

The beating rain ceased as if someone had turned a tap off, leaving only the steady dripping of water through the canopy. The sunlight streamed down in bright ribbons through the gaps. The Sergeant stooped, bringing her back to her feet and she lifted her head from his shoulder forcing herself to release his sturdy neck. Sonia shielded her eyes against the glare and looked around. She was back on the opposite side of the stream where she had made the cosmically stupid move of trying to follow a werewolf into the forest.

Lam stepped away. When her gaze met his, he just looked her up and down as if searching for injury. He lifted a hand toward her. She glanced at it but did not flinch. If he meant her bodily harm he had only to wait for her to drop off that log. Instead he had rescued her. His attention moved to her head as he pulled a stick complete with leaves from her hair. Her neat bun was now a tangled mess of tendrils that frizzed in all directions around her face and neck. She touched her head, realizing she'd lost her hat.

She lifted her hands and began to sign as she spoke. "Thank you for saving my life, Sergeant Lam."

He nodded his acknowledgment.

"I owe you one," she said while signing.

He nodded his agreement that, yes, she did. Johnny dipped a finger in the stream. He used the water to write on the flat gray stone, "Sorry."

She made a fist and then moved it in a circle over her heart. "Sorry," she repeated as she made the sign again.

He mimicked the sign perfectly. *Sorry.*

Johnny cupped a handful of water and used his opposite hand to gently tug her down to her knees beside the stream. He dabbed cold water on her cheek and she felt the sting of a cut. His touch was warm and tender. It made her throat ache even more so she took over using both hands to splash water on her stinging, scratched face.

A Jeep horn blared. Sonia shot to her feet, her face hot. She spun toward the drive, obscured by the house.

"Fucking motherfucking fuck!" she said, still signing out of habit. She glanced at Johnny. "That's the captain and just look at me!" She held out her arms to show him the whole muddy, bloody catastrophe. "*And* he's going to want to see your progress! I'm screwed."

The captain called. "Johnny? Private Touma?"

Johnny headed for the Jeep. Sonia looked back to the jungle staunching the irrational urge to turn and run the opposite way. She glanced down at her soaked clothing, torn muddy trousers and the scrapes that covered her hands.

"There you are," said the captain clearly speaking to Johnny. "Hour's up."

Sonia wiped her face and realized she'd likely just smeared more blood on it. She trailed around the house lifting one foot after the other. She couldn't manage to raise her chin until she cleared the house. She looked to Johnny as if for another rescue but he stood still as stone, his jaw locked, his big hairy arms motionless.

"How did it go?" asked the captain. His smile died a moment later as he stared at her, his eyes going wide as his gaze swept the entirety of her appearance.

Demerits she thought and then giggled. She slapped a hand over her mouth to stop the sound. Johnny looked at her and raised one tufted brow. He had long hairs growing from his eyebrows, like a sheepdog's.

"Not so well, I guess," said the captain, scowling now. "What happened to you?"

Sonia signed as she spoke. "I slipped."

"Are you all right?"

She nodded, although every muscle in her body ached. She hadn't felt this bad since basic training.

"Did Johnny have a lesson?" he asked.

Sonia's heart sank. For just one instant she thought her injuries might have caused a delay in sentencing but this judge had no mercy in his heart. She drew a breath to answer the question honestly when Johnny began to sign, perfectly and in quick succession. He signed, *Slipped. Sorry. I'm screwed. Fuck.*

The captain blinked. Sonia braced for the explosion. Then the captain smiled, a grin really. Wide and bright and some of the tension eased from Sonia's neck. She looked from the sergeant to the captain.

"Well, well," said Captain MacConnelly. "Looks like you learned a lot." His expression seemed to glimmer with relief. That's when she realized he had fully expected her to fail. "Good work, Private. I'd say you've had enough for today."

He waited for her to deny it and, to her shame, she didn't.

"Okay. Let's get you checked out and cleaned up back at base." He walked her to the Jeep with Johnny skulking along behind them as if he knew he wasn't welcome. But he was. She'd rather stay here with him than go with the captain and that realization made her gasp. Johnny noticed it. The captain didn't.

Johnny pointed at her and then lifted his brows and made the okay sign.

A question, she realized and smiled. His first question. She nodded then signed back without speaking, *Yes. I'm okay. Thank you.*

Johnny nodded and the captain had not even noticed the exchange as he swept into the Jeep and started the engine. "I'll bring her back tomorrow afternoon at thirteen hundred."

Sonia held her breath. Johnny gave her a long stare and then a single curt nod.

Sonia released her breath in a long sigh. She was coming back. Thank God. She had gotten another reprieve.

Sonia reported to the medical unit for a check. Nothing was broken but the bruises were everywhere. They'd let her shower there and got her a new uniform. She was discharged and returned to quarters to find her footlocker had been placed at the end of one bunk.

Progress, she thought.

She glanced at the concrete bunkerlike room. Her new home, courtesy of the U.S. Government. It didn't look a lot different than a prison cell. She glanced at the windows. No bars, she realized. That was one important difference. Still, leave it to the government to make a tropical paradise look like a group home. Sonia unpacked her belongings that were not really hers. Everything she now owned had been requisitioned. She reached the bottom of her bag and her fingers grazed the one personal item she still possessed. A photograph of her and her sister, Marianna, when she was six and Marianna four. Her sister's hearing aid looked gigantic back then and made her ears stick out. The image was made worse by the short pixie cut that matched her own, a result of the lice they had both had. Her mother had been told they had to stay home until the medication killed all the lice. Instead her mom had shaved their heads and sent them to school. Marianna had earned the name Dumbo that year and it had stuck until middle school.

Sonia stared down at the two skinny kids they had been, with arms looped over each other's shoulders like two vines growing together. Marianna had gotten out, though. Gallaudet University on a full ride. A whole college for the deaf. It was just amazing. And with Marianna taken care of, Sonia didn't have to steal anymore to keep them in that crappy apartment. Her mother came and went like the tide. Back in jail, back on the streets, back in her bedroom with money in her pocket that she'd spend on booze. She wasn't dependable. Marianna needed dependable. Maybe Sonia could get through the next four years, be honorably discharged and go live near Marianna. Maybe even with her sister. Get their own place. She'd find a job to help Marianna again, if she even needed help anymore.

Sonia kissed her index finger and then pressed it to her sister's image. Then she tucked the picture frame back in her empty bag. Someday, she'd have a bedside table or a mantle or a bureau of her own.

Something.

Someday.

She sat down to write Marianna a letter and then realized that she could not include anything about Johnny and that her letter would be inspected by strangers. So she described the scenery and all the annoying habits of her bunkmates. She didn't like sharing a room with a group of strangers any more than she liked sharing her private letters with censors. But then who would?

The following morning she tried to take a run before breakfast, but her muscles were too damned sore so she opted for a long hot shower and lunch with the perkiest and most irritating member of her quarters before reporting to the captain for transport to Johnny's home.

All the way up the mountain she told herself how immature and childish she had been. She couldn't call him furball or swear at him. It was so unprofessional. Today she'd do better. She'd set the guidelines and her expectations. They'd begin with the basics. Who. What. Where. When. She'd teach him the signs for time. Yesterday. Today. Tomorrow.

The captain did not get out of the Jeep this time. "I'll send Zeno up to get you in ninety minutes."

"Ninety?" she stammered. The sheer number of minutes between then and now stretched to the horizon. "I thought… I thought…"

But he already had the Jeep in Reverse.

She stood rooted to the spot as the vehicle disappeared. Sometime after the Jeep had vanished down the road she snapped herself out of her daze and turned toward the adorable house that happened to belong to a werewolf.

She called for Sergeant Lam repeatedly but got no response. Belatedly, she realized that he might not appreciate being summoned like a dog. If he were not a monster, how would she approach him? Sonia decided on the front door, climbed the steep steps and knocked.

Johnny opened the door. His dark visage filled the frame and this time she did not back up at the sight of him. Instead she snapped a salute which he returned and then stepped out onto the porch. It seemed she would not see the inside of Sergeant Lam's home today. Sonia found herself disappointed. She was curious about him and about how he lived.

He motioned her to the porch as she remembered

how he had carried her to safety while she'd wept like a child in his arms. She followed him across the spotless wide planking that had been stained a natural color. The railings were also wood.

He motioned to a table under the wide roof. Who had hung wind chimes from the beam above the rail? she wondered.

He sat on a long bench before a coffee table that fit him much better than the two adjoining chairs and made the sign for her to sit. She removed her cap and placed it on a chair and then sat beside him on the bench. He instantly moved away as his eyebrows lifted.

Sonia spotted the bag she'd left yesterday and busied herself removing the small dry-erase boards and markers of various colors and lining them up on the table. By the time she placed the eraser Johnny groaned. She was losing her audience.

Sonia was determined to keep control today. No swearing. No temper. Just cool professionalism and a lesson that she'd stayed up half the night going over. She tried to channel Mrs. Kappenhaur, her seventh grade music teacher, the only one she'd ever liked.

"Today's lesson is ninety minutes. We will be covering time and some words to express needs. For example, 'What time is the meeting?'" she signed.

Johnny signed more obscenities.

"Yes. I'm sorry I showed you that one. Let's begin with these." She signed as she spoke. "Who? What? Where? When?"

Johnny grabbed a board and uncapped the green marker. She sat fidgeting with her own board as he wrote with an unsteady hand. It was painful to watch and when he finished she could barely make out what he had written.

"Y R U here?"

Off topic already, she realized, hurrying along. "To teach you."

"Y U stay?"

Sonia scowled. "We aren't talking about me. I'm here to teach *you* to sign. That's all you need to know."

Sergeant Lam threw his dry-erase board off the porch.

They scowled at each other.

"You do not have the right to poke around in my private life. I'm your teacher." There. She'd been decisive without swearing at him and she hadn't lost her temper. But she could feel her pulse throbbing in her temples and Johnny was baring his teeth. She dug in her heels. This would only work if he kept his nose out of her business.

He lifted a blue marker and wrote "Trust me."

She laughed. "Trust? Why should I? Listen, Lam. You are not my therapist. I'm here to teach you sign. That's it. You don't get a free pass to all my secrets. Got it? So take it or leave it."

He gave her a hard look. She didn't care. This was nonnegotiable.

"I'll keep coming back and I'll teach you. But no personal questions." She signed as she spoke. "Understand?" She then lifted her eyebrows to indicate it was a question, repeating the sign. "Understand?"

He nodded, stood and then jumped off the porch. By the time she reached the rail he had disappeared into the green curtain beyond the yard.

She watched him go. "Well, that went well."

Sonia descended the steep stairs and crossed the yard, staring down at the jungle below her. She was not going back in there again.

"Sergeant Lam!" she called. She tried again and received no response. After several minutes she gave up.

"I'm going to keep it professional," she muttered in a mocking tone. "I'm going to set ground rules." She gave a mirthless laugh and began signing as she spoke. She threw her hat and felt no better.

Sonia waited twenty minutes. He didn't come back. She returned to the porch and replaced the caps on the markers.

She stared at Johnny's board. *Trust me.*

It was impossible. She didn't trust anyone but her sister. That's how she'd survived. It wasn't a fair request.

She walked to the edge of the clearing realizing that he didn't have to be fair. Life hadn't been fair to him. Besides who could he tell? And what secrets did she have that weren't already in that damned two-inch thick file the captain had? But it was different saying them aloud. So different. Besides it was a sucky story. Depressing and humiliating. She'd be sparing him by keeping her mouth shut.

Or she could tell him whatever he wanted to know and get his furry butt back in that chair.

She could keep her secrets or her freedom.

She gave a cry of frustration. This overgrown furball was going to get her locked up. If she didn't get him back here then the captain would find out and... Sonia marched to the porch rail and gripped it tight as she leaned out toward the yard and filled her lungs with air.

"All right!" she shouted to the jungle valley. "I give up! I'm here because if I don't teach you sign, I go back to jail. Do you hear me? I'm an ex-con and you learning sign is all that's keeping me from going in for six. Johnny! Damn it, do you hear me?"

Johnny opened his front door. She whirled to face him as he fixed her with a long steady look. He'd been in there all along, she realized. From his place in the door frame, he lifted his hands as if gripping bars and then lifted his brows.

"Yeah. Breaking and entering. Stupid. I tripped a silent alarm. Cops got me and locked me up. If you don't learn sign I go back there."

And there it was, the reason he couldn't run her off and the reason she'd come back.

"Can we start over?" she said, signing in synchronization.

Lam placed one fist on top of the other and lifted them as if preparing to swing an invisible bat. He made a smooth strike, his big, gnarled hands sweeping in a wide graceful arch from one shoulder to the other. Then he held up two fingers. She understood.

"Two strikes."

Their eyes met and this time she nodded.

"Okay, but how is this going to work? You just ask me any damned personal, prying question you like and I have to answer it?"

He nodded.

"Well, I don't like that plan."

He shrugged and stepped inside his threshold. The door began to close. She hurried after him.

"Wait!"

He did, but he kept one hand on the door, ready to slam it in her face. Behind him the television blared. Football, she realized.

"Okay, okay. Goddamn it okay!"

Lam made his fingers and thumb form a circle in a quick mimic of her sign of okay. There was nothing wrong with his brain. But those claws! Damn, they looked like tiny bayonets. Her shoulders sagged as she accepted yet another defeat. She was not going to be able to keep Lam at a distance. She was certain this werewolf was going to try to unlock every embarrassing secret and forbidden memory. Like Scheherazade, she was here only as long as she interested him. But unlike her, the stories would all be true. Sonia glared up at him with all the hatred in her soul. He'd trapped her the same way the U.S. Marines had trapped her. The same way the captain had trapped her. She was getting tired of being trapped.

Four years. That was what stood between her and a new life. Record expunged. Fresh start. Useful training. She wondered where she would be able to fit "tutored a werewolf" on her resume. She snorted.

"All right, Sergeant Lam. What do you want to know?"

Chapter 4

Sonia waited as Johnny returned to the porch, scooping up a red marker and a board. Then he walked past her and into his house, turning to motion her in. She crossed the threshold and her breath caught. His place was spotless and lovely as any magazine spread. The rattan couch looked as if it were never used. The low chairs and ottomans were way too small for Johnny and she couldn't picture him eating on a glass dinette with royal-purple place mats, cloth napkins and a green glass vase filled with several sprigs of orchids. Beyond the breakfast counter a spotless kitchen sparkled with natural wood cabinets and slate tiled counter tops. How did he keep it so clean and where did he eat? Better still, *what* did he eat?

"Do you even use this kitchen?" she asked.

In answer he opened the freezer to reveal it stuffed with frozen meat.

"Fruits and vegetables?" she asked.

He gave a shake, no.

So he ate meat, possibly raw, alone in this empty kitchen.

Suddenly the spotless house seemed as sterile as an anonymous, impersonal hotel room. From the outside it looked like a home. But from in here it seemed a different kind of prison.

She heard a football game and realized the living room had no television. She glanced toward the hallway that must lead to the bedrooms. Was that where he lived? Because he certainly didn't spend time here. He motioned to the couch and chose to sit on a leather ottoman that she thought might collapse under the strain.

She turned her attention back to Lam to find him watching her.

"Okay, Johnny. What do you want to know?"

He wrote "jail" on his slate.

She sagged into the hard, new cushions. "Oh, damn. Really?"

He continued to stare and she knew she wasn't weaseling out of this one but she tried. "I broke into a house. I got caught." She shrugged. "Arrested, fingerprinted, court date, a deal to serve four years with the U.S. Marines. That's it."

She waited for some reaction. He blinked and shook his head and reached for the board and wrote. He turned the board around and she read, "Why B and E?"

Sonia blew out a breath from her nose, a blast like one from a fire breathing dragon.

"Because I just was a bad kid. I got into a lot of trouble." She stopped talking and set her jaw as the burning started in her eyes. She didn't want to think about that now, but he was making her. She glared.

He motioned for her to continue.

"What do you want me to say? I'm not the good little soldier, John. Not even close."

He sat forward and nodded his encouragement and touched the word "why" on his board.

She showed him the sign and he copied it. *Why? Why? Why?*

Her head bowed and she looked at her hands laced and locked up tighter than her heart. She wasn't answering. She'd keep her fingers still and her mouth shut. Johnny stood, heading for the kitchen. When he reached the back door she realized he was leaving again and shot to her feet.

"Stop!" she ordered.

He did.

"Come back." Sonia admitted defeat.

Johnny resumed his place, staring at her with his eyes big and yellow and his expression placid. He still looked fearsome as hell but Johnny was nothing if not a good listener, she realized. He lifted his chin as if encouraging her.

Sonia signed slowly now as the words were coming from somewhere so deep she hardly recognized her own voice. Her fingers danced along with each sign as naturally as breathing. "Okay. My mother, she drinks—a lot. Been in rehab. Been in jail. For drinking mostly and for the crap she did when she was drunk. Driving, fighting, stealing, causing accidents, bringing home men, pissing in public places, passing out in public places, getting fired, getting pregnant and forgetting about the two kids she already had. Me and my sister, we don't look much alike, if you know what I mean." She couldn't look at Johnny now, not with the shame rushing up to burn her face, so she focused instead on the magazines fanned across the coffee table, all Martha Stewart and all five years old. "A mean drunk, that's what the landlord called my mama to her face, before he called protective services." She stared up at Johnny, feeling the burning in her eyes but she would be damned if she'd let him see her cry. She widened her eyes and willed the tears back.

Sonia kept signing. "So I wasn't a good kid. I got into fights. Kids made fun of Marianna, that's my kid sister, so I kicked the shit out of them. Then some parent advocate got ahold of my mother and said that the school district wasn't meeting my sister's needs. That Marianna had rights and Marianna needed a special program." She met his steady gaze. "My sister is deaf, Johnny. Born that way. They said it was because of my mom's drinking, but mom was in jail when she was carrying Marianna, so that wasn't it. Anyway. She was either born deaf or maybe she got sick and that made her deaf. Nobody ever bothered to tell me. So my kid sister is smart, but she can't really talk. Sounds funny, you know? When she was little we had our own signs. Then I found a book and taught her some real signs. Later, when she got in that special program, she taught me. Marianna got into a residential school, but it was up in Elmsford and that's like twenty miles from where we lived. They said I couldn't go there because I wasn't deaf. I didn't think she could get along by herself, so I cut school and took four buses and I found her. You know what? It was the best damned thing that could have happened to her. She lived in a big dorm. She got regular meals and had friends like her. She was wearing clothes I'd never seen before, clean clothes. The school officials called my mother and she came to get me. But she came drunk, of course, so the school called the cops and, long story short, Marianna graduated with honors and I went to a group home, for good that time. I dropped out of high school and ran away. I was a regular rebel without a clue. When you turn eighteen you age-out. That means no more foster care."

Johnny sat next to her on the couch, turning to face her. She shifted so he could see her sign, even though the words she formed didn't mean anything to him yet. It gave her comfort, like she was talking to her sister.

"I was on the streets for a while until I got assistance with housing. I even got my GED. Then I applied to community college and got in under probation. I didn't make it through the first semester. So, if you're not in school, you lose the subsidy. I got a job but it didn't pay enough to cover the bills so I…" She rubbed the back of her neck. "I robbed that house. Took a bus to a nice white neighborhood, picked a house with a nice private yard and threw a nice little cement rabbit through that nice shiny glass window. And you know what? I wasn't sorry. Why did this family have a house like this when I couldn't make rent? And the food they had in their kitchen. It could have fed me for six months. But they also had a silent alarm. Cops got me still in the house because instead of taking their cash and getting the hell out of there I stopped to eat a bowl of cereal with milk. I made a shitty burglar. But I wasn't a minor anymore and this was a felony."

Johnny lifted the board and wrote "You wanted to get caught."

"No, I sure didn't." She pressed her fingers into her eyes for a minute then went back to signing as she spoke. "Well, maybe I did, but I sure the hell didn't want to go to prison. What I did was stupid. I'm not a thief, I'm just…angry. Or I was. So my lawyer worked out a deal. Go to federal prison or join the U.S. Marines. Seemed like a no-brainer." She lifted her hands and then dropped them. "So I'm a marine. Wouldn't be if I didn't have to be. Wouldn't be here now but the captain said he'd lock me up again if I didn't teach you sign. I can't go back to prison, Johnny. I just can't."

The silence stretched.

"I'm sorry. I'm not like you. I'm not a good soldier. I didn't sign up to serve my country or protect people. I signed up to avoid a prison cell. So what do you say? Will you learn a few words to keep the captain off my back?"

He signed, *Yes*.

She blew out a breath, feeling somehow lighter than when she walked in. All that armor was heavy and he'd made her set some of it aside. She smiled at him and he lifted his brows. "Okay, then. Hey, Johnny, why didn't you want to learn? I mean it will make things so much easier…"

He stood up so abruptly that the ottoman slid back several inches. Whoa, what was that about? she wondered. Seemed Johnny had a few sore spots of his own. She recalled him breaking the first board and throwing the second and leaping off the porch and walking out on her. Johnny *really* didn't want to learn to sign. Her curiosity prickled and she watched him stare out the front window. Her not wanting to teach him made a lot of sense. Her not wanting to talk about her rotten childhood, she understood. But this confused and intrigued her. She walked over to stand beside him. He didn't look at her, but his ears moved and he turned toward the road.

A Jeep horn blared. Sonia jumped. He'd heard that way before she had, she realized.

She signed, *Time to go.*

He nodded and walked her to the door. For some stupid reason she didn't want to go, which made no sense at all. So she lingered inside the open door. The horn sounded again. Sonia stepped out onto the porch and realized it had rained again. The mist rose from the earth in tiny wisps. She was about to descend the steep steps, but Johnny took hold of her arm and walked her down. At the bottom she turned to the Jeep and found the driver was a dimple-faced man she'd never seen before. Her relief at not seeing the captain was palpable and she blew out a breath.

She used the wide stones to cross the stream and realized Johnny didn't follow her. She signed, *Goodbye* and he signed back, *See you tomorrow.*

She paused, impressed. Had she taught him that? She glanced at the bag she had left on his porch yesterday, recalling the book on sign language. Sonia considered the possibilities. Had he been studying?

The driver met her halfway and waved at Johnny. "See you tomorrow morning, buddy." His grin lasted only until he turned around and then his expression turned somber.

"I'm Carl Zeno," he told her offering his hand. "One of the Den Mothers. That's what we call ourselves. Beats Wounded Warriors, don't you think?"

Sonia murmured a greeting as she released his hand

and climbed into the passenger side. The corporal set them in motion. She glanced back to see Johnny lifting a hand in farewell. She waved back.

"Say," said Zeno, "were you *inside* Johnny's place?"

"Yes."

"He doesn't let anyone in there. How'd you do it?"

"He invited me."

"Just like that?"

She shrugged.

"What's it like?"

Somehow talking to Zeno about Johnny seemed wrong, so she opted for telling him it was nice.

"Maybe it's because you're a woman. He's never had a woman teacher. I was talking to the guys about it. They think it's a really bad idea. He's moody, you know? You might want to be careful in there. So, you got off-base permission yet? I could show you around."

She put on her seat belt realizing that she felt safer with Johnny than with his den mother. "Not yet."

Zeno nodded as he kept his attention on the road. "Did he attack you yesterday? Because a guy at the medical center said you were pretty banged up. The guys were saying that maybe we ought to be there when you're with him."

"Johnny didn't do it. I fell."

He gave her a look that told her that he didn't believe her. "Listen he's taken a swing at all of us. Threw a full can of beer at Dom once. But he never actually hit us. If he did that to you—" Zeno pointed at her bruised cheek and the scratch that she knew crossed her forehead "—then you should tell the captain. They've got ties but I think he'd listen."

"He didn't do anything."

"I think they should lock him up instead of locking us all up in this half-assed zoo. Lam's just a mess. Won't talk to us, ditches us nearly every day. The guy's not human anymore. I don't know why the captain doesn't see it."

That third lesson set up the pattern. Not the falling down the mountain and nearly dying part or the sitting on his pristine couch part, but the prying into her past part. Sonia had to endure a series of personal questions on whatever popped into the sergeant's brain and then he'd endure her lesson and learn a few more signs. He threw in a few she hadn't taught him so she was certain he was reading that book when she wasn't around. By the end of each lesson she was exhausted, wrung out emotionally, but at least she was not in the brig and the captain was off her ass.

But what would happen when she no longer interested Johnny?

He was such a good student. She still didn't know what the big fuss about not learning sign had been. A power play maybe or a pissing match. Men were funny about their pride and dignity and Johnny *was* a man, despite what those Den Mothers thought.

Over the first week he'd learned where she grew up and that her sister was at Gallaudet University outside of Washington, D.C. And she'd taught him colors, numbers, the alphabet and a series of action words, like walk, run, come, go, listen, do. Lam was now using both the board and sign language to communicate.

Lessons took place outside in nice weather and inside in the rain. It rained a lot here, but not for very long. Today they were on the porch and he had a pitcher of lemonade for her and it really tasted like he'd made it from fresh lemons.

She signed to him a question without speaking, *Did you make this?*

He asked her what the sign for make meant.

When she finger spelled *M-A-K-E* he flopped his arms, unwilling to answer.

She kept signing as she spoke. "Because this is really tasty. Just the right amount of tart with the sweet. You made it, didn't you?"

He rolled his eyes and nodded, admitting that he'd made it. She grinned, pleased at his efforts. Somehow she suspected that he didn't make this routinely for himself.

"Fruits." She smiled. "You having some?"

He shook his head and finger spelled *O-N-L-Y M-E-A-T*.

"That get boring?"

Does fruit? he signed.

She laughed and lifted the glass, now beading with condensation. "It's great. Thanks." She took another sip and set the glass aside.

The early lessons had been very difficult for her. His questions were like having dental work done. But like dental work, she found if she just relaxed, it wasn't quite as painful. Still, Sergeant Beast, as she'd come to think of him, was a whiz at finding her soft underbelly. He would have made a great interrogator.

"So what is it today? My sister. My mom?"

He signed, *Day off.*

"Great. So how about you give me a question."

He nodded.

"Why didn't you want to learn sign?"

Lam shook his head.

"Oh, come on!" she said. "I told you about my mom."

Don't like, he paused to finger spell the last word, *S-C-H-O-O-L.*

She sensed the lie in the quick reply.

"That's bull. I answer your questions and you don't tell me anything about yourself. If you want us to be friends it has to be a two way street. Otherwise I'm just your...your..." She struggled with the right word, coming up with "lab rat."

Lam straightened and she knew instantly that she'd said something wrong. She just didn't know what. He rose and walked swiftly away

"Sergeant?" She followed him. He allowed her to keep up but kept rubbing his neck and then his long wolfish jaw in turns. "Did I say something wrong?"

He turned and signed, *Lab rat,* then lifted his brows to make the words a question.

"Well, yes. I don't know how else to describe it. Or maybe like a criminal investigation with me playing the crook. Or a psychiatric appointment. You know, 'tell me about your problems,' but shrinks never share their own." She was babbling and her hands could barely keep up. At last she sighed and dropped her hands to her sides.

Lam's stare was mournful. He began signing. She tried to understand but his gestures were wild and fierce as his emotions spilled into his words.

No. Lab rat. No.

"One way street?" she tried.

Ask something else, he signed.

"Okay." She thought for a minute. "Everyone on this base is here for you, aren't they? They all know about you. And with all the security and the fences and stuff. Are you a prisoner, John?"

He nodded and then shook his head.

"I don't understand."

He lifted the pad of paper and wrote while she sipped her lemonade. "Everyone here is trying to find a cure for me to change back."

She lifted her head and gaped at him. "Is that possible?"

He nodded and then shrugged.

She continued reading. "But fence is not to keep me in but to keep intruders out."

"I don't understand."

He lifted his hands in exasperation as if to say *I can't help you with that.* Then signed, *Finish.*

"What's finished?"

Lesson. Today. Finish.

"We still have thirty minutes."

He signed, *Walk you down. Need meet woman.*

She didn't understand but agreed. "All right."

He waited by a trailhead that she had not noticed in her first and only excursion into the dense undergrowth.

"We aren't taking the road?"

Long, he signed. *Two many long.*

She wasn't sure if he meant it was too long to walk the road or if he meant that it was twice the time to walk the road. Either way she was dubious about stepping into the jungle again. Most of the trails she had taken in her life had sidewalks and street lights.

"Is it safe?" she asked.

With me. Safe. Yes. Come.

She nodded her acceptance. "You're not going to ditch me in there, are you?"

He frowned and looked disappointed in her again. It was a look she was getting used to.

"Okay, I'm sorry. It's hard for me to trust people," she signed.

She motioned to the green wall of ferns and palms and a multitude of plants and trees she didn't know the names of. "Okay. Let's go."

Lam hesitated and her stomach tightened. He got that look when he was preparing to drill particularly deep into her past and if he went there she knew he'd hit a nerve, so she just started walking, somehow finding the trail. The path angled down sharply and she had to lean back to keep from falling. Lam nudged past her, taking point. The jungle here seemed a perpetual twilight because the bright sun never found the forest floor. She could hear water dripping from the leaves about her and occasionally was hit with a large droplet. The birdsong filled the air but she also detected an occasional worrisome rustling in the undergrowth. Johnny turned his head often to check on her. The sound of water began to increase, gradually drowning out her plodding steps and the birds.

Lam followed the switchbacks so they zigzagged in manageable steps down the embankment that she nearly tumbled down. When the trail leveled off it also branched. Lam pointed to their left and made a swimming motion, sweeping his arms in graceful circles. She heard that waterfall again. The one she'd glimpsed from an inverted position. The hairs on her neck stood up.

"You swim there?"

He nodded.

"I don't swim."

A-F-R-A-I-D. His fingers spelled the letters perfectly.

"Yes. I sure am."

Of water?

"Of drowning."

I teach you, he signed.

"No thanks. I'd rather fall down the hill again."

He shrugged and headed along the main trail. It didn't stay level for long. As she walked she tried to imagine Lam teaching her to swim. He'd probably just throw her in the deep end and see what happened. Swimming seemed to be a big form of recreation on this island, which only made sense. She hadn't had a leave day yet, though Zeno kept pestering her about going to the beach which she might enjoy, but not with him. She imagined she'd go to the shore alone, lie on a towel and when she got too hot just wade into the surf to her knees and splash water on herself as she used to do all those years ago at Orchard Beach in the Bronx. What would it be like to dive into the waves?

Terrifying, she decided. Like slipping from her mother's arms at the pool and just making it to the edge. Mom laughing, clapping, drunk. She shivered. But the swimmers on the Long Island Sound seemed so happy.

Sonia was so busy imagining herself diving into an oncoming wave that she didn't see Johnny stop and so, when he did, she bounced off his broad back and fell to her butt in the trail.

He turned and regarded her as she sat in a heap. Then he extended his hand. She accepted his offer without thinking and without flinching finding his palm warm, dry and rough as the pad on the foot of a dog. She had to tug to get her hand back. Man, his claws looked vicious. She wiped her hand on her thigh and then saw him stiffen. Had she insulted him?

She glanced up at those unnatural yellow eyes seeing the hurt she'd caused and feeling her cheeks grow hot.

"Sorry," she murmured but he just kept staring until she felt a hitch in her breathing that surprised and confused her. His look told her without question that he was unhappy with her and for some reason that troubled her. Her instincts told her to move away. What was happening here?

"Why did we stop?"

Lam signed, *I stop for you see captain house. You stop because I stop.*

He made a joke. His first sign joke. She nodded, proud of his accomplishment and complete, if awkward, first sentences.

"Good one," she said, smiling.

He grinned in return. A grimace really, that disconcerted her because it showed his very dangerous-looking fangs. He noticed the direction of her gaze. His teeth disappeared behind black wolfish jowls. She tried to picture the man he had been and failed.

"Did you say the captain's house?"

He nodded.

"But that is twenty minutes or more from your place."

Lam pantomimed that he was driving a car and then walked in a circle.

"Faster on foot than driving. I see."

Lam practiced the sign for driving and walking.

"Can I see it?"

Lam took her to the edge of the clearing. Sonia paused seeing the place where she'd first met Sergeant

Lam from a different perspective. Who kept the trail between the two properties so pristine and how often did Lam or MacConnelly travel between their places? Sonia stared up at Lam wanting to ask the question about his relationship to the captain and decided not to pry. She had the uneasy feeling someone was watching her and turned to face the back of the house. A woman stood on the porch above them.

"That's her!" whispered Sonia, in awe.

Lam lifted a hand and waved. The red-haired beauty waved back. She was by far and without question the most beautiful woman Sonia had ever seen.

"I saw her that first day. Or I thought I saw her. She was at the window and then she vanished. They said she never leaves her house. Is she really the captain's wife?"

Lam nodded. *She R-E-A-S-O-N for F-E-N-C-E.*

"She? Why is she a prisoner?"

Johnny shook his head. *P-R-O-T-E-C-T.*

The woman retreated to her home. Sonia felt inexplicably bereft. Suddenly she wanted to follow her. "Can I meet her?"

He shook his head.

"Why not?"

He didn't answer and Sonia stared at the place where the red-haired woman had been.

"I thought she never left her house."

Lam regarded her for a moment. She had the feeling he was considering his response. Finally he lifted his hand and spelled out three letters. L-I-E.

"So I did see her?" she motioned to the house. "But it's impossible. She disappeared right before my eyes." At some point Sonia realized she was explaining this impossible feat to a nine-foot werewolf. Sonia pressed a hand over her racing heart and dropped her tone to a whisper. "What is she?"

Johnny shook his head and turned to go. Sonia followed but she took one look back at the house. The captain's wife was now standing on the far side of the stream. Sonia was startled at seeing her so close, so fast, and then hurried to follow Lam. That woman was creepy as hell and she suddenly did not want to meet her.

Sonia turned and ran to catch up with Lam. She pressed a hand to his shoulder and he stilled then turned to face her. He stared at the place where she touched him and Sonia drew back her hand.

"Is she like you?

No.

"Is she the one who did this to you?"

No. She is V-A-M-P-I-R-E.

Was he serious? She gaped at him and he held her gaze.

"Holy shit. Really?"

He nodded, grim as a mourner at a grave. Sonia felt a shiver travel down her spine. She stared at him in shock.

Her thoughts exploded with denial and then horror. It wasn't possible, but when she looked at Johnny she knew that it *was* possible. Anything was possible. She wobbled suddenly unsteady, but Johnny caught her elbow and held on until she nodded to him. She looked behind them, now having another reason to fear this jungle. There was a vampire living here.

"She was out in the daytime."

He nodded yes, as if this were nothing unusual.

Johnny glanced back toward the captain's home and then continued on down the incline. The dripping on the leaves got louder as the humidity rose. Her shirt stuck to her back and arms. Lam grabbed at a broad leaf and tore it from the plant by the stem but never stopped. He twirled it as they continued on. A few minutes later they broke from the jungle and stood at the edge of a gentle slope covered with narrow-leaved plants that grew waist high on her but barely brushed Lam's knees. The trail cut neatly through the center. She paused beneath the cover of the foliage as she realized it was pouring. Johnny motioned past the incline to the U.S. Marine base and the barracks where she lived. She recognized her surroundings now.

It seemed the entire mountain was fenced, for they never crossed through a perimeter.

"Johnny?" She didn't know what to say. She was frightened and didn't want to cross the fifty feet to her barracks alone. He handed her the leaf and motioned that she should use it as an umbrella. She held it over her head. Johnny took her elbow and continued on, seeing her to her door and then signing his farewell. She watched him until he vanished into the wall of green.

A vampire, she thought, and they were protecting her. But protecting her from what?

Chapter 5

Burne Farrell waited as his chaser, Hagan Dowling, finished checking the abandoned concrete bunker within the Marine Corps Mountain Warfare Training Center in California. The two male vampires had made no progress tracking Brianna Vittori since they lost her trail eighteen months ago. So Burne, the elder hunter, had resorted to returning to her last known residence. The female's disappearance with two werewolves nettled his professional pride but more importantly her absence had prevented him from making her his personal property. His eagerness to have her only increased his annoyance at his best chaser's failure to produce her. Each day Brianna remained free was like a growing blister on his plum-colored ass.

No female vampire had ever evaded him for so long. But Brianna was not your typical female. Like all vampires, she was descended from the fey. But Brianna's mother was a fairy, a true Leanan Sidhe. So unlike him, any male child born of Brianna would look normal enough not to draw immediate notice.

It was Burne's disturbing appearance, and not any reaction to sunlight, that kept him, and his fellows perpetually in the shadows. He had been told that his great-great grandfather once walked among men. But Burne was sixth generation and with each new legacy, their form departed farther and farther from their human parent. The most pure vampires he knew were fifth generation. Brianna was first.

Her male offspring would not turn purple as ripe plums and be ugly as the back end of a pig. So he wanted her first male child to be his. The females of their race already walked freely in the light, when he let them. No females drank blood and all were visions. That was why they made such good assassins after training was complete.

Burne's skin was becoming more discolored by the day, dotted with purple patches like an octogenarian's. His chaser, Hagan Dowling, still had the white cast of a corpse. It only made his blue veins more prominent beneath his transparent skin after feeding but that would change with the decades and his veins would leak like Burne's until his skin was cold as death and he could not hold the blood he drank. And then he would die. They all ended that way. Being a vampire did not make one immortal. Despite the legends, vampires were mortal, even though they carried the blood of fairies in their veins.

Hagan breathed deeply. "It still smells like dog in here."

"Wolves," corrected Burne.

"Yes."

"Where would you go, if you were trying to keep her from discovery?" Burne asked Hagan.

"Outside our territory, if he knows what that territory is."

"Exactly. That's why you haven't found her. She's not here to be found. Perhaps her mother told her that we do not like to cross water.

"There are U.S. Marine bases throughout Europe, Africa, the Middle East and the Pacific," Burne continued.

"We need to search each one. Start with the Pacific. Go island by island. Meanwhile, I will check with our colleagues in Europe and the Middle East."

Burne stared at his chaser. Hagan's lips were the ruby red of a vampire just fed. His fangs had grown so long that they no longer fit in his mouth. They didn't retract like a snake's, nor were they hollow like straws. Their purpose was to tear through flesh and rip open major blood vessels so they could drink.

Hagan stared at him through milky-white irises. They were already fading from their birth color. Burne smiled. It always started with the eyes. He knew Hagan's vision was perfect, but this discoloration made him look like he was quite blind or quite dead. One look at him and the human flight crew would panic. He needed to get them across the ocean, a dozen preferably, without any of them being seen. Night was their usual disguise, though for this journey, that would not be possible. But it was worth any risk to find Brianna. Still, if they were discovered it would mean their lives, not from the humans, of course. But to expose themselves to humans was one of the great unpardonables. Some heads of state knew of them, took advantage of their services for a price. But being detected by such a large group as the passengers and a flight crew on a commercial airline would mean their death. Of course, if they were seen on the plane, it would be necessary to kill all witnesses.

He thought of Brianna, with her waves of copper hair and eyes as green as a birch leaf. His loins tightened at the memory.

"Return to our base and assemble a team. I will arrange transport."

"When do we depart?"

"Forty-eight hours."

"And the humans will not see us?"

"For their sakes, I hope not."

"Yes, sir."

He stared down at a photo of Brianna, taken from her apartment last April. Her face could be that of an angel, she was so lovely, her skin smooth and pink. Burne felt his heart pitch and his loins twitch. If he could catch her, he would keep her for himself.

"I want this one," he muttered.

"Yes, sir."

Hagan's reply was too quick and far too eager. Burne cast a sideways glance at Hagan and caught him ogling the image Burne held. His eyes narrowed on Hagan. The younger vampire forced a smile and the sharp tips of his fangs grazed his lower lip. It was possible that Hagan had similar ideas where Brianna was concerned.

Perhaps it would be wiser to accompany this team and see to her capture personally.

* * *

The next day, Sonia waited for her ride. She was unhappily surprised when the captain pulled up and motioned her to get in. She saluted and climbed into the passenger seat. They rode through the base. Every-thing seemed so normal out here with marines drilling on the rifle range. She turned to watch men scaling the wall on the obstacle course, using the twin nylon ropes to reach the apex. But things weren't normal. Johnny was a werewolf and the captain's wife was a vampire.

"Johnny tells me that you are teaching him a lot."

She turned back to the captain. "I'm trying my best, sir."

"He also asked me to tell you about what happened to him in California. I'm not sure why he wants you to know this, but I agreed."

Something about the captain's tone brought her to complete attention. He pulled to the shoulder so she had a view of men crawling on all fours under the cargo net.

"When we came back from Afghanistan we were shipped to the Marine Corps Mountain Warfare Train-ing Center in the Sierra Nevada Mountains. We were told that they were trying to find a cure for Sergeant Lam. They did medical tests, oxygen levels, CT scans, blood work, but they did other things, too." Her cap-tain covered his hand with his mouth and stared out the window.

Sonia watched him. Tension vibrated from him so clearly she could almost hear it. He dragged his hand over his mouth and then glanced at her, then quickly returned his attention out the window. She instinctively braced for what he would tell her next.

"They used Johnny for target practice to test the durability of his hide."

Sonia gasped. Now she understood part of the sadness she had seen in the captain's eyes. Lam was his friend, his comrade and a member of his squad. And his own commanding officer had done this.

"They shot at him?" she asked.

"Yes. He's bulletproof."

Sonia shuddered.

"They also used grenades. He almost lost his hearing. But that's not the worst of it. They took…" The captain wiped one hand over his mouth before continuing. "They took Johnny's sperm. Trying to make more werewolves."

"What!" Sonia's fingers went wide as her arms braced as if she were warding off something thrown at her face. "Who did?"

"Our commanding officer. We thought we were to undergo training and testing to make Johnny human. The truth was quite the opposite. They were trying to reproduce werewolves."

"Why?"

"Classified."

"How could they?"

"They did. And used his sperm." The captain rubbed the bristle on the back of his neck with his knuckles. For a moment he seemed unable to speak. "We found this all out later. There is at least one child as a result. A boy. So far he is completely normal and two other women, both marines, are pregnant. The boy has been adopted by a very nice couple in Northern California, the husband is retired military and knows the deal. We're keeping an eye on the child and the other fetuses, of course. Johnny knows. He wants to see his son, but…"

But he couldn't, of course. Not as long as he was a werewolf.

"This is terrible."

"Yes, so you'll understand why you shouldn't tell Sergeant Lam that you feel like a lab rat because he actually was one."

Sonia sank down in her seat. "I had no idea."

"But we are trying to make him human. This whole place, is all here for Johnny." The captain lifted his arms indicating the compound. "Everyone here. It's our purpose."

They weren't all here only for Johnny, she thought, remembering what she knew about the captain's wife. She wanted to ask him about her, but didn't have the courage. They sat in silence for a time.

"Something on your mind?"

"Why the fencing? Johnny says he's not a prisoner and I'm sure he could jump it or tear it down."

The captain said nothing to this.

"Is it for your wife?"

The captain's eyes narrowed to slits. "What about my wife?"

"Johnny says that she's a—a vampire."

"He shouldn't have told you that."

"Is the fence for her?"

The captain looked away. "In a way. She's a target. I'm protecting her."

"From what?"

"Male vampires."

"A fence can keep them out?"

"No. It can alert me when they arrive. But only a werewolf is strong enough to kill a male vampire."

The realization came first and then a rising wave of indignation. She beat her fists on the dash.

"I knew it! You're keeping him here—like some guard dog, to protect her?" Her fists were clenched on her knees. She wanted to strike, but she held back.

He stared her down, matching the fury with a glare that made her stomach twist. The captain looked pissed and dangerous as hell.

"That's not his job," he said. "It's mine."

"You said only a werewolf could protect her." She meant the comment as accusation, but the moment she said it the captain's expression changed and she understood the truth.

They'd been together in Afghanistan, Johnny and her captain.

"You," she whispered.

He didn't deny it.

Who else? she wondered. The wounded warriors? The MPs? Who else were werewolves?

"Touma. For once in your life, follow your orders and stop thinking so much."

She sat back, sagging into the seat. She should have known all along.

"No lesson today. We need Johnny to come down to medical but after what happened in California he doesn't like to come in for tests."

"That's understandable."

"This is different. We've made a breakthrough. He needs to see." The captain pulled the Jeep back out onto the road. "I don't care what you have to promise him, just get him down here as quick as you can. That's an order, Private. Your ass if he doesn't show."

Now how exactly did he expect her to accomplish what no one else had been able to do? He gave her a lot more credit than she deserved. Johnny only learned the signs as payback for her little revelations. She didn't have a secret big enough to get him off that hill.

Her head sunk. Yes, she did. But damned if she'd talk about that to him when Marianna didn't even know.

Sonia set her teeth and hissed at the captain. He didn't seem to notice.

Her superior had no qualms about using her to get Johnny to do what he wanted. She didn't like being a tool, but she liked her other option even less. She responded as expected. "Sir, yes, sir."

When they passed the turnoff to the captain's home a dozen questions sprang on her like hungry tigers.

She danced around the subject that so occupied her. "Does your wife like living up on the hill?"

He glanced at her out of the side of his eyes and then returned his attention to the rough road. "She does, yes. And she's very protective of Johnny. They became friends in California. If you hurt him, I'll be the least of your problems."

She definitely did not need a vampire pissed at her.

The captain dropped her off a few minutes later. "Call for a pickup. Sooner is better."

Johnny greeted her on the porch and invited her inside to the immaculate living room that he never used. She sat and Johnny perched on the adjoining ottoman like a tiger on a toadstool, waiting with folded hands for her to begin the lesson. But there would be no lesson today. So did she just blurt it out or try to ease into the topic of the medical center? Subtlety was never her strong suit.

She drew a breath preparing to dive into deep water.

"Johnny, the captain told me about what happened in California and at the lab. I think it's terrible."

His brow descended and his posture went stiff. She reached for him and laid a hand on his forearm, giving a little squeeze but he wouldn't look at her.

"Thank you for asking him to tell me."

He glanced at her now, but his muscles remained rigid under her light touch.

"I understand you not wanting to go back to a lab. But the captain, well, he says he needs to show you something."

He started to rise but she pressed down on his shoulder, as if that could stop him, but it did. Instead of knocking her hand aside, he placed his over hers and looked up at her with wide yellow eyes that were as foreign as the surface of the moon.

"It's not a test. He told me it's not a test."

Johnny shook his head as his eyes asked her to understand.

She slid her hand free to allow her to sign. "He also said it's my ass if you don't show."

Johnny slapped an open hand on the coffee table and all four legs snapped as the top hit the floor. He rose like a wave and paced through the dining area to the windows that led to the back porch. There he pivoted and paced back, coming to a smooth stop before the collapsed table. Grace in motion, she thought.

"What are you going to do?"

He signed his answer. *You come?*

She nodded. "If you want me to."

He finger spelled *T-R-A-N-S-L-A-T-O-R*.

"You'll go?" She barely kept herself from wilting with relief. "Thank you."

Johnny did not look pleased but he nodded.

"May I use your phone?"

He nodded and pointed to the one mounted on the wall.

After calling for their ride she asked to use his bathroom. He led the way and she trailed down the hallway that bisected the other half of the house. He had a guest bedroom. She peeked in there as they passed and saw stereo equipment, a wide-screen plasma TV with surround-sound speakers mounted on the walls. Instead of carpets, the floor was covered with two very large futons. One spread like an area rug and the other folded in half and leaning against one wall like a headboard. Both showed the indentation of a large body and a prodigious amount of black hair. This, quite obviously, was where Johnny relaxed. His man cave, she decided as they passed by the door.

He stepped aside to allow her to pass before him into a room to the left. There was a king-size bed that was still not long enough for a giant. His coverlet was a tropical garden of interlacing bamboo. The pillows, all four, had the same matching design. He was either very careful at making his bed or he didn't sleep here.

The bedside table had a clock but nothing else. No photos, no electronics. The walls had paintings that you might see in a hotel, a palm tree, a spray of orchids. But unlike a hotel, there was no bureau and the walk-in closet was empty because, she realized, Johnny did not need any clothing.

Did he live in the movie theater room or in the forest? She wasn't sure. But she was sure he didn't stay in this room.

He halted at a narrow door and pointed, then turned and left her, closing the door to his bedroom as he went.

Sonia opened the door to find a huge bathroom that seemed to have been constructed in what would have been the third bedroom. Everything was adjusted for a nine-foot tall man. She turned in a circle, impressed that the military could get this right. Had Johnny chosen the modern fixtures or had the U.S. Marines done that? What about the overlarge towels and the woven rattan floor mat?

The toilet was so tall that, when she sat, her feet didn't touch the ground. After she finished she washed her hands in the sink, and realized that it was set so high that she had to raise her arms to shoulder level just to reach inside. The mirror gave her a perfect view of her forehead.

There was no soap on the sink, so she opened the medicine cabinet. The inside had a mirrored back so she could still see herself. She could also see the contents of the bottom shelf: mint mouthwash, dental floss, a toothbrush, whitening toothpaste, a bottle of liquid drain cleaner and a .44 Magnum. She frowned and lifted the drain cleaner. This didn't belong here. It should be under the sink, not near his toothbrush and mouthwash. Her gaze flicked back to the gun. That didn't belong here, either. A werewolf did not need a handgun for home defense.

So what were they doing in his bathroom?

Her eyes rounded at the realization.

They said his skin was bulletproof. But Sonia thought

if Johnny put that drain cleaner or the muzzle of that gun in his mouth…

Her skin flashed cold and gooseflesh rose on her arms as the truth hit her. Johnny wanted to die.

On the day she had arrived the captain had said Johnny was depressed and suicidal but she hadn't really believed it, until now.

Sonia stared at the evidence she could no longer deny.

She sensed him behind her. The moment she met his gaze in the mirror she saw him take in her horrified expression. His face went tight and his jaws locked. Then he lowered his snout and glared a challenge at her. She didn't pretend she didn't understand but met his cold stare.

Her heart hurt and she pressed a hand over the ache. "Oh, Johnny, no."

He reached past her and slammed the medicine cabinet door closed, removing the handgun from her line of sight. Then he took the drain cleaner from her trembling hands and placed it under his sink. Finally he grasped her wrist and pulled her from the bathroom.

"Johnny. You can't," she babbled. "You mustn't."

He kept walking and didn't stop until they were outside on the porch. The warm sunshine streamed down on the yard making everything look idyllic. It made what she had seen even more surreal. She tugged and he released her. They stood facing each other and then she threw herself at him, wrapping her arms about his middle as she burst into tears. He went still at that and then lifted his big heavy arms and patted her back. They gradually came to rest on her shoulders.

"Johnny!" she cried. "You can't kill yourself."

Wouldn't she if she were in his place? She didn't know. Her first thought was of Marianna and how hurt she would be. Johnny had a family, didn't he? What had the captain said? "You don't want to hurt your family. Your mom. Your sister. Julia…Joon." She rushed on, babbling now. "We have to go to the lab. They have something to show you. Maybe…" She didn't believe what she was about to say but she said it anyway. "Maybe they know how to fix you."

He blew out a breath. The air was a hot blast on her neck even in the warm sunshine. Then he peeled her away and stepped back. He descended the stairs with a heavy tread. At the bottom he looked back, with brows raised, as if to ask if she were coming or not.

Sonia charged after him. She had to get him to the captain.

Sonia and Johnny reached the back door of the medical building twenty minutes later. This entrance had an enclosed tunnel from the mountainside that allowed Johnny to come and go without drawing any notice. Johnny didn't like being the center of attention, according to her bunkmates. As the captain said, they all knew of Johnny, though not all had seen him. No one spoke of the captain's wife which made her wonder if they did not know what she was.

"Are you ready to go in?" she asked.

No. But go now.

The moment they passed the doors they received an escort through the facility and down into the basement. They passed several swooshing doors and signs that said Restricted. Finally they were led into a viewing room. Beyond the glass panels was a series of nine stainless steel doors about three feet square. They reminded Sonia of the dumbwaiters she had seen in a movie except these were three across and three down making a strange metal tic-tac-toe pattern. She noticed each door had a corresponding number painted above it.

Three men stood before the doors around a stainless-steel table that looked as if it were used for autopsies. The first was Captain MacConnelly. The second was the base commander, Major Paul Scofield. She had met him briefly on the day she arrived. She didn't know the third but he wore a lab coat. He was a paunchy clean-shaven man with a captain's bar on his collar, his double chin made more noticeable by the angle of his head. She glanced at Johnny who now rocked from side to side. Was it the lab coats or the place that made him uneasy?

"Just in there, Sergeant," said the shorter of their companions. The two marines clicked their heels and saluted. Johnny returned it and then headed for the door beside the glass viewing panels.

At the sound of the door opening MacConnelly's brow's lifted. Sonia wrinkled her nose at the odd combination of odors. There was antiseptic, bleach and the smell of urine. That last smell made her stomach cramp and her mind leaped back. It took a few moments to stop shaking. She glanced about in discomfort but all eyes were on Johnny.

"John." The captain extended his hand and Johnny shook it. There was no salute between them. Johnny did salute Scofield who returned the salute with a smile and a clap on Johnny's arm.

"Good to see you, son," said their commander.

Sonia held her salute but no one seemed to notice her. Finally the major turned to Sonia, flicking a quick salute and ending her misery. "I hear you've got our boy learning sign. Good work, Private."

He made it sound like she was training a pony to count. She forced a tight smile and wondered if she'd have a moment to speak to the captain about that gun in Johnny's bathroom.

MacConnelly extended a hand toward the other man as he spoke to Johnny. "You remember Dr. Dimitrie Zharov. Zharov has been experimenting with the blood you provided."

The two regarded each other warily. Sonia could see the tension between them. Was there history here or was Zharov just anxious around an unpredictable werewolf? Sonia understood it but realized she was no longer frightened of Johnny. Now she was frightened *for* him.

Johnny shifted from side to side, one arm across his middle as he gripped his opposite elbow. His nerves were understandable after what he'd been through.

Did the captain notice the horror in Johnny's eyes or the slow unconscious shaking of his head? She moved closer to him and grabbed his arm at the elbow, giving a little squeeze. He glanced down at her and she felt some of the tension ease from his muscles.

"We've given your blood to several types of animals," said Zharov. "It killed the rats, mice and rabbits. But the dogs tolerated it."

She felt his tension return at the word blood.

He signed, *How?*

She spoke up, interrupting Dr. Zharov. "He asked you, 'How?'"

The doctor cast her an annoyed glance then looked to MacConnelly.

The Captain motioned to her. "Doctor Zharov, Private Sonia Touma is Lam's translator."

Zharov looked down his nose at her and Johnny's arm went tense under her fingers.

"Please answer Sergeant Lam's question," said the captain.

"How what? It doesn't make any sense."

She turned to Johnny. He signed his question and she relayed it to Zharov. "He asks how his blood was given to them."

"Oh, well, by subcutaneous injection. The dogs changed immediately into a version of were…uh…species. You will see here." He walked to a panel of buttons, laid out like a telephone keypad and he pressed number nine. A perfectly adorable dog with short wiry white hair and deep brown eyes greeted them with a stretch that looked like a bow.

"This is subject number nine. It will receive the newest variation of the strain today. He should have had it earlier but I was instructed to wait for you."

And he didn't sound at all happy about that, thought Sonia.

The doctor turned to the panel and paused, finger poised above number eight. Sonia felt her stomach tighten in dread as she realized what was behind that next door.

"This subject received the last serum one week ago." The eighth small door slid open and Zharov stepped back. The creature inside leaped to its feet and began growling and throwing itself against the cage in a futile attempt to reach them. There were teeth marks on the steel, like punctures in soft wood. Sonia's mouth dropped open. The jaws where enormous and they snapped like a bear trap. The yellow eyes were familiar and the clawed front feet looked a lot like Johnny's. But there would be no mistaking it for anything but a were-creature. It spun in circles, biting the bars, vainly attempting to set its teeth into something, anything. It seemed mad.

Johnny signed, *Crazy.*

"Yes, I thought the same thing," she whispered and then raised her voice for the others. "He says it seems crazy."

Zharov answered, "Yes. They are all like that. Abnormal brain pattern. They attack anything they can reach. So I'm to show you the derivative of your blood that I've isolated. I've made two serums that show some promise." He pressed the second button revealing the next cage. Inside sat a mutt with a black muzzle and sandy fur. He trembled as he looked out at them with sad and hopeful eyes. "This is number seven. Received the first serum strain three weeks ago and I will be injecting number eight with the second serum, returning it to its original form. And I'll be using the first serum on number nine to create a were-dog. So, a very busy day."

He glanced to the captain who glared. The man acted as if informing Johnny was a nuisance. Zharov returned his attention to Lam. "We have mastered making were-dogs. Once in the were-form they stay that way without this." The doctor lifted a hypodermic needle filled with a clear orange liquid from the drawer beneath the table and then replaced it in favor of the shot that made were-creatures. Zharov hit the button to shut number eight. The were-dog made a final lunge for the bars before disappearing behind the descending door. The doctor then approached number nine, opening the cage and grabbing the dog's scruff to lift the skin from the body. When he raised the hypodermic Johnny grabbed Zharov's wrist. Zharov blanched. His fingers extended and the needle clattered to the floor. Johnny released the doctor and stooped to look at the dog. Why would the captain want Johnny to see a poor little dog go through what he had?

Johnny's hands flew into words.

She turned to the doctor. "He says, 'Change me back.'"

"Yes. That is what we all are working toward and I'd be one day closer if not for this interruption." The doctor massaged his wrist and then retrieved his needle, tucking it away in the drawer. Then he focused his attention on Johnny. "The captain wants you kept in the loop, so I've stopped my research to show you my progress." His tone radiated contempt. She wasn't sure if that was for the captain or if he resented having to show the lab rat his work. Either way she didn't like Zharov. The doctor regarded the panel of buttons and closed the gate to the ninth cage, trapping his subject again. That left only number seven. The gentle little dog that had apparently been a were-creature, though he showed no indication of it. Sonia glanced at door number nine and shuddered, knowing that sweet little dog had only received a stay of sentence and not a reprieve. But didn't they have to do this to find a cure for Johnny?

Zharov returned to the panel and faced them. "So here is my little dog and pony show. Would you like to see number eight injected and transformed? As you know, Sergeant Lam, I cannot inject the serum through the skin of a were-creature. So the injection goes in the mouth. It's not pleasant to watch. But you may stay if you wish." He turned his pale pitiless eyes on her now. "You might want to step out, Private."

She wanted to. She hated the cages and the needles and the smell of this place. Fear roiled in her stomach. She couldn't look at the cages without breaking into a sweat. Johnny noticed and grasped her elbow, giving it a squeeze. His brows lifted as he stared.

"I'm all right. This place…bad memories," she whispered. She wondered if the dogs were in the dark as she had been. She was trembling now, but she lifted her chin and met the doctor's gaze. It was his smile that tipped the scales. He expected her to run. She blew out a breath, still feeling nauseated.

"I'll stay." She spoke with a determination that she did not feel. She inched closer to Johnny who wrapped an arm about her.

She glanced at the captain who was staring at her with a strange look on his face. Zharov lifted a metal stick that had a short needle in the tip. He approached the were-dog's cage and opened the door. The dog lunged. Zharov was fast and efficient making a quick thrust with the pole which the dog immediately bit onto. Then he jabbed forward. Blood and saliva foamed from the creature's mouth. The animal fell back and went slack. The foaming got worse and the creature began to writhe and shake. The movements became less organized and grew into full-fledged convulsions. Sonia covered her mouth to stifle a cry.

"I warned you," said Zharov.

The creature went slack.

"Is it dead?" she whispered.

"No. Transition phase," said Zharov.

The dog now began to twitch as if in the throws

of some bad dream, but its eyes had rolled back in its head showing white bloodshot balls. The fur began to change with the size of the dog. It was shrinking before her eyes, deflating like a helium balloon. The claws retracted. The teeth drew back into the pink gums. Johnny stepped forward, peering at the dog that now seemed just an ordinary brown mutt. The whimpering started next and the sound broke Sonia's heart. The creature was obviously suffering. Johnny leaned so close he nearly pressed his head to the bars of the cage.

"Careful, Johnny," Sonia whispered.

Johnny reached in and touched its foot. The dog startled and its eyes popped open. It struggled to its feet and wobbled as it turned to bring its face near Johnny's.

"Step back," ordered Zharov.

The dog licked Johnny's face. Johnny reached a claw between the bars and scratched behind the dog's ears. He turned to MacConnelly, signing fast. The captain looked to her. What's he saying?

"He says, 'Now. Give me, now. Shot. Now.'"

Zharov threw up his hands and turned to the major. "I told you. What did you expect him to say?"

The commander stepped forward. "No, son. Not today. But soon. Mac here thought you should know how close we are, that all of us are working to bring you back. But we need a little more time. Can you give us that?"

Sonia held her breath. Did they know? Did they all know about that gun in his medicine cabinet?

All eyes turned to Johnny. His shoulders slumped and he signed to her.

"How long?" she repeated.

"I estimate a month," said Zharov. "Transformation is still unstable. I have variables to control, dosage amount to calculate. Too little and there is no effect. But too much damages the—"

"That's enough, Doc," said MacConnelly.

The doctor nodded. Damages the what? Sonia wondered. The nervous system? The brain? The heart? The possibilities were endless and each carried a different horror. Her stomach churned and she glanced to Johnny. But he did not seem to hear.

Johnny pointed to the other doors.

"Seven has remained transformed for three weeks," Zharov pointed to the next door as he continued speaking. "Six for four weeks and so forth."

Ten weeks of experiments, she realized.

Johnny stepped past him and pressed all the buttons.

"No," said Zharov.

"Johnny, wait," said MacConnelly.

But it was too late, the doors whooshed open. Number seven stood and stretched as the neighboring doors opened. But her attention passed over to the reclining creature in cage number six. The animal seemed to be barely breathing and blood leaked from his ears, nose and mouth. The rest of the cages were empty. A shiver went down her spine. Where were the dogs from weeks one to five?

"Damn it," said Zharov.

"Cover them!" ordered Scofield.

Mac scrambled to close the panel. All the doors swept down, dropping with the finality of a guillotine.

"Zharov, my office." Scofield stormed away with the good doctor trailing past.

Johnny stared at the closed stainless steel doors and then he looked at his captain.

"We'll figure it out, Johnny. We're close now. You have to believe me."

Johnny growled and lifted the steel table cleanly from the floor as easily as she might lift an aluminum folding chair. Then he threw it with such violence that it sailed across the room, crashing through the glass panels. He turned to cast one look at Captain MacConnelly before bounding out through the gaping hole he'd created and pushed open the door without using the knob. The panel sprang from its position taking part of the frame along with it. And then he was gone.

Sonia turned to her commanding officer. She wanted to shout at him for his stupidity but instead she did what was best for Johnny.

"Captain," Sonia said. He turned to her and she spilled her secret, about the drain cleaner and the gun. The captain's expression darkened and he nodded grimly.

"I've been seeing the signs. That's why we brought you in. Hoping a female could reach him." He dragged a hand over his cheek. "What a mess."

They stared at the wreckage Johnny had left.

The captain's voice was quiet now. "He won't even talk to me anymore. Does he talk to you?"

"Yes."

"Good. Go after him. You know the trail to his place?"

She nodded.

"Get a radio from security before you leave and call me on channel four if you find him. I'll follow in the Jeep."

"Yes, sir." Sonia hurried from the facility, stopping only to collect a new radio which she latched to her belt.

Then she set off up the hill along the trail she knew. She pushed herself to hurry, praying that Johnny did not do anything to hurt himself.

Chapter 6

By the time Sonia made it up the hill in the damp, humid air of midday, she was slick with sweat and puffing like a steam engine. At the first turnoff she headed to the right, thinking Johnny might have gone to the swimming lagoon to cool off. But she had miscalculated and instead of breaking out onto the large green grotto and the shimmering cascade of silvery water, she stumbled into the private yard of Captain MacConnelly and his vampire wife.

She staggered off the trail and found the woman in question on her mobile phone on the bridge that spanned the stream. Sonia now realized that the stream was the runoff from the swimming area that lay between the two homes. Brianna's gaze went to Sonia like a heat-seeking missile and Sonia heard her say, "She's here."

Sonia stilled as that prickling warning lifted the hairs

on her neck. She started to back out of the yard as Brianna held up a hand to stop her. Sonia disregarded this and retreated to cover. When she turned to run she found that the captain's wife stood on the path before her.

"Johnny told you about me, then." Brianna regarded Sonia with a furrowed brow and a tight expression. Was that grief shimmering in her leaf-green eyes?

Sonia felt a trickle of remorse that she didn't understand.

"I can see it in your eyes. Well, better that you know, I suppose."

Sonia swallowed hard as her gaze flicked to the trail and her escape and then back to meet Brianna's open stare.

Sonia's skin prickled a warning, but she remained still, suddenly unwilling to run. She couldn't out distance a vampire, that much was certain. Sonia had forgotten how beautiful this woman was. And now, at close range she could see the pure opal radiance of her skin and the sparkling clarity of her eyes. She'd pulled her fiery red hair back into a ponytail. The casual style only served to better reveal the perfect structure of her high cheekbones and heart-shaped face. Her lips were lush and full. Sonia stepped nearer.

"Close enough," said Brianna.

Sonia jolted to a stop having just realized she was creeping forward as one does with some beautiful wild animal they do not want to frighten but are desperate to touch.

"You're Sonia Touma, Johnny's teacher."

Sonia nodded, thinking Brianna's voice perfect for speaking. She should be on television or the radio.

"I'm Brianna. They told you I don't leave the house. That I don't like company."

"Yes, ma'am."

"A lie to protect humans, like you. I do like company and I work with humans, but for their safety my only contact with them is electronic."

Sonia began to wonder if Brianna was really that pretty or if this attraction was one of her powers. Sonia stared at the slight flush on Brianna's cheeks and took another step in her direction.

Brianna backed away. "You're doing it again."

Sonia stopped. "I'm sorry. I didn't realize.

"Happens all the time." She lifted the phone. "Travis just called. Asked me to search the mountain. Please wait here. I'll be right back."

That made no sense. It would take hours to search the mountain. Sonia opened her mouth to say so and Brianna disappeared right before her eyes. One moment she was there and the next, gone.

Sonia turned a complete circle and found no sign of her. Finally she lifted the radio and called her commanding officer. When Captain MacConnelly picked up she explained that someone named Travis had called his wife and that she had vanished.

"I'm Travis."

Of course he was. His real name wasn't Mac MacConnelly, she realized.

"Permission to continue to Sergeant Lam's quarters."

"No. She would have searched there by now. Just wait. Out." The radio when dead and she returned it to her belt.

Wait. Where? Should she go in and fix a sandwich or sit in the inviting hammock? Sonia crossed the bridge and had just set foot onto the grass on the opposite bank when Brianna MacConnelly reappeared.

Sonia clutched her heart and the bridge rail simultaneously. "Holy Mother of God!"

Brianna smiled. "Yeah, I get that from Travis, too. It's jarring."

"How do you disappear?"

"I don't. I just move too fast for you to see. So I found Johnny. He's at his place. He's upset. I asked him if he wanted me to stay with him. He said he wanted you."

Sonia felt that attraction for this woman stir again, the insistent pull to move closer. This time she resisted and it faded like smoke.

"He listened to me and nodded when I said you were on the way. He was signing but I can't read sign, only the alphabet. Maybe you should teach me and Travis, too. Especially if they can't change him back."

The realization struck Sonia so hard she jolted. Brianna stopped speaking and stared with concern. Of course! That's why Johnny didn't want to learn sign language. Learning sign was an admission that he wasn't turning back.

"It was so obvious," she muttered.

"What was?"

"If he learns sign, he won't turn back.

Brianna shook her head. "That doesn't make any sense."

"Yes, it does, because Lam only needs sign if he's a werewolf. His captain's insistence that he learn must have seemed like an admission that they can't help him. But he's stubborn. He's not giving up even if everyone else is, so that's why he has been so determined not to learn."

Brianna nodded. "Mac should have figured that out."

Sonia thought of the way the captain looked at Johnny when Johnny wasn't looking back. It was an expression riddled with such guilt it made Sonia wince just recalling it. "Why is the captain so pushy about this?"

Brianna drew a long breath and then released it, turning on the bridge to stare at the water flowing below them. "Is that how he comes across?"

Sonia didn't answer as she watched this vampire sweep a strand of copper-red hair from her pale face.

"They're alike, you know?" said Brianna.

"Alike?" Her earlier assumption regarding her captain returned to Sonia and she hugged herself and hunched bracing for Brianna's next words. Confirmation was quick.

"They are both werewolves."

Sonia shook her head, denying what her gut told her was true.

Brianna waited until Sonia met her gaze before continuing. "The thing that attacked Johnny also attacked my husband. At the same time. It bit him, too. He still has the scars." She made a circular sweep about her own shoulder and chest. "After that he began changing into the same thing that Johnny became, only his fur is gray like a timber wolf's. Oh, and his eyes are blue, not yellow."

"He's changing into a werewolf, too?"

"He *is* a werewolf. That's why he can be near me without suffering harm. He's no longer human. But Mac can change shape at will. All werewolves can, except Johnny."

"There are more of them?"

"Many. But none here. Just the two of them. The others work with various government agencies. Make perfect body guards as they are the only ones that can stop vampire assassins."

"Vampire what?"

Brianna blew out a breath. "Assassins. I thought you should know. I don't have security clearance to tell you things like the others, but you are up on this hillside and that means you're in danger, too."

"From Lam and your husband?"

"Not from them."

"They're after you? Male vampires?"

"Yes. They're called chasers. They capture the females. Usually they know where to find them as the males are required to register any sexual encounter with human females that don't result in a human's death. But I'm unusual even by vampire standards."

"Why do they want you?"

"They train their females as killers, too, though a different kind entirely. They're all mercenaries, hiring to the highest bidder. A female's kills are undetectable since the energy draw shows up as a stroke or heart attack. Sleeping with me is deadly, unless you're a werewolf."

Sonia found herself backing away.

"I know it's terrible. Unlike the males, we are hard to spot. They are ugly as vampire bats. But we have some vulnerabilities. Werewolves for one. Wounds inflicted by shifters don't heal. Neither do injuries caused by anything iron until the metal is removed. Then we regenerate zip-zap. I think that's where the folklore about stakes and crosses started. Really what you need is an iron stake, like a section of rebar."

"Why are you telling me this?"

"Because they're hunting me and they feed on human blood."

"Do you drink blood?"

"I'm a vegetarian."

"But you feed on energy."

"Not exactly. I don't need it. The draw is involuntary on my part. Just happens, like, uh…" She wiggled her fingers and glanced skyward as if searching for something. "Like oxygen. You don't intentionally draw it from the air. You just do. Same with me and a person's life force."

"That's terrible."

Brianna's smile faded. "Yes. It *is* terrible."

Sonia wondered why Johnny wanted to keep her alive? Then her earlier thought returned to her.

"So Johnny's up here to protect you?"

"No. That's my husband's job."

"Then why doesn't Johnny live down below with the rest of us?"

"He prefers it here on the hill."

Sonia admitted she did, as well.

"Johnny's mission is to keep fighting until they can get him to shift back voluntarily. Then he can have a more normal life, visit his family and…" She looked away.

"His son?"

"Johnny would like that. But he can't."

"They'll make him into a bodyguard?"

"Assign him, yes. He wants that. It's a prestigious post. Protecting the president or other vital American targets. He told me he'd be honored. And I know he hates vampires. It's instinctive."

"All vampires?"

"Yes, well, initially. He's made me an exception, thankfully. Now you'd best go check on Johnny."

Sonia was about to agree, but Brianna disappeared.

Sonia reached Johnny's home a little after twelve-hundred, hot, thirsty and worried. Upon entering the clearing about his home, the first thing she noticed was one of the patio chairs lodged in the top of a palm tree at the side of the yard. The second thing was the eerie silence.

"Johnny?" she called but received no answer. Brianna's earlier assurance did not relieve the tiny heartbeat of panic in her throat so she crossed the yard at a run. Her mind filled with terrible images of a pistol placed in Johnny's mouth and liquid drain cleaner eating away the lining of his stomach. She hit a dead run as she charged up the porch stairs.

She heaved open the front door and stumbled in to find Johnny in the kitchen lifting a glass to his lips. Sonia charged across the room and slapped the glass from his hand. The plastic tumbler bounced as clear fluid splashed over the wide boards of his kitchen.

He lifted both his palms up with a clear question on his face.

"What is that?"

He reached for the faucet over the sink and turned the stream on and then off.

Water, she realized. Sonia grabbed the counter and dropped her forehead to her hand. "I'm sorry. I thought… I thought…" She turned her head and stared up at him. "It was horrible, wasn't it?"

He nodded.

She told herself not to, but somehow she needed his touch. Sonia stepped forward arms extended and he opened for her, gathering her up and rocking her as she clung tight. She started talking, babbling about the dogs and the empty cages. But how they were making progress. They needed more time. Johnny held her close and rubbed her back.

A voice came from the open door. "Johnny!"

Sonia sprang from Johnny's arms as if pulled by a bungee and snapped a salute. They both turned to see the captain standing in the door.

"Oh." His eyes swept from her to Johnny and back to her again. He returned Sonia's salute. "At ease, Touma. You both all right?"

"Yes. That is, I think so." She deferred to Johnny.

The captain came forward. "I had no idea those dogs were dying. But Zharov says that it has something to do with their anatomy which is different than a man's. I don't know." He rubbed his neck. "Anyway, we're close. Really close. You have to hang in there, buddy."

Johnny nodded.

"I'll stop back if I have more information." The captain turned to her. "You're staying awhile?"

She wasn't sure if it was an order or a suggestion but she nodded. "Yes."

"I'll tell them not to expect you. Call for a pickup if you need one."

If?

Sonia's brow furrowed. It wasn't an order, but she got the impression the captain didn't want Johnny left alone. "I'm heading out." He thumbed over his shoulder and backed from the room as if it might be rigged with trip wires. Seeing him flustered made him seem more human to Sonia which was ironic because now she knew that he wasn't human at all.

Did it hurt to change forms?

Johnny lifted a finger to her and then followed the captain, snatching the whiteboard from the counter as he went. He was gone long enough for Sonia to realize she had been hugging Johnny and the captain had seen them. She felt sick to her stomach wondering what would happen next. A reprimand at least. She was blowing it again. She felt it—getting too personal. Sonia looked to the back door and wondered if she should just leave. Johnny seemed all right. But what if he wasn't?

Sonia grabbed a roll of paper towels from under the sink and began sopping up the spill. The door opened and closed. Sonia hoped Johnny was alone. She heard his huffing sound and realized he could not see her behind the counter.

"In here."

A moment later he was squatting before her, dish towel in hand, helping her clean up.

"Is he gone?"

Johnny confirmed that with the sign for yes, rather than a nod.

"Am I in trouble?"

Why?

"He caught me hugging you."

No trouble. More lab tomorrow at noon.

"Both of us?"

Yes.

She was squatting there before him when she spilled her other worry.

"I met her."

Johnny fixed Sonia with his steady gaze and nodded. Had Brianna told him, then?

"She told me about the chasers. Johnny, do you think
the captain is trying to help you or keep you like this
as a watchdog for his wife?"

Johnny's eyes went hard and he shook his head. He
signed, *I trust Captain.*

"All right."

"What do you think about the experiments?"

Sad. They try.

"Yes. And they can change them back but…" Best
not finish that train of thought. "But I'm sure they will
figure out what went wrong. I hope it's soon." She
drummed her fingers on the counter and then recognized what she was doing and stopped.

"This is impossible. All of it."

Johnny cocked his head as if to say, *really?* He
scratched beneath his furry extended jaw as evidence
that it was all happening, all real.

"So the captain is a werewolf, a gray one, who can
change at will." Her eyebrows lifted as she gasped. "Is
he naked when he transforms?"

Johnny nodded.

"Does it hurt?"

He signed, *Don't know. Think so. Look like pain.*

But Johnny couldn't know himself because he had
never changed from this form. He'd been this shaggy
fearsome looking creature since he'd been attacked in
Afghanistan. Where had the creature bitten him? She
could not see any scars, but then his shaggy coat covered him from nose to toes. She wouldn't dwell on this.
If she expected Johnny to move past it, she needed to,
as well. But it wasn't fair. She breathed deeply. *Let it go.*

Sonia folded her arms around her middle and stared out the kitchen window at the dense jungle that flowed up the hill.

After a moment, she realized she was searching for movement. Were the vampires out there right now? If they were would she even see them coming? Brianna moved too fast to see. What if they killed Johnny? She found that prospect brought a sharp stab of pain to her heart.

"I'm frightened for you and for the captain."

Johnny left his seat and rummaged in the kitchen junk drawer for a pen and pad. Then he wrote, "Natural enemies. We kill them. I'm a marine, Sonia. I might not look it but I'm a marine and marine's protect people."

"Yes. I know you are."

He was a werewolf and his neighbor was a vampire. But what Sonia had learned about the mercenary males, it made her skin go cold. Her smile faded.

"Brianna said the males are ugly."

Johnny nodded and then drew a quick sketch of a thing with pointed ears, slanted eyes. Slitted nostrils and needlelike canines. She stared in horror at the line drawing and then at him.

"Really?"

He nodded.

"No wonder they only come out at night."

He shook his head and signed, *Any time.*

She stared back at the drawing. Johnny nudged her and she had to take a fast side step to keep from falling over.

Don't worry. I keep you safe.

"Yes. I know that." She set aside the sketch and

rubbed her hands together. "Are you hungry? I can fix you something?"

Not hungry.

"Johnny, they are going to figure it out. And when they do you are taking me out for dinner and dancing."

His gaze snapped to hers and his brow lifted as if he was checking to see if she was making fun of him. She wasn't.

"I'm serious. When you turn back, I want you to take me out."

He nodded slowly. *A D-A-T-E.* Then he lifted his brows.

"Yes. A date." She took his hand, happy to see the hope in his eyes and feel the warm reassurance of his big, strong hand. "And Johnny? Learning to sign isn't going to keep you from turning back. It will just make the waiting easier."

He did a double take at her words and straightened. His jaw bunched but he nodded his understanding.

They stared at each other. That's what this was about really. Overcoming fear. He was afraid of waiting for a cure that would never come. She was afraid of screwing up again.

"I'm going to stick this out and so are you."

This time he drew her into his arms and held her. She closed her eyes, feeling safe and hopeful. How ridiculous, she thought. She'd never been in more danger in her life. And then one of those moments from her past sprang into her mind with the subtly of a popping jack-in-the-box. She shoved it back down, acknowledging that she'd been in real jeopardy then, too. Not all monsters had fangs and fur. Some came in a bottle.

She pushed away as she muttered that she was hungry. Turning to Johnny for comfort was just a bad idea. He wasn't some overgrown teddy bear and she knew she was blurring the lines between them again. Maybe Johnny needed comfort as much as she did but that wasn't somewhere she was willing to go.

They busied themselves fixing a meal and then eating it at the counter. After that she made a call to the captain who sent a driver to pick her up. A few minutes later the horn blared. Sonia said goodbye hesitant now to leave him alone.

"You'll be all right?"

He nodded, keeping his moonlike eyes on her. She hesitated wanting to go, feeling the need to stay. The horn sounded again.

"Damn it," she muttered. "I'll see you tomorrow. Right?"

He looked weary as he nodded again and guided her out. He stood on the porch as she descended to the driveway. When she looked back she could not see him in the dark, but she could see the strange green glow of his eyes. They glimmered like an animal just outside the circle of light. A chill went up her spine as she waved and jogged to the comfort of glowing headlights.

She knew how long the nights could be. Would he be all right alone?

The next day, Sonia called for a ride before breakfast. She hadn't slept thinking of Johnny alone with that damned gun. When she got to his place it was to find his house empty. She pounded and called and peeked in the windows.

Why had she left him alone? Why hadn't the captain sent someone to stay with him last night?

As she grabbed the phone that called the MPs and flipped it open, she heard a familiar huffing. She spun and saw Johnny striding across the yard.

She pounded down the stairs to meet him halfway and then started shouting at him like a maniac.

"Where the hell were you? You scared me half to death. I thought you were dead in there." She pointed toward his home.

Johnny lowered his snout and his brow simultaneously as she finally stopped yelling. Her lower lip began to quiver. He patted her shoulder and she sidled closer resting her forehead on the massive hairy plane of his chest.

Finally she drew back and signed that she was sorry.

Johnny blew out a breath that made his gums flap. Then he signed that they should go swimming.

She began shaking her head before he even finished the sign, her skin flashing cold in dread.

"I don't swim."

W-A-D-E.

She didn't want to, but she agreed just to please him. Damn she didn't even have a bathing suit.

Twenty minutes later she was up to her neck in the lovely deep pool which seemed less serene with her flapping about in the water like a whirligig.

Somehow over the course of the morning, Sonia learned to keep the water from going up her nose as she made slow, steady progress across the pool. The water had become a cool refuge from the tropical heat. Her olive green tank top and bikini briefs made an acceptable bathing suit and paddling in a grotto sure beat waiting for an open shower at the barracks. Johnny was a patient teacher and in just one morning had straightened out her kick and taught her the arm motion for the breast stroke.

She reached the volcanic rock that edged the pool near the falls. Puffing and gasping, she laughed at the sheer joy of her accomplishment. Johnny had kept pace with her on the journey, but this time she had not clung to him midcourse. She'd made it all the way without help.

He lifted a hand offering her a high five. She slapped his hand hard.

"I did it."

Again.

"No way. I'm going to soak my sore muscles in that waterfall and then I'm going to sunbathe. Lesson over."

Johnny offered a hand and then helped her into a spot where the water gently cascaded over her like a warm shower.

"All I need is soap."

He grinned. The horror of yesterday seemed to have faded for them both. The water worked its magic massaging away the soreness from her neck and back. Johnny swam as she enjoyed the falls. Afterward, she stretched out on the towel Johnny had given her and gazed up at the patch of blue sky. He left the pool and lounged beside her, water running in rivulets off his wet coat. It took a moment to realize what she was feeling, it had been so long.

She was happy. She felt secure and did not worry where her next meal would come from or if the cops would be at her house. She didn't worry if her little sister was safe or if her mother had drunk their rent away. Everything was all right.

It was an unfamiliar feeling, light and airy. She thought she might float right up there into the blue sky.

Something brushed her arm. She turned her head to see Johnny lying on his back. The sun made his wet black fur glisten with a glossy gleam. With his fur matted to his skin, it was easier to see his form. His musculature was more gladiator than average Joe, but he did not seem animal to her until she looked at his face. In profile his snout, nose and canine jaws were startling. He did not look human, but she was becoming more accustomed to his appearance. As if sensing her scrutiny, he opened one yellow eye.

He patted his chest with both hands in the sign for happy and then lifted a tufted brow.

"Yes. Very. I'm afraid someone will come and snatch it away again."

Again? His brows lifted.

She rested one forearm across her brow and glanced at the sky, letting the sun warm her damp skin. She held back a moment longer and then let it out. She'd never told a soul. But she already knew that she'd tell Johnny. The decision made, she rolled to her side, propping herself up on an elbow. Sonia thought back and the tension crept back into her joints as she wondered if he'd use this later to humiliate her.

She rolled to a seated position, folding her legs like a meditating yogi so she could use both hands to sign.

"All right. Remember when I told you I was in foster care?" She didn't wait for an answer, just kept signing and speaking, the signs flowing as she forced herself to release this secret. He nodded that he remembered. She didn't want to look at him when she told him, so she stared at the falls and the water cascading in ribbons onto the rocks as she spoke. "Well, I want to tell you why."

Johnny stretched out on his side. It was hard telling him that her mom had not been a very good mother. Sonia had learned from birth that this was not a topic that was to be mentioned, so she danced around the problem like a matador sticking the bull a few times to weaken it. Her mention of not having enough food caused one of her eyes to twitch. She glanced at him to find his jaw locked and his gaze steady. Sonia looked away again, speaking to the pool before her and then taking a quick glimpse at him when the anxiety grew too much. When she told him that she'd often eaten her Cheerios as her mom poured herself a tall glass of gin, no ice, Johnny tapped his front teeth. The gesture seemed unconscious. She pressed her lips together then watched the water falling and falling. Letting go at the top, regrouping into calm depths below. She let go, too.

"She wasn't too bad when I was little. Mostly just coming home drunk and falling asleep on the sofa. But she wasn't really asleep. You know?"

Johnny's nod was barely perceptible and there was a tension in his shoulders now, a quiet, deadly stillness.

"Then she got fired. That first time really upset her and she said she'd stopped drinking, but then I realized she was just putting it in her juice. I got Marianna up and dressed for school because Mama wasn't ever up at that hour. She got work in a bar. Well, she got worse. Child services came a few times. Marianna and I tried to clean up, but they saw the bottles on the curb in the recycling. It was the wrong day for recycling. That was the first time they took us."

Johnny reached over and grasped her hand. The

warmth and the pressure gave her courage. She held on a minute and then thought she'd just stop right there. The rest seared her insides. But Johnny released her hand and signed for her to go on. She didn't want to but she did.

She continued to sign. "But it wasn't the last. Mama got us back and then showed up drunk at school. I was in third grade. She tried to pick up Marianna, too, but she ran and Mama couldn't catch her. When we heard the sirens, Mama left her and took me. I found out later that the school called the cops but they didn't have the right address because Mama had moved us to a hotel. It was a bad hotel. Not the kind you stay on vacation but where people live all the time. The room smelled like cigarettes and there was stuff in the dressers that wasn't ours. It took them two days to find us. Mama…" Sonia's voice broke. She swallowed, forcing the lump down with the shame. "It took them two days." Sonia looked away. "I was screaming that she couldn't leave Marianna at the school. We had to find her and she said if I was going to tell the school counselor that she was an unfit mother then maybe I didn't need a mother anymore." Sonia bowed her head. "She locked me in a dog cage that was in the room. The big kind that you keep animals in at night. It was cream-colored plastic on the sides and the front and back had a grate that you opened from the outside but I couldn't reach the latch. She left me so I tried to claw through the plastic." She looked at her own fingers remembering the ragged nails and bloody tips. "And I was screaming. It smelled like a dog in there and I got…well, I still don't like closed spaces. I can't stand them. Then those dogs at the lab were in those little cages and I could smell them."

Johnny lifted a finger and scooped a tear from her cheek. She rolled against him, her back to his front. He held her tight, just tight enough to make her feel safe.

She stopped speaking, sharing this part only in sign. She felt him bend to look over her shoulder, focusing on her hands.

They smelled like piss and fear, just like me.... The police found me. I don't remember all of it. I was kind of a mess. Still am, I guess. So I don't tell people about it and I don't let people get inside. It's too risky. But then, you've had a rough time, too, and I decided...

Johnny finished the sentence for her.

He signed, *To trust me.*

Sonia gave a shuttering sob and nodded. She spun to face him, speaking in a strained voice as she signed, "I didn't know you when I came here. I was just afraid. Anything seemed better than prison, even teaching a werewolf. But you're not a werewolf. Not to me. But when I think of that cell, I can't breathe. I get dizzy and sick. It's like I'll never be free of that damned cage."

That's why you stayed.

"Yes." Sonia smiled. "But not why I'm staying now. The captain knows. I'm sure of it. He must have seen it in my file and knew I couldn't quit. Anyway, my mama lost us for the second time then. We became wards of the state of New York for almost a year. Foster care sucked but no one forgot to feed me. Mama cleaned up and they sent us back to her again, but that didn't last. The next time she showed up drunk at our school, Marianna got a golden ticket out of there and I got placed in a group home 'til eighteen. I wonder what she'll do after college. College." She sighed at the wonder of it. "I thought I'd be out of the Marines the same time she got out of school. We could get a place together, like a home. Just an apartment, but ours, you know? I don't know. It's hard to make plans. Life is unpredictable, right?"

Yes, he signed. If anyone knew how unpredictable life could be it was Sergeant John Loc Lam. *Won't let you go to jail.*

Gratitude squeezed her heart and she stared up at his big, lovable face. "I believe you." She lifted a hand and stroked his cheek.

His eyes drifted closed.

"And you're still taking me dancing?"

His eyes opened and they seemed sad and she realized in that moment that he didn't believe it would ever happen.

"We *are* going dancing, Johnny. Believe it."

Okay.

Her fingers slid down his strong neck and came to rest in the soft hair of his chest. She remembered something Brianna said and drew back to sign as she spoke.

"Hey? Have you seen the captain's scars from the werewolf attack?"

He nodded, his expression curious now, as if he didn't know where she was going with this.

"So where are yours?"

He frowned and he stared at her a long silent moment before signing that he didn't know.

"But you must have scars. Where did it bite you?"

Johnny lifted his index finger to his chest.

I, she read.

Then he crossed his hands at the wrist and swept them in opposite directions.

Don't.

Now he had his thumb at his forehead an instant before he swept it down to contact his other thumb, tapping them once.

Remember.

"You don't remember?"

Chapter 7

Hagan Dowling sat before his laptop's web camera as his superior's face came on his screen. Burne Farrell lifted his chin, revealing the distended blue ropelike arteries branching out over his throat. Their engorged appearance showed that he had recently fed.

Looking at his own hands seemed preferable to looking at his superior's slitted nose and spiny rodentlike teeth punctuated by two menacing fangs protruding from his liver-colored lips.

Hagan tried not to stare at the new purple blood spots that had appeared on his superior's neck and forehead since their last meeting only two weeks ago. When they had met ten years ago, Burne Farrell was in his prime, his skin an admirable lavender shade that seemed preferable to the white cast of his own dermis. But now that middle age had taken a firm grip on him, he grew more hideous with each meeting.

"So you have arrived," said Burne.

Hagan nodded, superstitiously checking his own hands for any sign of the dreaded purple stains before reducing the size of his superior's image to that of a matchbook. "Yes, sir. We are on the main island of Hawaii. The team's initial sweep located one female."

Farrell rose so quickly his face disappeared from view and the camera now relayed a view of his mint-green dress shirt and the black belt with gold buckle that held up his gray trousers. "Vittori?"

"No, sir. Just an ordinary female. Vampire. Tenth generation from her scent."

Farrell sank back to his chair, his expression peevish now.

"She is perhaps two years past her womanhood. Her father reported her conception but at the time of her first bleed, her mother went into hiding. She was easy to track."

"Then why the two years lost? She might have had a babe twice already."

"It is the backlog of missing vampires. My MV list is growing longer because of the hunt for Brianna Vittori." He glanced up now, not wanting to be obvious in his distaste. Burne's condition awaited them all unless they fell to the brutish werewolves.

His superior smiled, showing his two rodent incisors. "But she will be worth the trouble. First generation. Who knows what her male children might look like?"

Hagan knew from the obsession that Burne Farrell showed for Brianna Vitorri that his supervisor wanted her personally. But Hagan planned to be the first to locate her and first to impregnate her. If he was virile and she fertile than they might make a son whose skin did not speak of death and whose face that, if not comely, might not be so hideous that he was condemned to walk only in darkness.

"This latest capture is secured. I ask permission to let my men have this female capture as it will be some weeks before they can report to the training facility and several days before she can be safely transported for formal indoctrination."

"Granted. See that they don't feed on her. Such entertainment needs preparation. Just sex. You understand?"

"Of course, sir."

Farrell aimed a blotchy finger at the camera. "Find me Vitorri, Dowling. Find her."

His superior clicked a button, swore and then disappeared from his computer screen.

"Oh, I certainly intend to find her—for myself."

Over the next ten days, Sonia taught Johnny to sign in the afternoons and stayed for supper most evenings. Johnny had kept her secret and had not mentioned her disclosure again. He also rarely used his compliance as a weapon to get her to tell him personal information, which was a relief.

She might have actually begun to feel comfortable here until she recalled they could transfer her in an eyeblink. It was wiser not to lower her guard. Johnny liked her and that was good only because it ensured she could stay a little longer. But this was no more permanent than any of her other living situations.

No more permanent than anything had ever been in her life.

Still, he was a good student and his progress made her proud.

His sign vocabulary was progressing very fast now and he could carry on a conversation without breaking to finger spell words. He finally admitted that he was using the book and the websites she recommended to study at night after she had gone. When Johnny discovered that nicknames were common among the deaf community, to keep from having to finger spell out their names, he took to calling her Kitten. Kitten was the sign for baby and cat combined. At his suggestion, she called him Wolf, the sign that involved drawing her fingers outward from her face and nose to simulate his long snout.

On some occasions Brianna appeared in the late afternoon, seeming to enjoy chatting with Johnny now that he had a translator and their conversations were no longer one-sided. The captain's wife even started picking up some signs herself.

He had not told Sonia anymore about the werewolf attack or why he could not remember, but he wanted to talk about her. She permitted his questions glad that they no longer seemed an inquisition but simple interest in her.

Today, as they sat side by side on the mossy bank of his swimming spot, Johnny asked about her mom's current location which was in Fishkill Correctional Facility in Upstate New York. Sonia did not write her mom but her sister did and kept her abreast of more information than she wanted to hear. All Sonia wanted was to pretend she had a normal childhood that didn't involve her mother putting her in a dog carrier. She'd told Johnny as much and he said he thought she should talk to someone about it.

"You are someone," she reminded him.

When he pressed, she said she would if he would and he let the matter drop.

They had made their way back up the trail as the afternoon crept toward evening. Tomorrow was a big day. The doctors wanted to show Johnny something at the lab again and she'd been ordered to get Johnny to the medical facility tomorrow. She planned to walk up to get him and he'd agreed to go with her but after the last time, they were both dreading what might happen. She knew this because they were both avoiding speaking about the appointment. Perhaps that was why Johnny chose the walk back up the hill as the time to tell her about his family. He had a sister, Julia, which Sonia knew from her briefing, but she didn't know that Julia was planning to attend the University of California, Berkeley, come fall and Johnny was worried about the cost and strain to his mother's shaky finances.

He also said his mom was a widow who had tried to manage their family's Chinese restaurant after his dad's heart attack, but had failed, nearly losing the house with the business. He'd used his signing bonus to settle that debt, but their house was still underwater and there was no money for Julia's schooling. Sonia began to see why Johnny was so eager to get back in action. Combat duty came with more pay.

Too many D-E-B-T, he signed.

"So I'm a marine because I broke into a house and you're a marine because you wanted to help your mother keep hers."

And serve my country.

"That makes you a saint and me…well, not a saint."

He gave her a little pat on the shoulder that she found comforting. He had a way of making her feel hopeful.

As if it would all be okay even when she knew better. This was one of those plateaus that came before she fell back into a valley. At least this time she saw it coming. She was sick of thinking things would be different because they never were. Not for her, anyway.

On the walk from the swimming spot to his home, he looked out for her, helping her where she needed and letting her alone when she didn't. She'd never had someone who listened as intently as Johnny or who seemed to understand her quite so well. He accepted her, she realized, warts and all. He might not be all human, but he didn't have the fears that she carried about like some thorny armor.

When they reached his house, he convinced her to stay for supper. That wasn't difficult as she was tempted by his gentle presence as much as the chance to skip another meal served on a tray. Three square meals the military promised and they were square, unless you were in the field and then they came in sturdy little plastic packets.

Back inside his quarters, they found themselves to be ravenous. She rummaged in his cupboards, taking out plates and silverware. She excused herself to use his bathroom and could not resist looking in his medicine cabinet. No gun, no drain cleaner. Where had he put them?

She was tempted to search, but instead she returned to him. His quarters were so cozy that all she needed was her kit and she could move right in. Sonia stilled at the thought. This wasn't her home. It was Johnny's. She didn't have a home. Had never had one.

Johnny gave her a toothy smile and pointed to the

grill. He had a whole fish on there that had turned red with the cooking.

"What in the world? It's still got its head."

He flipped the fish in one smooth motion.

"I've never eaten a whole fish on the bone before. Just fish sticks."

Johnny made a pained face and shook his head in disgust.

"I know, you learned to cook from your dad, right? He must have been something."

Johnny had a nostalgic look in his eyes when he nodded this time.

"Never knew my dad. Marianna and I, we have different fathers. I asked to see a picture of mine once and, oh, never mind, it's too sad."

Johnny motioned for her to continue.

"She didn't have a picture. So I asked her when she was drunk and she said she wasn't sure who my father was. But she knew Marianna's and he was a mean son of a bitch. Trucker, she said. I was just an accident."

B-L-E-S-S-I-N-G, he signed.

She gave a mirthless laugh. "To who?"

To me.

She felt herself warming up inside like a flower coated in frost when the sun is finally strong enough to melt the crystals. The warning bells sounded next. *Don't get attached. It will only make it harder when they transfer you.*

He lifted the wine bottle.

She shook her head. "I don't drink. Too many drunks on my mother's side for me to take a chance."

He set the bottle out of sight.

He explained with sign and finger spelling that he

couldn't get drunk since the attack. Something had happened in the change. After supper, Johnny suggested a movie. He had an online video package and he let her pick. She hadn't been to a movie in months.

"We should go to a movie, too. Do they have a movie theater in town."

He nodded yes and signed, *Off island.*

They settled in, she on the couch while he sprawled on wide cushions on the floor, his broad head propped up against the couch just a few inches from her. He lay so close that she could have reached out to stroke his head from where she lay on the sofa and she found it a struggle not to do so. Why did she always want to touch him?

The movie she selected popped on.

She grinned. "So much better than fighting for computer time."

Write sister here. My computer.

The movie was a romantic comedy with that blonde actress who had such great comedic timing. She felt warm and peaceful and happier than she could remember. Johnny had given her something that she had been avoiding for so long she hadn't even realized she was missing it—friendship. But she didn't make friends. Too much risk. She yawned. Still, it would be nice. She hadn't planned to doze off but she did and the next thing she knew the sun was in her face and she found herself stretched out under a coverlet on Johnny's couch.

She threw herself upright and scrambled to her feet. "Holy shit!"

A moment later Johnny charged down the hall looking frightening as hell. He glanced past her and she realized he was searching for whatever it was that made her yell. She stilled, realizing he was searching for vampires. She'd actually forgotten that there were monsters out hunting for the captain's wife.

She lifted her hands. "I'm fine. It's okay."

Johnny skidded to a halt.

"But I fell asleep! I was here all night. Oh, God. What are they going to do to me now?"

Johnny signed, *Nothing. You with me.*

"I don't have permission to come and go as I please. The captain said I could spend the day. Oh, I have to report in."

She asked to use Johnny's phone and failed to reach her sergeant. *Screwed,* she realized as she made quick use of the bathroom before reemerging a few moments later, her face wet from the water she's splashed over it.

Breakfast? he asked.

"No. I'll see you at noon, Wolf, at the lab. If I'm not there come find me please."

Sonia hit the trail and headed back to the base at a full out run. Once there she could not find her supervisor and knew she'd catch hell later but she had to get to the lab for Johnny. She missed breakfast and had time only to grab a shower and change into her uniform before it was time to report. When she reached the medical facility it was to find her captain waiting for her like a one-man firing squad. Her stomach turned a full twisting somersault as she realized he had been looking for her. She snapped to attention.

"Where is he?" he asked as he returned her salute with a slashing motion that reminded her of a machete slicing through the air.

Her stomach dropped an inch as she realized that

Johnny was a no-show. She'd been so caught up on her unplanned sleepover that she'd forgotten her job was to get Johnny's furry ass to the medical facility.

"He said he'd meet me here." Had he? She wasn't exactly sure what he'd said beyond offering her breakfast.

"Do you not remember me telling you yesterday to bring him along, Private?"

"I'll call him, sir."

"He won't answer," he muttered as he reached for his cell phone and dialed. And he was right. Johnny didn't.

"He might be on his way." Or she might just be done for.

The captain stared her down. As she studied her toes waiting for whatever consequences the captain might deem appropriate his phone jangled. He snapped it on and lifted it to his ear.

"MacConnelly," he barked. His gaze flicked to her as he listened. "Got it." He disconnected the call, his eyes still on her. "He's here." His tone changed, not friendly exactly but more respectful. "I don't know how you do it."

Neither did she, but he seemed in a mood less likely to result in him tearing her a new asshole. Now the captain's gaze turned speculative.

She shifted under his scrutiny. Sonia needed to get something off her chest. Johnny's revelation about the attack troubled her and she was pretty sure there would never be a good time to tell her captain about it. So she could either keep her mouth shut, which was better for her or she could speak up, which might be better for Johnny.

"Sir?"

"Touma?" His tone became cautious and his eyes narrowed.

She swallowed back her uncertainty and ignored the voice that warned that she should just mind her own business.

"Johnny told me he doesn't remember the attack."

His familiar frown deepened the lines on his face.

"Of course he does. He was there."

"He doesn't, sir. He told me he doesn't."

"Amnesia?"

"I don't know, sir. Just wanted to bring it to your attention is all."

"I'll look into it. Now meet Johnny at the lab. He's on his way. I'll see you there."

She saluted and when he returned it, she did an about-face but did not get far before his words stopped her.

"Thank you, Private."

She glanced back, surprised to see the sincerity of his expression.

"Yes, sir."

She reported to security and was guided to a different part of the facility and directly into one of the lab's examination rooms. She'd expected to find Johnny but the room was vacant. It could have come straight from any doctor's office except there were no windows. The heavy metal door swung shut behind her. The moment the door clicked she felt trapped. Cold sweat covered her as she tried to breathe, but the walls seemed to close in on her and she found herself panting like a dog.

She pounded on the door until her arms ached. Finally the door swung open and a marine stood there, one hand on the latch and his eyes on her.

She flung herself at him and he wrapped his arms around her while she shook like the last leaf on the tree.

"Hey," he cooed. "What's wrong?"

She gasped as the tears welled from her eyes and streamed down her face.

He made a shushing sound and stroked her back. She pushed back and felt a moment's resistance before he let her go.

Sonia heard the growl first. An instant later the marine flew away from her and landed on the opposite side of the examining room, crumpling in a heap. Johnny glared at her and she shrank against the wall, suddenly afraid of the fury she read in his yellow eyes. Johnny's gaze flicked back to the young man.

A lightning bolt of terror went through her as she realized that Johnny was out of control. She knew in her pounding heart that Johnny would kill that marine because he had touched her.

"Johnny, no!"

Johnny stopped and turned to her. She signed as she spoke. "It wasn't him. I was scared and I threw myself at him." She had to get him to believe her. Had to stop him from hurting this man. "It was me, do you hear me? *I* did it, not him."

Johnny stilled. His body trembled and she read the betrayal in his eyes. The marine scrambled to his feet. Johnny turned and ripped the steel door from its hinges and threw it toward the marine but it went wide. Intentionally, she thought. The marine ducked and then ran for the opening, streaking between them and tearing down the hallway, screaming as he fled. "Help! He'll kill her. Help!"

She turned to face the angry werewolf. Then her blood went cold as Johnny's gaze flicked from the retreating marine to her. She tried to speak but the look he gave her froze her blood and her larynx all at once. She lifted a hand and signed, *Sorry*.

Johnny roared. Sonia clamped her hands over her ears. It was a sound she hoped never to hear again, a long agonizing cry, full of anguish. Then he turned to the table bolted to the floor and ripped it from its attachments before hurling it against the concrete wall opposite her. He threw the stainless-steel side table. The wheels exploded from their casings on contact with the wall and the frame collapsed as if made from aluminum foil. The counter fell next, torn from the wall, sink and all. Water now poured onto the floor and out the open door. Sonia watched Johnny attack the large surgical light as if it were a serpent. He paused a moment to look at her and then lifted the door, throwing it halfway down the corridor.

Just like her mother's rages, she realized, curling into a ball and whimpering. Sonia looked at the open door and Johnny lifting the ruined examining table over his head to beat it against the floor again and again.

Sonia ran. She ran from her past and from her future and from Johnny's pain, but got no farther than the hall before her legs gave way and the shaking started. In her heart, she had known that what he felt for her was more than friendship. She'd let him give her comfort, disregarding the warning signs, so she could have dinner in her make-believe house with a man whom she didn't have to fear would get too close. But he had. What had she done?

She'd crossed some line, screwed this up, too. Now the captain or Johnny would send her away.

This was why she didn't let people in. She couldn't save them. Not her mother or her sister or Johnny. God, she couldn't even save herself.

The captain rushed past her and she rose to follow but Scofield grabbed her arm, halting her.

"What's going on?"

Captain MacConnelly charged down the hall at a run.

"I've never seen Johnny lose control," said Scofield. "What set him off?"

It grew quiet except for the pounding of her heart slamming into her ribs. She knew exactly. Her eyes met Johnny's and she saw the question in his eyes.

"Touma. I asked you a question. What happened?"

They'd blame her. She knew it and she knew they'd be right. She had turned to another man for comfort. No, that wasn't it. Did his rage stem from knowing that comfort was all he could give her, all she could accept while he was a wolf? He knew it. She knew it and…oh, she had to get out of there. Before the captain found out and called the MPs.

The major's hand slipped from her wrist as he turned toward the crashing coming from the examining room. She saw a flash of gray fur, the captain, she knew and then Johnny's black coat as the two spun in circles like all-star wrestlers.

She couldn't stay to see how she had disappointed one more person. She never meant to hurt him. But she had.

She kept going, out of the lab, the hall, the waiting area and out of the building. She kept moving, a walk at first and then finally a full-out run. She had to get away.

* * *

Johnny wanted to kill Webb for touching Sonia, for doing what he had dreamed of doing every day since he had met her. Last night, when she was sleeping on his couch and he had covered her with a blanket he had leaned over, wanting to kiss her. Only he couldn't kiss anyone. He couldn't because he had a snout instead of a mouth.

Mac had him from behind. It didn't stop him from lifting the table and throwing it again, taking out a row of ceiling tiles.

Mac's growl rumbled through him. Johnny's arms when slack. His shoulders drooped. Mac released him and stepped back.

He couldn't have her, not as long as he was stuck like this. He had to face it sooner or later. They were teaching him sign because he wasn't coming back. They all knew it. All these tests and research, it was just to keep him busy. They didn't have the first damned clue.

Mac watched him. Johnny punched both fists through the cement wall which collapsed into powder. The rough edges of the hole did not even scratch his skin. It didn't even hurt. He couldn't break his hand or cut his skin or put a bullet through his temple, because his hide was too damned tough. He could still put the barrel in his mouth, pierce that soft palate and then on to the squishy tangle of his brain. Sonia had forbidden it. Then she had turned to a stranger.

Johnny threw back his head and howled again, pouring out all his rage and pain.

Since Sonia arrived in his life, he hadn't thought about putting that pistol in his mouth. He hadn't thought of the poison that he had kept beside his mouthwash.

Instead, he occupied his mind with Sonia, what she looked like with the sun on her face or the ocean mist beading on her dark hair. He spent his time away from her trying to learn as many signs as possible so his conversations with her might flow naturally. He'd cooked for her. He'd taken her on walks, gone swimming with her and watched movies into the night. But she didn't see him as a man. More like her pet Cocker Spaniel. He was crazy for her. But now she'd seen what he really was and she had left him, too.

He knew his father hadn't left on purpose. He'd died, but he was still gone, leaving Johnny to pick up the pieces alone, care for his mom. Johnny dropped to his knees. Care for his sister.

His dad was gone. He couldn't see his mom or his sister or that baby, the one they'd made from his sperm. Now Sonia was gone, too, and he was here, alone, a monster. Still. Always.

He covered his face with his hands, hating the long wolfish slope of his snout.

It wasn't her fault. Who could blame her if she turned to a man for comfort and it wasn't him? Because he wasn't a man. Johnny felt sick to his stomach. He wrapped his arms about his middle and let his head sink. Mac draped a long furry arm about him. Johnny did not resist as they sat side by side.

He'd thought she was different because Sonia had managed to look past the beast he had become and see him there underneath. He'd let her in and she'd let him in. It had been a battle and he wasn't proud of his tactics, but he'd cracked open that tough shell. She had been closed up tighter than a walnut and now he understood why. She'd been through a lot.

Johnny dragged his claws over the floor again and again in a restless repetitive motion and only stopped when he realized he'd ripped through the floor tiles and a half inch into the concrete subfloor.

She was gone like a lovely dream that fades in the light.

The captain's arms fell away and he gave Johnny's back a pat.

Johnny made a fist and rubbed it in a circle over his aching heart. *Sorry. Sorry.* So damned sorry for all of it.

But the captain lifted his brows in confusion. He couldn't understand him. Only Sonia could do that.

Chapter 8

Sonia kept running. Acting on instinct now, using her lizard brain, she called it, as she did when things got too frightening. Her lizard brain told her to run. So she ran. She didn't plan or notice what direction she headed. Somehow she was outside while her mind played a video loop of that marine crumbled on the floor. Just like her mother, Sonia thought, picturing her mama sprawled out drunk on the floor of the kitchen or the bathroom or the hallway and once on the front steps. She'd run then, too. To the park or the library or the YMCA. Somewhere, anywhere where she could blend in and act as if she was there for some benign purpose other than escaping her miserable, drunken mother and her own miserable sober life. She'd run many places but she'd never run to the bottle.

Sonia's sprint ebbed with her energy. She glanced

behind at the way she had come, trying to orient herself, trying to think. She couldn't go back. They'd lock her up if she went off base. But if they blamed her for Johnny's outburst, then they might send her back to prison anyway. She hurt Johnny, her fear becoming his pain. She knew something like this would happen. Nothing ever worked right for her. He'd gotten attached, so had she, but what was she supposed to do about it?

She was just his teacher, wasn't she?

And perhaps his only friend. Sonia swiped at the tears.

Johnny obviously saw their relationship as something more than friendship. What he wanted, she could not provide. Had she given him mixed signals? Was this her fault, too?

She'd screwed it up, as usual. Like with her mother.

She knew her mother didn't drink because of her. Her mind knew it. But in her heart she always felt that she had never been enough. Not enough to keep her sober. Not enough to fill those holes—in her mother and she sure the hell was not enough to fill them in Johnny.

Sonia didn't get far. She didn't even make the main gate before a Jeep with two imposing, chisel-jawed marines with MP bands on their arms cut her off. The one in the passenger's side swung gracefully out of his seat and strode to her. Only her wobbling legs kept her from turning tail and running again.

"You Private Touma?" he asked.

She nodded, trying not to fold in half and grasp her thighs as she sucked in the oxygen she lacked from her run. Instead she placed a hand on the hood of the Jeep for support and burned her hand before retracting it.

"You're to report to Captain MacConnelly's office ASAP," said the burly MP.

Sonia glanced toward the road. The closed gate and guard booth did not stop her from looking beyond to the open road. How many times in her life had she thought of running away? How many times had she actually gone? And how many times had her situation gotten worse as a result? She frowned, recalling being returned to her mother in a squad car. The cops had taken one look at her mother wobbling on her heels, wreaking of booze and called protective services. Two months in foster care that time. Worse. Run—caught— worse problems. Not this time.

Sonia dragged her feet as she walked beside the Jeep. Her silent companion tipped his seat forward and indicated that she should crawl in the back like a child. On the short drive to the captain's office, she rehearsed several ways to explain. Maybe if she set it out correctly he'd give her another chance. Then she thought of all the damage to that room and grimaced.

She had just enough time to wear a groove in the rug in the captain's office before he arrived. As she held her salute she wondered where he kept little stashes of clothing. He bared down on her, leaning close and scowled so hard that the furrows in his forehead turned white.

"You want to tell me what the hell happened in there?"

She really, really didn't.

Finally, he returned her salute and she dropped her weary arm to her side, but remained at attention as the captain began to add to the groove she'd started. He spun and marched and spun and marched.

"Start talking, Touma, because I'd like to know why

Johnny, who has never shown violence without provocation, would suddenly go crazy and trash an examining room."

Sonia's throat went dry as she opened and closed her mouth like a goldfish who suddenly found herself on the kitchen counter instead of in her bowl.

"Webb said Johnny threw him across the room. If Johnny had bitten that marine, Webb would be turning werewolf right now. And Johnny would be responsible for that forever, for changing a man to a monster."

She'd never seen the captain look so fierce. His eyes were changing from sapphire blue to the ice blue of a wolf. The tint rising to overtake his natural coloration. Was he transforming?

It occurred to Sonia suddenly that the captain had unintentionally changed Johnny to a werewolf and that this situation must be striking him close to the bone. She started backing toward the door.

"Do you know how difficult it is for a werewolf to control the impulse to attack when angry? So I'll ask again, if you know what provoked him, you had better speak up."

She didn't. Instead she clamped her lips together as her chin began to tremble.

The captain folded his arms across his chest. To Sonia, he seemed to be holding himself in. When he spoke, his voice seemed different, harsher, like a growl.

"Was it Webb or you or Johnny, because someone is responsible. Start talking, Touma."

Sonia considered saying that she didn't know what had set Johnny off because the captain was intimidating as hell on a good day but when he was angry, like now, and the veins in his throat and forehead pulsed with blood, he was positively terrifying.

But if she tried to pull that, then they might think that something was wrong with Johnny. They might put *him* in the cage and she absolutely could not let that happen.

"Sir, they told me to wait for Johnny in exam room one." There, she'd gotten that part out and her voice only trembled a little. Maybe he didn't even notice. "Then the door shut behind me and I couldn't get out."

The captain's scowl deepened so that his brow was so furrowed that she thought she might want to plant some vegetable seeds along the rows.

"Locked in?" He shook his head in confusion. "Those doors work with a panic button so they can be opened without using your hands. Didn't your escort show you the red button beside the door?"

Sonia went still. "Button?" Why hadn't she seen a big red button beside the door? "No, sir."

"Was Sergeant Lam trying to get you out?"

"No, sir, Corporal Webb opened the door from the outside." She lifted her hands to glance at the bruises and cuts there from her efforts to escape. Why hadn't she seen that button? "I wasn't thinking and I just threw myself at him."

"You attacked Webb?"

She dropped her head to stare at the rounded toe of her shiny shoes. "No, sir."

"Ah. What happened then?"

"Webb held me and I was crying and hugging him and…"

Her captain made a sound that fell between a groan and a growl.

"Johnny dragged Webb off me. It was my fault, sir.

It just happened and Johnny moves so fast. But Captain MacConnelly, sir, I didn't understand how Johnny felt. I thought we were becoming friends, but I never knew how he…"

She lifted her head and saw the captain's face flushed with blood.

"I wasn't thinking and Johnny saw us."

"Holy shit." The captain raked a hand over the stubble at his temple. "You're saying he did this because he was jealous?"

Sonia lowered her head as she fought the tears at facing yet another failure. She'd really wanted to help Johnny deal with this but it was too much. Instead of making his life easier she was complicating it and as much as she liked him, she was not prepared to take their relationship any further. He knew her well enough to know that sticking to anything wasn't her strong point. Why he even wanted her was baffling; she was such a screwup.

"I've failed to keep our relationship professional, sir. Johnny is lonely and I'm female and he seems to think he has feelings for me, which he might very well have." This was so embarrassing. "I'm not helping him, so I think I should go."

"True to form," muttered the captain. He pinned her with a gaze so cold she shivered. "Private, we are a hair's breadth away from fixing this mess. But we need Johnny's cooperation. In the last month he has been ordered to the lab a dozen times but he only showed up twice, both times with you. You haven't failed. He'll get over it. So will you."

"Sir, he could have killed Webb."

"That might just keep me from doing so." He rested

the knuckles of his right fist on his desk and leaned toward her. "The day you came I told you that your file said you were cautious about entering new relationships. Well, Touma, let me be the first to tell you that you are in one. You have managed to reach Sergeant Lam when no one else could and you have kept him from doing anything to hurt himself. So I don't give a shit about the exam room."

She blinked at him.

"The day you arrived I also told you that Lam needed understanding and not a woman who would hit and run. So this time, Touma, you are not running."

She swallowed before she spoke aloud her other reservations. "Sir, Sergeant Lam sometimes cooks supper for me."

"So?"

"And lunch."

He gave her a look that showed confusion blended with irritation.

"And breakfast."

The captain's brows shot up. "Are you saying you are sleeping with him?"

The shock straightened her spine. "No, sir. But I did spend last night on his couch and we watched a movie together."

"On his couch?"

"I fell asleep during the movie. But, sir, I didn't report back to base until oh nine hundred. But I couldn't find my supervisor, sir."

"She noticed your absence and she reported it to me. How I proceed depends a great deal on your actions moving forward, Touma."

Her stomach squeezed and twisted as if being consumed by a boa constrictor. "Sir, I've screwed this all up. I don't know what I'm doing. I can't tell if I'm teaching him or he's teaching me."

"What exactly is he teaching you?"

How to trust. "Swimming."

"My wife told me you spend downtime together. Also that you eat meals together."

A shiver went down her back as she thought of Brianna, not just appearing to talk, but also sneaking about without either of them knowing.

"I asked her to keep tabs on you. Johnny knows. He can smell her whenever she enters his territory."

"I'm not a good teacher."

"Really?" The captain rounded his desk and sat in his chair. "So your complaint is that you are getting to eat really good food, swim in a lush tropical paradise and watch movies. What, is the couch lumpy?"

Sonia was not letting go so easily. "It's not a professional relationship. I tried but…" She let her insecurities pour from her with the perspiration. "He knows signs that I never even showed him. He's learning on his own from the book I left him so I don't even know if he needs me to teach him. I didn't tell you because I like Johnny. I tried to be firm and professional but it didn't work. The only thing that did work was if I answered his personal questions. If I answered, he stayed. If I didn't, he took off. I've mismanaged everything. That first day when he showed you his signs—" she lifted her gaze to peek up at him as the fear made her stomach ache "—those were curse words, sir." She dropped her gaze to the carpet. "That's what I taught him because I lost my temper. I've been walking on egg shells afraid you'd find out what a terrible job I've been doing. It's completely out of control."

"What is, Private?"

"My relationship with him. He obviously thinks it's personal."

"And you don't."

She threw up her hands. "I do, too. But it wasn't supposed to be. I tried to keep him out, but I couldn't because I had to show progress or you'd…" She sighed. "You'd follow through on your threat, sir."

"I don't make threats, Private. And, I'll admit that I expected you to fail."

And she had. Her shoulders rounded and her throat began a familiar burn.

"But my wife was right. She told me to choose someone who couldn't quit and you didn't."

A tiny pearl of hope bubbled up inside her.

"Let me lay this out for you, Touma. Johnny needs to learn sign, but that's not your job. Never has been. Your job is to give him hope and make damned sure that he is occupied, engaged and interested. I don't give a fart if you sleep over and get breakfast in bed. I don't care if he knows how to swear in sign."

She winced, realizing that the captain had known all along what Johnny had said that first day.

"Johnny is happier than I've seen him since he was attacked. So you must be doing something right."

"I'm not sure what I'm doing at all, sir. Sometimes I feel like I'm drowning and I don't want to hurt him."

"We are close to a treatment, Touma. I am telling you. We nearly got this nailed. We've isolated the protein Johnny needs to be human again. So let me be very clear. You have my permission to eat Cheerios on his porch and learn how to cliff dive if you want to. Just stay with him. That's your job. Johnny's big and burly. He might look solid as a rock, but there are cracks, Touma. Serious cracks. So don't break him."

Knowing what the captain expected momentarily filled her with relief until the weight of his expectations pressed down on her. This was worse than being his teacher. She was responsible for so much more than teaching him sign language. She lifted her hand to salute. "Yes, sir."

"We've got another series of tests this week. So don't hug anyone else until then."

Her face went hot at his words but she nodded her understanding.

He rose. "And now, Private, you and I are going to see Johnny because he won't use the white board with me and I can't understand a thing he is signing." He rummaged in his drawer and retrieved a flip phone. He tossed it to her. "My number is in there with some others. My wife has asked that her number be included on your phone. Brianna wants you to call her. Seems you've made an impression all around."

The mention of his vampire wife's name made her skin tingle. Suddenly all she wanted to do was to get Johnny and get back up the hill.

"Yes, sir."

"Follow me."

They walked in silence down corridors and through automatic doors, each of which had a bright red button the size of a grapefruit that was used to open them. Panic did funny things to a person. It made her brain stop working. She'd been sweating and it was hard to breathe. Right now she had a cramp in her belly just thinking of Johnny. Was he still upset?

The captain stopped at a door that was clearly an exterior exit judging from the solid steel and the panic bar. He peered down at her.

"Upbeat, Touma. Upbeat and optimistic," said Mac-Connelly. "We nearly have this."

She nodded and he opened the door and held it. She passed through first and out into a central grassy courtyard that ringed a Koi pond. Wooden benches sat nestled before sprays of palm fronds and blooming tropical plants. A place of serenity in the center of the medical research lab. It seemed as out of place as an orchid in the middle of a gravel quarry.

"This was created at my wife's insistence. She said Johnny should have somewhere peaceful to wait before tests and lab work. You know when we draw blood we have to take it from his mouth because it's impossible to puncture his skin?"

She didn't, but the information just made the entire testing process more horrific. They'd been at this for six months? No wonder he was depressed. She began scanning for him. The door clicked shut behind them and Johnny emerged on the opposite bank, straightening from where he seemed to have been feeding the fish, judging from the number of the bright yellow, orange-and-white Koi swimming practically up onto the bank.

Why weren't they afraid of him?

Probably because they didn't know how much fish he ate. She smiled and started toward him, taking the fastest route over the high-arching foot bridge that spanned the narrowest part of the pool.

He was signing already. *Sorry. So sorry. Not try scare you.*

The captain's shoes rapped smartly on the wooden planking behind her. "What's he saying?"

She signed to Johnny. *It's okay now.*

She started signing and speaking in unison. "I was afraid. I thought I was locked in that exam room and you weren't there. I just panicked."

"And Webb is an idiot," added MacConnelly.

Johnny signed to his captain and Sonia spoke nearly in time.

"He says, 'I just lost it. It was stupid. I know how strong we are. No excuses.'"

"You did hold back," said the captain. "If you didn't you would have killed him. It's easy to kill a man now. And you didn't bite him. I know that took restraint."

Johnny closed the distance to her and then paused looking uncertain. His hands moved with the grace of a dancer. *Forgive me, please. Don't want to lose you, too.*

He had lost so much already, his family, his squad, his old life and even his body.

"What did he say?"

"Apologies again."

"All right, Johnny. No more of that." He turned to the sergeant. "Touma isn't yours. She is a translator and a teacher. You need to check that territoriality. You got me?"

Johnny nodded.

The captain swiped both hands over his face and then drew a breath as if preparing to launch a missile strike.

"Johnny, is it true you can't remember the attack?"

Johnny stilled and then glanced at Sonia as he gave a slow nod. Her gaze dropped. Why did she feel like a traitor? He'd never shared any of her secrets, but she had shared his.

"What *do* you remember?"

Johnny began to sign and Sonia translated.

"He says it doesn't make sense because—" she paused waiting for more signs and then continued "—he saw the wolf jump but you stepped in front of him. He saw it bite you." She pointed to her shoulder a moment after Johnny. "Here."

Johnny kept signing and Sonia drew a startled breath at his words.

"Next he was on the helicopter. But, sir, he says he thinks he was still human. He saw you change, sir."

"Maybe he just hadn't changed yet."

Johnny's hands continued to move.

"He said he was uninjured, sir."

"That doesn't make any sense," said the captain. "We both changed. We're both werewolves. I bit him. I saw the report."

Sonia turned to watch Johnny and then began to speak. "He says his memory isn't clear. Maybe he's wrong, but that's what he remembers." She stared at one and then the other. "Haven't you ever talked about this?"

They both shook their heads. *Men,* she thought. They sucked at communication.

"I'm ordering an investigation," said her captain. "Anything else you want to tell me, Johnny, before I send you home?"

Johnny nodded and began to sign. Sonia found her words stuck as she tried to speak. "He says, 'I was prepared to die that day, Mac. But I wasn't prepared for this.'"

Johnny finished by sweeping a hand over his face and form.

Who could have ever been prepared for this?

"Give us a few more days. We are on to something now. The dogs aren't dying and they are still changing. Just hold on."

Sonia watched Johnny lift a fist.

"He says he's holding on."

The captain glanced from one to the other. "Dismissed, you two. Touma, call my wife." He rested a hand on Johnny's shoulder and Johnny pulled him in for a hug. The men clapped each other on the back. She heard the captain say, "I'll make it right for you. Swear to God."

Then the captain was retreating with a hasty step.

Sonia moved in to the place the captain had been. She wrapped her arms around Johnny's middle. "Let's get you home."

They walked side by side up the narrow winding path. Sonia fell into step with him. Johnny could probably climb the hill in a matter of minutes but he slowed his pace to match hers and did not hurry her.

Once back at his quarters he stopped and grinned at her signing.

We are home.

She cast him a sad smile. "When I was a girl I imagined a house of our own with a swing in the yard. Now I just want a place I can heat without turning on the oven."

Johnny stared down at her. Had she said all that aloud? She'd never told anyone that before.

"I'm sorry. I didn't mean to be such a bummer."

He signed to her. *This home, my home is your home. Make it yours.*

She laughed at that. "Don't be silly."

Captain says you stay here or at base. You choose. Come. Go. Up to you. So, this your home now, too.

It was sweet of him to say. But it wasn't true. A home, well that wasn't just a place it was… Sonia stilled as she realized that a home was where you wanted to be. Where you felt safe and where you were with the ones you cared most about. By that definition she was indeed already home and that scared the crap out of her. She pulled back, staring, stunned, at Johnny.

What?

"It's not my home."

It could be.

"No. I'm not playing house, Wolf. I stay or go at someone else's whim. It's not up to me. So I'm not unpacking or settling in because I know what this is. It's a job."

He cocked his head. *Scared.*

"Hell, yes, I am most of the time."

That night Johnny cooked short ribs, the best she'd ever tasted. After supper he gave her the master bedroom with that enormous bed he never used. She stayed the night and the next morning she woke to an empty house. Johnny left a note that he was training with his assigned friends, the wounded warriors. Beside the note he'd left three things: a glass of juice, a bagel and a magazine with a scrap of paper set between the pages on an article about the decorative touches that make a house a home.

She pushed the magazine aside in favor of the bagel.

Damned if she was going to be his interior decorator, too.

Over the course of the next three weeks their lives fell into a pattern. She had the mornings to herself. Sometimes Brianna came for a visit, always keeping a distance and never touching Sonia. The more time she spent with Brianna, the more she liked her. She wasn't frightening or distant, just cautious. She knew the harm she could do to humans by simple contact. Being a vampire that drew energy from other beings made her a prisoner of sorts. She was isolated just like Johnny, but unlike him she had no hope of recovery. Sonia felt terrible as she realized Brianna would spend her life in a self-imposed isolation to protect others from her powers. It would make for a lonely life. Thank goodness that werewolves were immune. That meant she had at least one friend in Johnny and a husband who could hold her in his arms. Better than many. Better than herself, she realized.

Johnny seemed distracted and she knew there was a shadow hanging over them both. He was still in werewolf form. Each day of waiting, the unspoken hung between them. Could they fix him? Because if they couldn't she would rather have him as he was than lose him in a failed attempt to make him human.

Sonia went still as she realized how much she feared the end might come at anytime. What if she lost him, too?

The call came the next morning just as they sat down to breakfast on the patio. The messenger surprised her. It was Brianna who appeared from nowhere on the lawn below the porch.

"They want Johnny at the facility at fourteen hundred to run a trial. And they want you there, as well, to act as his translator." Brianna smiled at Johnny. "This could be it, Johnny. They believe this will change you back."

Johnny signed and Sonia translated.

"He says, 'Will you come?'"

Brianna smiled, but shook her head no. "I'd have to be too close to the others. I'll wait here." She turned to Sonia. "Perhaps you can call me to let me know how it goes and if all is well, perhaps you two might have dinner with us soon?"

Johnny nodded his acceptance.

Brianna lifted a hand in farewell and vanished.

Sonia shivered. "I hate it when she does that." She faced Johnny who offered her a ginger-pineapple muffin grinning broadly.

For her, this news was like preparing to hear a jury verdict and she didn't know if Johnny would win his freedom or be sentenced to death. Either way she'd lose him.

His wide grin faded as he dropped his black jowls over his white teeth.

"What if something goes wrong?"

Already went wrong.

"But something might happen to you."

Worth the risk.

She disagreed but it was not her decision.

"I'd rather have you as you are than see you…" Her words trailed off. She couldn't bring herself to say what was in her mind as if keeping from speaking that word would somehow keep him safe.

Die, he supplied. Then he took her hand before releasing it to sign. *I would rather die than live like this.*

"Is it so bad?" she asked, tears welled in her eyes, making his image swim.

Yes.

Her little fantasy bubble burst. Had she really thought that she and Johnny could live together in this bungalow on the hill forever? That he would be content with her companionship and nothing more?

Chapter 9

Sonia watched as Dr. Zharov stroked his tie speaking to Johnny who lay on the surgical table. There were lead lines from his body to various machines taking his heart rate and reading brain function. The machines scared her silly. Zharov had six assistants. If it was safe, why did he need so many doctors and why was there a crash cart behind the table?

"I've isolated the absent protein from Captain Mac-Connelly's blood. My team inserted the protein into your own blood cells to prevent the kind of rejection you witnessed. The injection works on dogs and monkeys. We have had zero fatalities with this new procedure. I have advised that we wait another two months. That is twice the time that we saw any negative outcomes but unfortunately that is not my call."

Johnny shifted in a nervous gesture as if trying to get comfortable on the stainless-steel surface.

"Do you have any questions?" the doctor asked.

Johnny shook his head and retracted his gums, silently asking for the injection. He had already signed the releases holding the U.S. Marines blameless if anything happened.

Captain MacConnelly stepped forward. "I'm right here, Johnny. Don't worry."

Johnny nodded.

Zharov drew a long breath and lifted the needle. The fluid inside looked like blood. Sonia felt her entire body tense. Would it hurt him?

"Private, please step out," said Zharov.

Johnny grasped her hand and then signed.

"'My translator. She'll report what I feel,'" Sonia said.

Zharov grimaced. "This won't be pleasant, Lam. Just bringing this to your attention."

Johnny held his hand palm up and bent his fingers.

"He's ready," she said, finding her voice as harsh as coarse sandpaper on metal.

The doctor told Johnny to open his mouth and then he stuck the needle into the pink flesh between the upper and lower jaw as if Johnny were a dental patient being prepped for a root canal.

Sonia felt a hysterical bubble of laughter rising inside her. Johnny lifted his hand toward her and she took it gladly. She had the irrational thought that if she just held him tightly enough, it would keep him safe. He squeezed her hand and winked. She squeezed back looking at his familiar yellow eyes as her heart thumped in her throat so hard that it hurt to breathe.

She signed with one hand. *So afraid to lose you. I am right here.*

What happens next? Do you feel anything?

Johnny's eyes fluttered closed. He drew a long sharp breath. His eyes popped open and Sonia stared. They were no longer yellow, but brown. Deep as dark chocolate, so dark that she could not see his irises.

"Johnny?"

His fingers went slack but she held on. Then his body slumped. His mouth gaped and he gasped as if suddenly struck in the stomach. His back arched.

"Step away." Zharov pushed her aside. Johnny's hand slipped from hers. "The transformation takes several minutes," the doctor said to her.

Sonia was breathing so fast she felt dizzy. But she refused to faint. Johnny's eyes rolled back so she could see only white and his muscles spasmed into one long rigor followed by a seizure.

"Normal," said the doctor staring at the monitor on the EKG. Johnny's heart rate was fast and the usual up and down of the heart monitor's moving line seemed to be flattening out. Sonia looked back to Johnny to see the fur on his arms dropping away in great hairy clumps leaving patches of perfect smooth skin.

"That doesn't happen when I change," said Mac-Connelly to the doctor.

"Normal," he repeated. "Just like the subjects we studied."

"Not normal," said MacConnelly. "I don't lose my coat. It just changes with the rest of me."

"You and Johnny are different. You make the necessary protein to allow you to change back and forth."

Johnny's teeth receded into his bleeding gums as his jaw bone retracted with a cracking sound that turned Sonia's stomach. Johnny arched and the leads attached to his head fell away with the ones on his chest. The straps were now too big as his entire body contracted. Muscles corded. She could see his muscles.

Johnny cried out once and she realized it was a sound she had never heard. A sound of agony but the sound made by a man with the vocal cords of a human being.

She couldn't watch him writhe, so she threw herself across his body, gripping him tight as he bucked beneath her.

"Oh, God, make it stop."

"Get her out of here," ordered Zharov.

Sonia was bustled from the room. The door clicked shut behind her. She stood gasping and panting as she stared through the small window. They surrounded him. Fur fell from the table in black clumps landing at their feet like hair on the floor of a beauty salon.

She could see only the men's backs and the jumping line of the EKG. It was spiking impossibly fast. Her knees gave way. Someone caught her.

"Hold on, Touma." That sounded like the captain's voice, but it was so far away. Why couldn't she see anything?

Dora Morton huddled in the filthy packing crate. Shouting did not bring help. Banging on the solid padded walls brought no rescue. Soundproof they had said and so it was. Dora shifted her weight and groaned. Even her remarkable ability to heal did not bring her full recovery from her capture by the male vampires.

She thought of their pitiless leader. He had malevolent cloudy eyes and freakish white skin that looked waxy as a beluga whale's. Her shoulders shook as she wept. They had taken her in Hawaii. The miles of ocean water had not protected her after all. Her mother had been wrong about that, but not wrong when she had told her daughter that vampires were ugly, but, oh, even her terrible descriptions had not done them justice.

Her poor mother had done nothing but try to protect her child and their terrible secret. And for that, they had attacked her. Had her mother survived?

Dora's clothing still stank of them. But that was better than what awaited her. She'd met a female years ago, one who had been through it. She had explained it to Dora's mother. The ones who hunted her were vampires. Her daughter was a vampire, too, with the power to self-heal and to inspire greatness in mortal men. And she was fast as the wind. But not, she now knew, faster than the males.

Dora shifted in the foam padding and tried again to claw through the steel beneath. The metal burned her skin, forcing her to retreat again to the protection of the foam. Even through the padding, the metal made her head pound and her stomach heave. It was like being buried alive in a crypt. The long rectangular box was large from the outside. She had seen it. But inside it was a steel coffin. They shipped her as a dead body. She wasn't dead. No vampire was. Just other than human. If they went underground, it was only to hide from mortal eyes. That's what the woman had told them. A different species. A parasite. A predator. The bile rose in her throat and she went still.

"Please don't be sick." There was no telling how long she would be in this box. Would the air last? If she survived this trip, when they took her out she knew what would be waiting. The vampire woman had told them.

Ten years in their underground hive. Ten years of indoctrination, bearing children and then, finally, if she learned her lessons well, she might be set out on mortal men as an elite assassin, able to kill merely by spending a night with a man. Ten years without the sun. She'd be twenty-five then.

God help her and God help any female they captured.

Sonia came around to find herself stretched out on an orange vinyl couch. The ceiling tiles and lights shone relentlessly down on her and she blinked as she glanced about. She seemed to be in a waiting room of some kind. What was she doing here?

The answer swept down on her with such a rush that she felt as if she were under attack.

"Johnny!"

Sonia pushed herself up to a seated position and her head swam again. Had she fainted? Heat flooded her face with the shame. She was a marine, for God sakes, but a poor one. Johnny asked her to stay with him and she had fainted like a little girl who was afraid of blood.

But she wasn't afraid of blood. She was afraid of that heart monitor and those electrodes. She scanned the room, surprised to find herself alone. Well, they had more important things to deal with than her. A moment later a marine stepped into the room chewing on a chocolate bar. His eyes snapped to hers as he froze and then glanced behind him. He definitely looked as if she had caught him doing something he wasn't supposed to be doing. Was he told to watch her?

"You're awake," he said, trying for a friendly smile, but the lump of candy bar in his cheek ruined the effect. He quickly choked it down and stowed the rest, torn wrapper and all, in his pants pocket. "I'm Corporal Gail. How are you feeling?"

She'd lost her hat, she realized and her neat bun had come loose. Where were her hair ties? Sonia pushed herself to a stand and then grasped the couch back for a moment as she swayed.

Gail came forward reaching. "Take it easy now."

She lifted a hand to stop him. "Where is Lam?"

"Moved to Recovery."

"Alive?" She held her breath.

He nodded. "Last I knew."

"Where?"

"They told me to send word to the captain when you were awake."

"You do that, Corporal. I'm going to Recovery." She walked past him and she saw his hand snake out. She glared at him. He changed his mind and motioned down the hall. "This way."

He stopped at the recovery room door before the large sign that read Authorized Personnel Only. Do Not Enter.

Sonia pushed the door open and stepped inside. There was activity at only one of the curtained cubbies. She headed for the sound of the beeping heart monitor. Her steady, hurried step slowed as she crossed the large white floor tiles. Her heartbeat pulsed in her ears as she saw Zharov standing at the foot of a bed beside the captain and Major Scofield. All three stood grave and silent. But the monitor beeped so Johnny's heart was beating. Wasn't it?

But what if he was on life support? She imagined the machines keeping him alive and listened for the hiss of a respirator. *Please, God, don't let him be brain-dead.*

Scofield saw her first and offered her a smile, looking both tired and worried. She came to stand beside the major forgetting to salute in her hurry to see Johnny.

Zharov spoke. "None of the test subjects lost consciousness."

She glanced at the bed, her eyes moving up the white sheets that covered him from his feet to his waist. His arms rested still beside his hips, as if placed there. Human arms, arms that were well muscled and had just a dusting of black hair on the forearms. There was a monitor on his index finger and an IV taped to the back of both hands. His broad, muscular chest looked like a circuit box with all the electrodes running every which way. The sight of him so still and helpless made her throat go tight and her breath catch.

They'd managed to put a needle into him, so his skin was normal again. That was good, wasn't it? And Johnny was very definitely a man. He wore no hospital gown and so she noted the clean line of his collar bones as it swept from his muscular shoulders to the V below his Adam's apple. She inhaled quick and sharp as her body reacted to the sight of him. His skin was smooth and slightly lighter than her own light brown Latina coloring. And then she looked at his face, first taking in the dark shock of straight chin length black hair that fell back to the snowy pillows. Her fingers itched to rake through that thick hair. Johnny no longer had a G.I. haircut. She next studied his face. He had a strong jawline, broad forehead and thick arched brows. His eyelashes were full and feathery against his cheeks. His face was square with a long nose and a wide generous mouth. It was a striking face. A stranger's face.

Sonia frowned. She knew Johnny well, but she did not know this man.

"It worked," she whispered.

MacConnelly glanced at her and then back at his comrade. "They don't know why he won't wake up."

Zharov tapped the tip of his pen to his lower lip as he stared at his patient as if he were some puzzle. "There's nothing wrong with him. He's perfect."

The captain motioned toward the bed. "He's out."

"Brain activity normal, everything normal."

"Except his eyes are closed," reminded the captain.

Sonia inched past the men.

Scofield rested a hand on her shoulder. "Why don't you speak to him, Touma. Let him know you're here."

She wanted to say that she didn't know this man. That she wanted Johnny back. But that notion was so completely ridiculous she merely nodded and leaned forward.

"Johnny? You in there? It's time for your lesson."

Johnny did not move but his heart rate increased. She lifted his slack hand and turned it palm up. Then she began to finger spell into his palm as she spoke.

"Come on now. Lesson then swimming."

His eyeballs moved beneath his closed lids and then he went slack again.

"Say something else," ordered Zharov, his body tense, his gaze alert.

Sonia gripped Johnny's hand and leaned forward whispering into his normal, well-shaped ear as she signed into his palm. "Johnny, wake up. You promised to take me dancing."

His fingers threaded with hers. She drew back enough to see his eyes snap open. Brown eyes, she realized, deep, dark, lovely eyes. Where were the yellow ones she had grown so accustomed to?

He seemed to be struggling to focus but at last he flicked from her to the men behind her and then back to rest on her face. The corner of his mouth twitched and her stomach fluttered. Her visceral reaction to him so startled her that she had to press a hand to her chest in a vain attempt to slow her racing heart. She reminded herself that this was Johnny.

Johnny's voice came as a hoarse whisper, his vocal cords likely weak from disuse. "Is it done? Am I human?"

"Yes. And as soon as you are up to it, you are taking me out on a date."

He lifted their clasped hands and stared at his own. "That's my hand." He pressed his free hand to his chest and then glanced up to see the three sentinels at his foot rail.

"Welcome back, son," said Major Scofield.

"I told you I could do it," said Zharov.

"Johnny." The captain's voice cracked as he moved up the opposite side of the bed. Sonia stepped back as the two men embraced. Johnny's finger monitor slipped off and the machine shrieked. The two drew apart and Zharov replaced the monitor and reset the machine.

Johnny turned to his doctor. "When can I get out of here?"

Sonia laughed and brushed the tears from her face. Her captain's Adam's apple bobbed.

"Tomorrow," said Zharov.

"Tonight," said Johnny.

"It's nearly midnight, son," said the major. "You need

sleep and look at Touma. She's practically swaying on her feet."

Johnny looked at her, really looked. She pushed her hair back from her face and smiled.

"You all right?" His voice was rich and low and did funny things to her insides.

She nodded and dropped her gaze but her skin still tingled from that look.

"Tired?"

"We're all tired, Johnny." She signed, *Stay the night. I'll stay too.*

He pursed his lips and looked to Zharov. "I'm leaving tomorrow. I have a date."

Johnny grinned at Sonia and her stomach did a funny little quiver. She had been fond of the wolf. But what she was feeling for Sergeant John Lam was something else entirely. Something strong and exciting and scary stirred inside her. Funny to be more afraid of him now than when he was a werewolf.

She'd failed to keep her distance from him then. What chance did she have now? But a promise was a promise and he was taking her out tomorrow night.

She needed a dress.

Sonia startled awake at the alarm, confused by her surroundings and disoriented with fatigue. The barracks, she realized. Johnny insisted she find a bed and it didn't seem right to sleep at his place any longer. He wasn't there and when he returned, he'd be a man. That changed everything.

He was a man again, and one that made her insides curl up like a ribbon on a birthday gift. She'd seen his photo, of course. The captain had showed it to her, but that photo wasn't Johnny, or a least not this Johnny. The boy in the photo had been a young marine before he'd ever seen action. Then his face was more angular, his body more lithe. Now his mouth was pure sensuality. And his body had bulk, mass and a power that she suspected came from his werewolf side. And his hair, well instead of the short bristle of a man in uniform, he now had long sweeping straight black hair that reminded her of an Asian Antonio Banderas. It was long enough to draw back at the nape of his neck, a look that she found sexy as hell.

But there was something else, something dark. His eyes reflected a palpable danger. Time, experience and his injuries had changed him. He had transformed to human form but held on to that sharp edge of the wolf.

Sonia stretched and rose with the other women in her barracks. They went about their business casting her odd looks as if they'd found a toadstool growing in the center of the room. She had the fastest shower of her life and then reported to the medical facility, feeling oddly uncomfortable in her fatigues. But Johnny wasn't there. They said they had him running some physical tests and she was not going to see him until they released him at seventeen hundred hours. She couldn't believe they were releasing him at all. He'd left her a note that was written in a crisp, bold, unfamiliar hand. His transformation would change so many things between them. She felt lost and sick to her stomach as she read that he would pick her up for their date at eighteen hundred and to leave him a message as to where to find her. She scribbled her reply on the bottom of the page explaining that she would be at Brianna's home, then returned the note with the messenger. Then she checked to see if there was anything she was supposed to be doing. No one knew.

She was Johnny's translator, only he didn't need one any longer.

Sonia recognized that she was about as necessary as a fur coat on a weasel. John Lam no longer needed a teacher or a companion. He no longer needed his private entourage and he no longer needed her. How long until they sent her packing? Suddenly the nervous excitement of their date was replaced with a twisting anxiety. She knew how things worked. She had top secret clearance for a job that had just disappeared. What would they do with her now?

Sonia left the base and walked up the hill to the home of Brianna and Captain MacConnelly. Brianna greeted her warmly and asked for news of Johnny. Sonia told her what she could and right there in the middle of her description of Johnny's transformation she began to cry. She sat on Brianna's white couch beside the arrangement of birds of paradise as her shoulders jumped like a semiautomatic rifle, her breath coming in short uneven gasps. Brianna did not come to sit beside her or wrap a comforting arm around her shoulders.

Sonia's embarrassment grew as she continued until she glanced up and saw Brianna pale and wide-eyed, gripping her hands together so tightly that her knuckles had gone white. Then Sonia recalled that Brianna couldn't go to her, couldn't offer physical comfort without also causing Sonia physical harm. Brianna nudged a box of tissues in her direction and then fetched a glass of water.

Her hostess set the water on the black lacquer coffee table before Sonia. "Travis says Johnny is doing really well today. Strong as a bull, that's part of the condition. They retain that strength, acute hearing and enhanced sense of smell even when in human form. But no one is sure if Johnny has reversed back into human form permanently or if he will be able to change between forms. I know he still smells like a wolf."

Sonia lifted her face from the tissues and gave a questioning look.

"It is one of my powers, the sense of smell. I can also see in the dark."

Sonia knew her eyes must be the size of saucers but she could think of nothing to say, so she reached for her water and took a sip.

"Did you see him?"

Brianna rubbed her palms together and stared absently at the floor and then met Sonia's eyes, forcing a smile. "Last night. No one saw me. He seemed human but there is that darkness clinging to him. I only feel that around werewolves. Travis says that it is because they are my natural enemy that I sense them. In any case, no one is sure if it is possible to make a werewolf truly human again."

Sonia's disquiet grew as the unease rippled over her like a hot breeze and she availed herself of a tissue to wipe her eyes.

"Travis is going to try to teach Johnny how to transform today. At first it takes a few minutes and it is not pleasant to watch.

Sonia remembered witnessing Johnny's change and shivered.

"Travis can change very fast now. I asked him once if it hurt and he said, 'Hell, yes.'"

"If Johnny learns to change at will then he won't need sign language anymore," said Sonia.

"That's right," she said brightly. "He won't." Brianna's smile faded as she regarded Sonia's glum expression. "Oh, I see. Has anyone spoken to you regarding your future?"

Sonia's breath hitched. "Do you know something?"

"No. But I understand your concern."

Sonia shifted uncomfortably on the pristine white sofa. With no visitors it might always look this sterile and new, she realized. There were no children here, no pets, no life other than the vampire and her werewolf husband.

"Johnny seems very comfortable with you and you seem fond of him. I don't think his new condition will change that."

"It will if I'm reassigned. I don't expect them to keep me here with no job to do."

There was an awkward pause and Sonia realized Brianna was glancing at the door. She hurried to get to the reason for her visit before this strange woman sent her away.

"We have a date tonight. I promised him that when he changed back he could take me dancing."

Brianna smiled brightly. "How romantic." Her smile flickered and faded. "But I didn't think marines were allowed to date one another."

And they weren't. Sonia groaned. Why hadn't she remembered that rule when she had promised Johnny that they would go dancing.

She cradled her head in her hands and exhaled. "He was so angry after the last lab failure. I was just trying to cheer him up." It wasn't exactly true. She was trying to give them both hope.

"Well, I suppose you could get permission. Does Travis know?"

"He must. I was talking about it when Johnny was unconscious." Sonia wondered how she was going to get out of this one and then felt a sharp tug in her heart. That's when she realized she didn't want to get out of it. She wanted to go out with Johnny so much it hurt. She lifted her gaze to Brianna issuing a silent plea.

"I'll call Travis. These are hardly ordinary circumstances. He'll have to understand."

When Sonia didn't return her smile Brianna cocked her head.

Sonia rose and took a step toward Brianna, thinking to throw her arms about her and the vampire lifted a hand again to stop her. Sonia halted.

"I'm sorry. I forgot again." Just thinking of going out with Johnny made her heart ache and her blood rush and she knew that marines weren't allowed to fraternize, but she was thinking of fraternizing him right out of the clothing that he now needed. Her original problem now rose in her mind. She rubbed her neck and said, "I have nothing to wear."

"I'll handle that. Is that the only reason for the long face?"

Sonia shook her head. "He's so different, like another person."

Brianna's brows swept lower. "Sonia, I never knew him before he was a werewolf. But I know he is the same inside."

"But not outside. You've seen him. He's gorgeous.

And he doesn't need a translator and as for a date, he could have his pick."

"And he picked you."

"I don't know what will happen next."

"If you mean what will happen tonight, that will be up to you. He's been in wolf form a long time, but he is still a gentleman. You only need to say no."

If she *could* say no. Johnny was so appealing it frightened her more than the first time she'd seen him.

"Sonia?"

She glanced up and noticed that she had torn several tissues into tiny little pieces.

"Oh! I'm sorry. I'll clean that up."

"You *have* dated men before. Haven't you?"

She didn't really consider them dates. She'd met men in a variety of places. She'd even slept with a few. But she never went back for seconds and made sure that they couldn't, either.

"Not exactly a date."

"What exactly?"

Sonia held it in a while longer and then decided that Brianna was as good a sounding board as she'd likely find.

"I'm not a virgin. But I've never had a steady boyfriend by choice." She was careful and always very clear that she was not interested in a relationship. In that way she had satisfied her needs. "I don't like the idea of being trapped in a bad relationship and I don't like the idea of being vulnerable. I've got baggage. Bad home, yada, yada. Anyway, it feels safer to just keep to myself but sometimes..." She glanced up and saw the pain reflected in Brianna's eyes. If anyone understood the need to keep apart, it was this vampire. She chose her own company, as well, but for different reasons, selfless reasons.

Brianna nodded. "Funny, before I knew, I was just the opposite. I'd do just about anything to switch places with you, be able to have friends, go out in public. I'm lucky my husband is immune or I'd have no one. And here you are able to make connections and you don't."

"Maybe I just haven't found the right guy."

"Or you prefer to be safe and alone. But Johnny slipped under your radar because he wasn't really a man, more like a nine-foot Labrador Retriever right?"

"I never thought of him like that."

"Well you clearly didn't see him as a man or you would have kept him at arm's length."

"That wasn't possible with Johnny. He wouldn't… I didn't… Well, he was very stubborn. And he knows stuff about me that no one else does."

"You can trust him with those secrets, Sonia. He'll never betray them." She rubbed her hands together in anticipation. "So, what time is the date?"

Sonia glanced at her watch. "At six. I hope you don't mind, I told him to pick me up here."

"We have to get you ready!"

Brianna herded Sonia into the bedroom and had her try on a series of a half-dozen dresses. Demure midnight blue, sleek short black, shimmering silver sequins, elegant gold halter, regal purple, a crazy black and white shredded silk number and then a slim, high-waisted poppy-red cocktail dress.

"Why do you have so many dresses when you…" Sonia stopped herself too late.

"When I don't go out?" Brianna's smile never reached her eyes. "Travis does my shopping. He likes to see me in dresses. We have date night at home, order in."

Sonia thought her captain would also like to show off his beautiful wife. But he couldn't.

"That's the one," said Brianna pointing at the red. "It looks lovely with your skin tone and with a red lip you'll look like the kind of woman that every marine in the world wants to take out for dinner and dancing."

What kind of woman, Sonia wondered, did Johnny want her to be? As she stared at her reflection in the full-length mirror it suddenly hit home that Johnny had not been with a woman for many months. Did he hope that she and he… Sonia blanched, not because she could not imagine sleeping with Johnny but because she could imagine it in great detail and it made her skin flush and her body grow damp.

She wanted to sleep with him. What she didn't want was a relationship because a relationship meant trust and she didn't trust her heart to anyone. Besides, it couldn't last. He was a war hero and she was, well, the opposite of all that. Johnny didn't need her anymore and she'd be stupid to let herself need him. Sonia knew she was many things but stupid was not one of them. Realist, pessimist, whatever you called it, she knew it wouldn't work out between them. So she told herself to keep it light and casual. So why did her heart ache with the dread at their impending breakup? And how did she get out of here with her dignity? She didn't do relationships, but now, because of her work with Johnny, she already had one and it was about to get complicated. Johnny's condition had caused her to lose her secrets. He knew her deep down and now he was a man, an alluring man who wanted to take her out.

She closed her eyes and imagined Johnny's hand low at the center of her back.

Brianna's voice came from behind her. "Sonia, are you all right? You look a little flushed."

She met Brianna's gaze in the mirror. "What if he wants to…"

Brianna's eyebrows lifted. "It's up to you to decide if and when you and Johnny do more than dance." She turned toward the door and paused in the opening. "Feel free to use any of the makeup in that drawer."

"Yes, ma'am."

The flutter of excitement in her stomach told her she really wanted to have Johnny's arms about her and not just on the dance floor. But she'd never been with someone she really cared about.

Brianna returned with three perfumes. Sonia gave her a panicky look.

"It's only a date," said Brianna.

"Yeah. Just a date."

Chapter 10

Just a date, Sonia thought as she returned to Brianna's home hours later to prepare for her evening with Johnny.

But it was more, much, much more. Sonia felt the truth of that in her heart. He was tall, dangerous and his very presence threatened her nice, safe world. And now that he was human, Johnny stirred all her sexual fantasies.

He'd come through this nightmare. But his experiences must have scorched him. Had it been too much? Had they ruined him the way the drink had ruined her mother?

Some hurts are too big to heal, her mother had once said. *Your only chance is to drown them.*

Weren't Johnny's sorrows bigger than her mother's, bigger than her own? She knew Johnny and respected him. But now he was human and her confidence fled.

Whatever happened tonight, there would be consequences. She just didn't know what they would be.

Sonia went to work applying eyeliner and curling her eyelashes. Then she applied a red lip that made her mouth look lush. Brianna insisted she tuck the tube of lipstick in her borrowed clutch.

When her makeup was finished, Sonia began pacing in her silver high heels, borrowed from Brianna, as well. They shared a similar foot size, dress size and an affinity for werewolves.

But Brianna had sought and had achieved a lasting relationship with the captain. That took a kind of optimism Sonia had never had.

She paused to regard her reflection in a full length mirror. Their dress size might be the same but their body type was not. Sonia was sure that the dress that looked elegant on Brianna's willowy form but it looked like an invitation on her curves.

What would Johnny think? He'd seen her in a bathing suit, but not in makeup and red lipstick. He deserved a pretty, feminine date. Besides, Sonia wasn't a girl to be dressed in pink, but neither was she the confident sexy woman who stared back. She'd never wore red before in her life and now she knew why. Brianna's reflection appeared behind her in the mirror. Sonia met her gaze but did not return her encouraging smile.

"I feel like the cape that the matador waves before a bull," she said to Brianna.

Brianna chuckled. "Yes, I can see that. I reached Travis. He's given his permission." Brianna searched Sonia's expression and opened her mouth to say something before cocking her head. "They're here."

Sonia stopped as if suddenly frozen and her heart jolted along at a gallop.

"I don't hear them."

Brianna shrugged and tapped one ear. "Super hearing," she muttered and headed for the door but she paused close to Sonia and smiled. "Have a wonderful evening and please come and see me again soon. You're welcome anytime."

Sonia felt a welling of gratitude and a sense of how very few people Brianna would welcome into her home.

"I will. And thank you for the dress and, well, everything."

Brianna smiled, reached toward Sonia and then drew her hands back, folding them tightly before her. "I hope they play a slow dance." Then she opened the door to an empty driveway, but a few moments later a Jeep appeared. Brianna waved her inside. "Go into the bedroom. Make an entrance for goodness' sake."

Sonia did as she was told but watched from the window as the captain emerged from the driver's seat, wearing his beige cammies. Her gaze flipped to the passenger seat but the glare prevented her from seeing Johnny until he stepped out. His dark head appeared first, his hair pulled back at the nape of his neck. Her breath caught at the sight of him. Tiny sparks of electricity fired inside her belly as he straightened. He was still tall, over six feet, surely. The last time she'd seen him he was in a hospital bed attached to various machinery. Now he stood in a charcoal-gray suit and crisp white dress shirt that made his skin look dark by comparison. His tie was red and he stroked it once as he glanced toward the house. She held her breath and backed away from the window. Had he seen her? Sonia checked her lipstick and added more. Her lips and mouth felt so dry all of a sudden. Then she checked the contents of her borrowed bag and found everything in order, brush, lipstick, tissues, money, credit cards and— Her fingers brushed something cold and unfamiliar. She drew out a green foil packet and realized it was a condom. Several condoms that Brianna had added to the bag. Sonia pictured sliding the rubber sheath over Johnny's erection and felt dizzy all of a sudden. She sank to the bed and fanned her hot skin belatedly realizing she held the spread of three condoms like a fan. She tucked them deep into the purse and exhaled.

"Just a date."

There was a gentle tap on the door. Brianna stepped in and Sonia made an attempt to fiddle with the silver buckle on the high-heeled sandals.

"He brought flowers!" the vampire squealed in a hushed voice. "Red roses. Are you ready? Sonia, pinch your cheeks you've gone pale again."

"First time I've ever gone out with a man who knows my last name."

Brianna's brow wrinkled and she chuckled, then glanced at Sonia and stopped as she must have realized Sonia wasn't joking. "Well, not the only first tonight, I suppose." She worried one hand with the other until Sonia stood and made for the open door. She preceded Brianna out and found the men in the living room. Johnny spoke to the captain who spotted her first and frowned. Her commanding officer did not look happy as he shook his head and glanced to his wife who shrugged. Johnny stopped speaking and turned in her direction. He was so handsome in his new suit she felt her throat close. She stopped and Johnny came to her, hands extended and a smile growing on his generous mouth.

"Sonia, you look so beautiful."

She didn't need to pinch her cheeks because she felt the heat flooding them now. "And you look very handsome." She reached for his tie, straightened the knot then slid her fingers down the silken fabric. When she lifted her gaze to his she found his eyes blazing and his stare intense. He leaned in and kissed her cheek, lingering as his warm mouth brushed her skin. She flushed right down to her toes. His rich spicy scent lingered after he drew away.

"Don't forget these," said Brianna handing the roses over to Johnny.

He presented them to her and she cradled them as if she was Miss America. The florist had arranged them in a spray intended for carrying and had mixed in just enough tropical greenery that she would not forget that she was now on an island paradise.

"They are lovely, Johnny. Thank you."

"Ready?" He offered his arm.

She clamped the tiny silver shoulder bag against her side and nodded, wondering why all she could think about was those damned green foil packets. Brianna handed her a brightly colored shawl at the door and kissed Johnny goodbye. The captain drew her aside and leaned in.

"Put this phone in your purse. Call me directly if you need me. I'll be close and get him back here safe." He straightened and gave her a forced smile.

Sonia swallowed back her anxiety, gripping the phone. He'd be close? What did that mean exactly?

Johnny helped her over the rough ground and guided

her into the Jeep, shutting the door and then dashing about the front with such speed she could almost believe he was half vampire.

The captain stood stiff with disapproval as Brianna waved from the steps. Johnny helped Sonia into the passenger seat and then took the wheel, backing out and then left the captain and his vampire wife behind as they headed down the mountain. The silence between them was new and unfamiliar. Finally she asked about his day and discovered that he had failed at changing back to his werewolf form.

"What does that mean, exactly?"

"Mac thinks I don't want to change. Might be right, too."

Their conversation died away again. Sonia stared out the window and noticed they were not heading for the security checkpoint. When it became clear that they were heading across base she had a sudden flash of panic that they were aiming for the mess hall, a move that neither of them would ever live down, but Johnny drove them to the docks and carefully escorted her onto one of the boats where Sergeant Domingo Cavillo, one of Johnny's exercise companions, ferried them the ten miles to West Maui and the oceanfront resort where he had made reservations. She wondered if the sergeant would wait for them, but her stiletto heel no sooner hit the dock than the boat headed away.

"I can call him for a pick up."

Can? She lifted an eyebrow because she realized that he could just as easily not call him for a pick up and they were at a resort with palm trees, blooming jasmine, newlyweds and many, many vacant bedrooms. The possibilities stirred her blood and she stopped walking as she glanced up into Johnny's intent brown eyes. The captain wanted her to get John back safe while she wanted to wake to mimosas and a rumpled bed.

His mouth stretched into a wicked smile and she forgot how to breathe. He placed a hand on her lower back, ushering her along as she tried not to dwell on the warmth of his hand or the strength of his graceful stride, slowed now to match her smaller one.

They walked slowly along the dock in the early evening, past the snorkelers on the beach and the poolside restaurant.

"Lots of honeymooners here," he commented, his voice and his implication making her skin tingle.

His hand slid from her back and he offered his elbow. She clung to his arm more tightly as they left the dock for the brick walkway. Beneath the fine fabric of his jacket she could feel the steel of his muscles.

They strolled past the bar and families enjoying casual dining. Johnny was the only person in a suit and their appearance turned more than one head.

"We're overdressed," she whispered.

"We're not eating here."

Inside the hotel lobby Johnny strolled with the casualness of a confident man. He nodded at the concierge and continued on through the etched glass entrance of the Waterfront Steakhouse, pausing to open the door for her and then again at the hostess station. Johnny spoke to a young woman wearing a red hibiscus in her hair while Sonia admired the tropical fish in a large saltwater tank.

A hostess escorted them to the restaurant's interior and a table with a killer view of the sun setting over the

Pacific Ocean. She even took Sonia's flowers and returned with them in a lovely arrangement for their table.

Johnny glanced at the wine list and then set it aside asking for sparkling water and two nonalcoholic frozen drinks. The drinks arrived a few moments later with huge glasses topped with orchids and a skewer of fresh fruit. She sipped a sweet icy strawberry drink and smiled up at Johnny.

"Perfect."

He nodded. They watched the sun dip toward the water, a huge orange ball that gradually melted into the sea. As it set, the sky blazed with streaks of orange fire that turned the clouds violet and gold.

"I've never seen anything so beautiful," she whispered.

"I have," he said and she glanced up to see he was staring at her.

The compliment pleased her and she beamed. "You've seen me before."

"Not at sunset. Not at my table in a dress like that."

"I liked the meals you cooked for us at your bungalow."

"I'll be glad to cook for you for as long as you like."

"That's good news because you've spoiled me for the mess hall forever."

The silence between them seemed more complicated now and she was relieved to see the appetizers arrive. She tried the potstickers which turned out to be delicious little dumplings with a salty brown sauce. She'd never had to struggle to find a topic of conversation with Johnny before, but as she crunched her way through her salad she stretched to think of something, anything to say. The tension between them made her stomach ache and she had trouble eating the special, a pecan-crusted tilapia fillet with a mango and pineapple chutney. Johnny's appetite was epic as he polished off his favorite, very rare steak and potatoes and the entire bread basket.

During the main course, the recorded music ceased as a band set up on the large balcony. The steel drums' ringing rhythms drifted in on the Pacific breeze, exotic and alluring. Still she wished they were back at Johnny's place. Alone, instead of here in the open with his goons across the room watching her as if she and Johnny were on pay-per-view.

"You seem nervous," he said.

She snapped her eyes back to him, wondering how it was possible that he hadn't seen his wounded warriors yet. "I suppose I am."

"Why?"

She watched Corporal Del Tabron give her a small nod before lifting his beer glass. They knew she was aware of them.

"Hmm? Oh, I never really go on dates. Just one-nighters mostly. I don't even tell them my real name." This was met with silence and she snapped her gaze to his to see his brow low over his dark eyes and a definite edge of danger in his expression. What the hell had she been thinking?

But she hadn't been. She'd been so busy looking at his wounded warriors, she hadn't censored her reply.

"Sonia, what does that mean?"

Her shoulders dropped with her spirits.

"Just that. I told you I don't like people. I don't trust them. They either want too much or I want too much.

Relationships are complicated. I like to keep things simple."

"You mean sex."

She pursed her lips for one long intake and exhale. Then she answered. "Yeah. Sex. Sex with guys I don't know and never wanted to know. Scratch the itch. Move on."

She'd shocked him speechless.

"You think I'm bad."

"I think you're broken."

"Yeah. That's about right."

Right then, in the middle of his deciding she was as dysfunctional as a car on blocks, the band played their first slow dance.

Perfect timing, she thought.

"Listen, John, you can take me home. I'll understand."

Instead, he set aside his napkin and offered his hand. Sonia sat poised between wanting to leave the room and wanting to be wrapped in John's strong arms.

"May I have this dance?"

"Are you sure?"

"Never more certain."

She accepted his hand, surprised at the thrill of excitement that rippled from the point of contact.

He walked her past the other tables to the dance floor surrounded by brightly burning torches. When they got there, they were by no means the only couple enjoying the trade winds and starry night.

Johnny laced his fingers with hers and splayed his other hand on her back before sweeping them into a slow circle.

Magic, she thought, as she moved in time with his

steps on the most romantic of all dance floors. So why was her heart jackhammering so loudly that she could barely hear the music? He didn't draw her closer, just moved with a grace that rippled with sensuality. She was acutely aware of the sway of his hips. The second dance was slower and couples around them seemed to melt into their partner's embrace, moving in perfect synchronization, obviously relaxed and at ease in each other's company. Sonia felt awkward and uncertain as she edged closer resting her cheek on his shoulder. She was unwilling to press her body to his mainly because she wanted to so badly. This was a dangerous road, she realized. Her skin tingled and her breasts ached. She knew the signs. Sonia sighed as his cheek brushed the top of her head and closed her eyes. Sonia let the music and John Lam take her deeper into the enchantment of the night.

She wanted Johnny's body, but in the morning there would be no escaping him because unlike the rest of the men she had slept with, Johnny knew where she lived. He knew other things, too, secret intimate things. Things she never expected another person in this world to know about her. She shivered in excitement as she rocked her hips from side to side, matching his lead, wanting to let him lead.

What was she doing and where would this end?

Johnny breathed in her fragrance. The tiny capillaries beneath her skin opened wide bringing a beguiling pink flush to her cheeks and the scent of the rose petals that she had carried all the way from the base. Johnny's sense of smell remained acute and despite his inability or unwillingness to change, he felt the wolf still inside him. It hadn't disappeared as the doctors feared. It had just gone deep.

How long had he dreamed of this night? How many nights had he imagined holding her in his arms and having her see the man that he had always been instead of that monster that still lurked within?

Now she was here with him but instead of the easy falling together he had dreamed it would be, Sonia revealed a new hesitancy in conversation and a reluctance that troubled him. Why had she never had a second date and what did that mean for them? He knew her name. He knew her secrets. He knew Sonia and he wanted more. Would she be willing to sleep with him knowing that she couldn't just disappear in the morning?

He scented her arousal but also her fear. Now that he was a man, she no longer trusted him. Or did she just not find him appealing. Didn't she like his looks?

Every time he moved closer, she stepped back. His hips were a tantalizing inch from hers, her breasts nearly brushed against his chest but she kept just out of reach. It was all he could do not to drag her against him. He didn't want to frighten her but he'd never wanted a woman more. Not just any woman. He wanted this woman.

Johnny had broken off with his high school steady when he joined up and had only had occasional companionship since then. Now all he could think about was kissing Sonia everywhere and of seeing her lying naked in his bed by candle light and then again in the morning, her long hair tangled in the rumbled bedding. His insides squeezed and the steady thrum of blood beat insistently within him. He wanted this woman.

He glanced down to see her eyes closed as her cheek

rested on his chest. Even with her eyes closed, her expression looked pained as if she wanted to be anywhere but here. Well, that was exactly what he wanted, but now he worried that Sonia did not imagine this night ending as he did. He glanced around the room, seeing other couples, ladies clinging to their men, pressing hip-to-hip or gazing longingly into each other's eyes.

Honeymooners, he realized, now recognizing his mistake. He'd taken a woman who was terrified of commitment on their first date and dropped her into the center of a room full of committed couples. How stupid could he get?

She didn't press herself against him like the other women draped like boneless cats against their new husbands. Sonia wasn't a bride in the arms of the man she loved. She was a young marine on her first date with a werewolf. It was a wonder she didn't fly screaming from the room. And then it hit him. She couldn't. She couldn't say no to this date any more than she could quit teaching him. She was stuck because she'd robbed a house, so now if she didn't make him happy, they'd send her back where she came from. Back to jail, back to that damned dog cage.

No wonder she barely touched her dinner.

Suddenly Johnny felt sick. He didn't want her here against her will. He drew back.

The song ended and the band played a faster number, with steel drums and a Caribbean sound. Sonia looked up at him with eyes that asked for rescue. He felt the same aching need he always felt when she looked at him and then as now he wouldn't act on it because he'd never know if she wanted to or felt she must. He knew she'd do anything to keep from going back to jail, even, apparently, go out with him.

He hated the idea of taking her upstairs now. Would she look at him as she did on the dance floor as if he were some distasteful obligation to be discharged as quickly as possible? He'd bought her flowers, put on a suit and she'd dressed in red. But it was all a lie.

"Are you all right?" she asked as he held her chair back at their table.

"Yes." He said it a little too quickly.

"You look as if you are in pain." Her eyes went wide. "Johnny, you'd know if you were about to change. Wouldn't you? Because the captain said…"

God, he hadn't even thought of that. No wonder the captain and the major had been so against his coming out and why she was tense as a newbie at boot camp. Why had they let him go? He had another thought and glanced about the room, finding the bar and three familiar backs perched like crows on a wire. He met the eyes of Carver, Zeno and Kiang in the mirror. Apparently the major hadn't let him off the leash after all. They'd just made it a little longer. His mood darkened. Had they enjoyed his awkward little dance with Sonia?

Sonia noticed the direction of his gaze and he heard her groan.

His gaze narrowed on the men.

"Yeah. Maybe I'll just go say hello."

She clasped his arm and he stopped as suspicion grew.

"Why don't we just order our desert?"

He was in a fishbowl. Had anything really changed?

"Did you know?"

She lowered the menu. "They're here for your protection and to protect all the people here."

"Did you all think I'd go crazy?"

She lowered the menu. "They can't know what will happen next any more than you do."

He knew she was right but the situation now stuck in his throat like an overlarge piece of steak. "I wanted to be alone with you."

"Then we should have stayed at your place on Molokai." She reached across the table and rested her hand on his. "Johnny, we've had a lovely meal and you are an excellent dancer. Let's have desert."

"And then head back?"

"If you'd like."

Johnny glanced at his three escorts. His bodyguards and the realization that Sonia might not be here by choice made the evening about as romantic as a frontal assault. Johnny ordered an espresso and Sonia had a crème brûlée. She seemed relieved to be escorted back to the dock where the boat he hadn't called was waiting. Johnny wanted to kick someone's ass. Instead, he helped Sonia aboard and then handed her the vase of red roses. He felt stupid and betrayed all at once.

Sonia wrapped the shawl over her shoulders and huddled about her flowers protecting them from the wind.

Back on Molokai, he drove her to the barracks and walked her to the entrance.

"John, I know that the evening didn't go as you would have liked. But I had a lovely time and I want to thank you."

He stared down at her, his heart so full of hope and despair he could not even summon a single word.

"Please be patient with me. I just need a little time."

"Time," he parroted. How much time? Time to do what? He'd had too much damned time—time alone, time as a monster, time with her when she couldn't see how he felt. Now she wanted more of it. Finally, he nodded because he had no other choice. "All right."

"Will I see you tomorrow?"

"Sure. Come up in the afternoon. You can teach me some more signs." Like frustrated, sullen and pissed-off, he thought.

She lifted on her toes and tried to kiss him. He turned so her lips met his cheek accepting it for what it was, a mercy kiss.

"Thank you for the flowers."

He made a fast retreat and headed off base. Behind him he saw the lights of a Jeep which he had no trouble ditching. He ended up in one of the three places he'd heard his groupies mention and just as he'd expected there were single women at the bar, working girls who didn't care who you were and didn't expect you to be patient. He looked over the bunch and picked the one who had dark hair and mocha skin. She was native but she had Sonia's coloring. She smiled an invitation but Johnny recognized the feral glint in her eye, the look of a wolf hunting.

"Hi, handsome," she said. "You want some company?"

He stood his ground and she slid from the stool and sidled over, swaying her hips as she approached. The moment she brushed her hand over his cheek he knew coming here was a mistake. He thought this was what he needed, one of them beneath him. He'd just close his eyes and pretend it was Sonia. Now instead of the flush of heat and lust, he felt stone cold.

"Damn it," he muttered.

"You got a ride, soldier? We could take a ride." She licked her sticky pink lips. "Or take a walk in the moonlight."

He could have her and be done. But somehow he knew he'd never be done. Not since he'd first set eyes on Sonia. The woman wrapped her arms around his neck and pressed her small breasts against him. Cigarette smoke clung to her hair and her soft body only reminded him of how Sonia held back. Johnny dragged the woman's arms from his neck because he didn't want her. He wanted the woman he'd been dreaming of and lusting after for weeks and weeks. He'd spent too many nights imagining Sonia to settle for this clinging woman who smelled like stale beer and male sweat. He pulled her off and moved to the other end of the bar.

He didn't want sex with this stranger. He wanted Sonia.

She'd asked him to be patient. Damn her.

He ordered a whiskey and then threw it back. The burn in his throat was familiar but there was no second kick.

The front door opened and in walked his captain, dressed in jeans, running shoes and a marine sweatshirt on inside out. Johnny just knew he'd gotten him out of bed, that nice warm bed he shared with his bride. Johnny snorted, not feeling one bit guilty. If he had to sleep alone, the captain could, too.

"Waste of money," said Mac, nodding toward the empty whiskey glass.

Johnny stared sullenly at him.

"You can finally talk and you got nothing to say?"

Oh, no. He had plenty. But he was pretty sure the captain didn't want to hear it.

"You remember when I found you and Brianna together in my bed?" asked Johnny.

Mac winced. Suddenly it was the captain who had nothing to say. He ordered two beers just to have something to do and pushed one at Johnny before taking a long pull of his own. Finally he banged the long-necked bottle on the bar and turned to him. "I remember."

"I was pissed she picked you. Hoped she had feelings for me but she couldn't see me so I never had a chance. Not with my…condition."

"Johnny…." Mac stopped there and had another swallow of his beer.

"Did you pick Sonia to be my companion? To keep me company while I waited for this?" he swept a hand over his form.

Mac's fingers tightened on the neck of his bottle and his jaw muscles twitched. "What if I did? She kept you from using that gun, didn't she?"

Johnny scowled.

"You think I didn't know about it? Well, I did."

Johnny released his beer and made several gestures.

Mac watched in silence and then said, "Say it to my face."

"I said you're a fucking asshole and Sonia is treating me as if I've got the clap."

Mac stared at Johnny's hands. "What's the sign for clap?" he asked.

"You have to finger spell it."

Mac exhaled through his nose and made a face as if he didn't have the time or energy. Johnny finished his beer in several long swallows. Mac signaled the bartender by raising two fingers then returned his attention to Johnny.

"She's treating you like someone she just met. John, look at you." Mac gestured toward the mirror. "She doesn't know you."

"The hell she doesn't."

"You look different. Give her time. She asked you to be patient, didn't she?"

Johnny slammed his empty bottle on the table. "How do you know that?" Had he bugged the restaurant? Was their date scripted?

"She said it right in front of me." He rubbed the back of his neck. "Did I have eyes in that room? Yes. I couldn't let you go out alone. There are too many variables. You don't know how to control the wolf yet. Strong emotion triggers the change. I couldn't have you going all furry in public."

"Strong emotion? Then I ought to be wearing a fur coat right now."

"Listen, John, I'll teach you how to control it. You'll get the hang of it and if Sonia is right for you, she'll come around."

"What if she doesn't?"

"Well, she won't if you keep acting like an asshole and chase her away. Do you know about her mom?"

Johnny nodded.

"Her sister?"

Another nod.

"Then you know she's cautious. So what is wrong with going slow? Her usual M.O. is a one-night stand. Would you rather have her only once. Slow might mean she's, I don't know, interested. So go slow."

"Do I have a choice?"

"Yeah, you do. Go slow or fuck it up. Now can we go home?"

Chapter 11

Johnny woke alone in his king-size bed to the ringing phone. The bedsheets still smelled of Sonia, who had slept here, just not with him. He checked the phone's screen and saw Mac's image. He groaned, almost wishing he was in wolf form just so he wouldn't have to pick up the damned phone.

He was at the medical center an hour later. Despite Johnny's best efforts, he was still unable to change to wolf form. The team of doctors revealed that some of the earlier canine test subjects faired the same. Most changed back, some didn't and they were at a loss to determine why. His sight and vision remained acute. He picked up an uneasy vibe from the group as if not changing was a bad thing. He couldn't say he was the least bit sorry about that until he looked into Mac's eyes and saw the worry there. Then he remembered the vampires stalking Mac's wife. Now his captain would have no help protecting her. Mac had lost his wing man and Brianna had lost one of the only two werewolves in the world who were willing to protect a vampire from her own kind. Most of the werewolves would have gladly turned her over or killed her on sight.

Johnny met his friend's troubled stare and knew he'd be worse than useless against vampires now, like a toddler with a butter knife going against a medieval knight.

"I'm sorry," he said.

Mac's brow furrowed in question.

"I can't help you protect Brianna," said Johnny.

Mac dropped his gaze but recovered quickly and pressed a hand to Johnny's shoulder. "I told you when we came here, that was never your job. She's not your responsibility. She's mine."

Easy to say, but Johnny knew that when the vamps came, they came together and one werewolf might not be enough. They'd need to get her to the lock-in facility.

"Johnny, if you're human again, mostly human, then you can live a normal life. See your sister and your mother. I'll keep my wife safe. We have the entire secure perimeter right here. I'll scent them in plenty of time to get her to safety."

Johnny gave him a long look and Mac nodded. The weight of that responsibility ebbed away. He smiled.

"I would have defended her."

"I know it. We're both happy for you. Eventually Sonia will be happy that you won't be going all furry on her, too. Give her time."

"I haven't seen her since last night."

Mac rubbed his neck. "You want me to have her report to your place?"

"For what, a lesson?" Then it hit him. Sonia must have realized it right away. Of course she would have.

"What's going to happen with her?"

Mac shrugged. "Not sure. She'll keep her clearance but…"

But he didn't need a translator. Holy shit, they'd be reassigning her. "No, I want her here."

Mac nodded. "I know you do, buddy. But it might not be up to you. And besides, if you stay human you can have your combat assignment. You'll be leaving anyway, just like you wanted."

Leaving Mac and Brianna behind. Leaving Sonia behind. He'd been badgering Mac to get him back to combat duty for months. Now he could go, but where did that leave Sonia? Uncertainty oscillated inside him like water sloshing in a bucket.

"Yeah, like I wanted," said Johnny and rubbed his jaw, not sure he wanted to leave the island and realizing it wasn't the island he didn't wish to leave, but Sonia.

"Well, not so fast. The doctors want to observe you awhile. You still have your sense of smell and you're too damn strong for a human. So some part of you is still wolf."

"What about Sonia?" asked Johnny. "Her assignment?"

"She can stay awhile."

But she was leaving or he was. Johnny felt sick. How long did they have?

Johnny left Mac and headed for his quarters. He was halfway up the hill when he scented something familiar and froze to the spot as if he had just realized he'd stepped on a land mine.

Vampire. Had to be. But not Brianna. This was sweet

and cloying, like heavy perfume mixed with the tang of spilled blood.

Johnny changed direction, running to Mac's home. As he went the scent grew fainter and fainter until he was not sure he had smelled it at all. He drew out his phone as he ran and called Mac. Johnny arrived in Brianna's yard to find her standing in her garden, where she had obviously been working. She would have heard his approach as he crashed from the undergrowth. Her welcoming smile faded as she looked at his wild expression and she clutched her other hand over the first.

"What is it?" she asked, but already her gaze was flitting about for any sign of the vampires and she was vibrating as she did before she vanished from his sight. Brianna could move so quickly that even he could not track her movements.

"I smelled something down the hill. I called Mac." He no sooner said the words then she was at his side, clinging to him. Then she gave a cry and pushed off and away staggering backward.

"I forgot. You're human again. I can't touch you."

He'd forgotten, too. What did he do now—stay with her, wait for Mac, take her to lockdown or send her down alone? She could be there in five seconds but if they were here that would not be fast enough. For the first time since the change, Johnny felt powerless. He motioned away from the house. It would be better not to be where they would expect to find her.

They did not have long to wait. Mac roared into the yard in his gray werewolf form a few minutes later. He huffed from his exertions. Johnny realized he must have fairly flown up that hill. And as an odd turn about now Johnny could speak and Mac could not.

Mac moved to stand beside Brianna who collapsed against her husband as naturally as if he were in human form. She did not cringe or show any sign at all that his fearsome appearance troubled her. In fact she looked damned relieved.

"Did you scent them?" Johnny asked.

Mac shook his head.

"It was down the hill before that second turn. Very faint. Do you want to bring her down?"

Mac gave another nod.

"Walk or drive?"

Mac lifted his hands as if on a steering wheel then pointed to Johnny. He wanted him to drive. Johnny motioned to the Jeep and Brianna climbed into the back seat leaving the larger passenger seat for her nine-foot werewolf husband. Johnny drove fast but not crazy fast. At the bottom they drove straight into the secure facility built to study one werewolf and protect one female vampire. The metal doors shut behind them.

Johnny now began to wonder if the vamps were inside the base or if his senses were screwy. The perimeter fence included their houses above the base and were rigged with special motion detectors sensitive enough to detect male vamps. The high-speed cameras recorded everything that moved. If intruders broke perimeter, they'd know it. That meant they weren't on base...yet.

Major Scofield waited inside the lockdown facility, meeting both Mac and Brianna.

"Where's Sonia?" Johnny asked.

Mac pointed up the hill and Johnny's heart shuttered as cold terror flashed through him like flood water.

"I've got to get her," he told his commanding officer and took off without waiting for approval. Ten minutes later he roared into his driveway. It bothered him that he could not run the distance, that it was now faster to drive. What if the vampires were at his house? Mac was down below with Brianna and Johnny would no longer be a match for them. He left the Jeep and raced into the yard, charging up the stairs. He threw open the door to his place so hard the knob crashed through the sheet rock. Sonia, in the kitchen, turned and screamed. She took one look at him and ran in his direction. He didn't explain, just grabbed her and turned, running with her in his arms, holding her like a tackle dummy as he tore across the yard and back to the Jeep. When she was seated and he had the Jeep in Reverse she asked him what was happening.

"One of them is here," he said, eyes on the road as he threw it into gear.

"Vampires?" she whispered.

"Yes. Down the hill."

"Brianna!" called Sonia as they flew past her driveway.

"Already at the base in lockdown."

Sonia clicked on her belt and held on as they sped down the road and into the fenced compound.

"Did they trip the perimeter alarms?"

They hadn't. So they'd beaten the perimeter or they were still outside the fence.

"No. I smelled one."

It wasn't until they reached lock-in and he stopped the Jeep that he allowed himself to believe Sonia was truly safe. He reached across the seat and dragged her into his lap.

She threw her arms about his neck and their lips met in a fierce kiss. His mouth slanted over hers and she held him tighter as she gave a cry deep in her throat and opened her mouth. His tongue slid along hers as they deepened the kiss. She was safe, he realized and pulled her closer, so thankful she was out of harm's way that his eyes drifted closed. Fear melted to relief and the kiss changed from frantic to fire. Pure liquid heat ignited in his core and his body hardened. Her fingers raked through his hair, those trimmed nails leaving a tingling path in their wake. She rubbed against him and he felt the aching pressure of her soft, round breasts pressed to him in a way that he'd imagined many times. But this was better. So good. She writhed against him and he angled her closer so that she sat between the wheel and his chest, with her bottom planted firmly on his erection. She sighed and shifted, rocking against him as he deepened the kiss. The horn blared and they both jumped. Sonia broke away staring at him in shock, her lips parted and pink. He tried to kiss her again but she slithered back to her seat.

He shook himself, trying to drive away the arousal and the aching need. Nothing in his imagining could ever compare to that kiss. She had a hand on her forehead as she breathed heavily through her open mouth.

"Wow," she said at last.

He blew out a breath and nodded.

"Should we report?" she asked, glancing toward the entrance and the surveillance cameras

He should, but not in his condition. If strong emotions triggered the change than he was definitely not changing to wolf form any time soon because he had never felt an emotional tsunami like that one. He swallowed.

"I need a minute."

She glanced at the long ridge of male flesh sheathed in his beige cammies. "Oh, sure." She straightened in her seat tugging at her shirt and her face flushed.

"What were you doing at my place?" he asked. Not really caring, but fighting hard against the urge to drag her back onto his lap.

"Oh, well, I thought we should talk." She sagged in her seat and then turned to face him, picking up with sign language, only this time she didn't accompany each word with speech.

I am so sorry I ruined the evening. I'm confused and afraid. What will happen to me now? Her eyebrows tented at the question. *You don't need a translator or any of the sign language I taught you. You don't need me.*

He made his response in slow careful movements. *I need you now more than ever.*

Her bottom lip trembled and she reached for him, throwing herself into his arms. "I knew this would happen," she said.

"What?"

"I didn't want to get attached. Then I wouldn't care about leaving. But now." She sniffed. "I knew something like this would happen the minute I did."

He felt a spark of hope that died as he took in her bereft expression. He stroked her hair. "Sonia, it's going to be all right."

Someone banged on the driver's-side window. Sonia sprang back to her seat, wiping her eyes. Johnny turned to the jerk who interrupted them and saw Major Scofield.

"Need you both inside, son," said the major.

Johnny nodded and opened the door, but hesitated as he looked back to Sonia.

"Johnny," urged Scofield.

He exited the vehicle as Sonia scrambled out the other side, her face now red as she saluted.

The major motioned with his head. "Touma, you're coming with me. Lam, you've got perimeter with Mac-Connelly."

She gave Johnny one long beseeching look before scrambling after the retreating major.

She signed, *Be careful.*

Johnny found Mac, still in werewolf form. They spent the rest of the afternoon sweeping the hillside and surrounding area but found no trace of the scent of vampires.

"False alarm?" asked Mac that evening.

"Might have been. It was faint. But I could swear I smelled them." Were his senses playing tricks on him, leaving him all together? "I was sure."

"But then why can't we track him? And why no perimeter alarms or surveillance footage?"

Johnny couldn't answer but the doubts crept in. He could no longer trust his senses.

Everyone stayed at the compound that evening. Johnny checked on Sonia, finding her eating alone in the mess hall. She said she was fine but she seemed nervous and upset. He wanted to linger, but he had a duty to Mac and the others here, so they swept the hillside again that evening and once more the following day. He and Mac remained on patrol, one or the other, circling the compound and scenting for vampires.

The base remained in lockdown one more night before calling an all clear. Scofield put extra security details on assignment and patrols on the hill. Johnny didn't like the company, but he could see that it relieved Brianna. *It shouldn't,* he thought. Marines were no match for vampires. The volcanic hillside was steep and impassible in places, even for a vampire. That was why they selected this spot. It allowed Brianna the distance from others, while affording them a defensible position. Despite their assurance that no vampires could attack from above them, they still had a perimeter fence, high speed cameras, infrared trip wires. All had been checked and all came up empty. Which made him wonder if he'd imagined the entire thing.

The only one here who stood a chance against them was Mac and he was all set to face however many they sent for Brianna. Once they found her, that might be a lot. If he were hunting her, he'd be damned sure he came with more vampires the next time.

Johnny heard the Jeep when he was in the shower and assumed it was Mac. He threw on jeans and a T-shirt before coming out onto the porch, then paused as her scent came to him on the breeze.

Sonia.

She'd come back to him at last. Over the days and nights of searching for some trace of the vampire his mind kept wandering back to that kiss in front of headquarters. Johnny closed the door and retreated into the house flicking off the overhead lights, leaving only the lamps on the end table illuminated and the lights beneath the cupboards in the kitchen. He didn't want to meet her in the driveway or the stairs or his porch. He wanted to meet her in his bedroom. He might not manage that, but he could at least greet her in his living room beside the couch that had always been too small for him—until now. Now, it was just the right size for two with one stretched out on top of the other. His skin tingled as the sound of her footfalls upon the stairs reached him.

She rapped on the door and he came to her. The breeze carried no hint of danger as he opened his arms. Thankfully she stepped into his embrace kissing him quickly on the cheek before stepping inside. Not what he'd been hoping for, he thought, but better than nothing.

He glanced past her to the hillside. His night vision was still good and he scanned the yard in twilight wondering if he were still strong enough to kill a vampire if one appeared.

Johnny inhaled once more and, finding nothing unusual, he followed her inside. He managed to hold his smile, trying to pretend that he wasn't already burning for her. She'd asked him to wait and he had waited. Was the longing now too much for her, as well? Did she want him, but only for one night?

Sonia shifted restlessly before him, rocking from side to side as she stood in a pair of tight-fitting jeans and a pretty pink sleeveless top. The cut of the garment showed her toned arms and the pale brown perfection of her skin.

"How are you?" she asked, peeking at him from beneath thick lowered lashes.

He breathed deeply. She'd put on a light body spray at her throat and her stomach. He smiled and inclined his chin. "Better now that you're here. I've been missing you."

He watched her swallow as if nervous. She rubbed

her hands together absently and glanced around the living room.

"Have you?" Her eyes met his in an expression that he thought was hopeful. Then she cast a look toward the door as she pressed her lips together. He grasped her elbow and guided her farther into the house, farther from the front door.

"Come sit down," he said, bringing her attention back to him.

"Oh, I can't stay."

He moved back, giving her space and hoping to bring her farther into the room. He'd never seen her so nervous before and it made him wonder if she was here for what he hoped or for what he feared.

"I'm making you some tea. Iced green oolong with ginseng."

He thumbed over his shoulder toward the kitchen and she nodded, following him. She perched on one of the stools that faced the counter and watched him work. He set the kettle on the gas burner. Tea was a ritual, a comfort and an art form. He set out a small ceramic teapot and threw the dried leaves in with the crushed ginseng powder. He had made her tea before, many times. Now he felt her eyes upon him as he worked. The silence buzzed between them louder than the peepers outside.

He waited for her to speak first.

She cleared her throat. "You'll be able to see your mother and sister again soon. Won't you?"

He smiled imagining that reunion and then thinking of bringing Sonia to meet his mother. What would these two women think of one another?

"I guess I can."

"And you can fly on an airplane and go out in public." Something about her tone drew his complete attention because it was flat, lacking the usual passion her words so often conveyed. Where was she going with this?

She stared at the teapot and blew out a long breath. "Talk on the telephone. Have dinner in the mess hall. All the normal things you've missed."

He missed seeing her sign as she spoke.

"Yes. Sonia what are you saying?"

"You can do all those things now and more. You can talk Johnny. You can date anyone you want. You can get that assignment you've wanted. Make that higher pay grade."

He met her gaze and saw the sorrow reflected in her light brown eyes. She was trying to say goodbye. Well, he'd be damned if he'd let her. He was keeping Sonia, one way or another. She was the one who took the time to get to know him, to cheer him and to understand him. Yes, he'd had to play hardball at first, but he wasn't letting her go before they finished this. He needed to know. She needed to know what it was like to be with someone you cared about, someone who knew you like nobody else.

His hands stilled on the bag of dried leaves. He set it carefully on the counter and continued his deliberate movements, lifting the boiling kettle and pouring water into the small ceramic teapot. He filled two tall glasses with ice as the tea steeped in the little pot. Then he brought the glasses and teapot to her, setting them on the counter between them.

"This isn't because of that kiss," he asked.

Her denial was quick. "Of course not."

He'd shaken her. And she'd shaken him. Only he

wanted more and she was turning tail. Well, he wasn't going to let her run until she knew good and well what she was leaving behind. Then if she wanted to run, he'd let her.

"Maybe against your best efforts you've grown attached to me. Maybe that kiss scared you because it was so damn good. So now you want to go."

Her eyes widened and she pushed back from the counter so that her hands gripped the lip of the marble surface and her arms were stiff before her.

"I did my job but it's over, John."

He signed to her. *And you did it well.* "Are you afraid of me?" he asked.

"I wasn't before. Now I am."

He nodded. "Ah, I see. Then you're afraid of us."

"I liked it the way it was, when we could talk and just…" She shrugged one shoulder.

"So you came up here at night, alone to tell me that you wish I was still a werewolf."

She absently ran her index finger along the smooth edge of the counter. He watched the rhythmic stroking, tracking each tiny movement like a cat watching a water bug. Her finger stilled and he lifted his gaze to find her motionless as a paused image on his television, except for the widening of her eyes and the pulse that pounded at her throat.

"I don't want you to still be a werewolf. But I don't want this, either. I didn't want to come here. Now I don't want to leave."

"I don't want you to leave, either."

She made a fist and pounded it on the counter. "But I will be leaving. Any day now." She lowered her head. "I'm sorry. Is the tea ready?"

He opened the lid of the teapot to allow the steam to escape.

"Are you always this nervous around men?" he asked, trying to make the question casual as he reminded her that he was now a man.

"I never was before. But that was because they only touched me here." She pressed a hand over one breast cupping herself and he watched riveted as her fingers sank into soft flesh.

He gripped the handle of the ceramic teapot and he realized he was dangerously close to snapping the clay handle like a piece of chalk.

"I never let them in here." Her hand shifted so that it lay flat over her heart.

Did she know he could hear it beating in her chest, the throb of blood surging and the valves snapping shut?

"You're trying to shut me out again."

She nodded, not trying to deny it. "You're a marine trying for combat duty. I'm a marine trying for a nice safe spot on the sidelines until I'm discharged. I don't see a whole lot of options for us."

He poured the hot tea over the ice cubes in each glass. They cracked and hissed as they dissolved. He stirred the fluid in each container with a long necked spoon until the glasses and Sonia both began to sweat. Then he added more ice to each glass and handed one to her, being certain that their fingers brushed. Here they had no escorts, no prying eyes to watch them together. They were not parked before headquarters. She was right to be nervous because her words of caution did not mesh with the gleam in her eyes or the flush of her cheeks.

He watched her as he lifted his tea and downed the

contents in three long gulps. Then he wiped the remaining moisture from his lips with the back of his hand. Her mouth dropped open as she clutched her own glass.

"Aren't you thirsty?" he asked.

She lifted the glass and took a sip. Her hand was shaking, but not from fear. Arousal, he realized, scenting her desire. His pulse jumped and his body hardened, ready for her.

"The way I see it, you have two choices. You can cast off and run, which I know you are damn good at doing, or..." He lifted a brow as he plucked the glass from her fingers with one hand and captured hers with the other. He gave her a lazy grin.

"Or?" she asked, leaning toward him.

"Or you can get the answers to all those questions."

She cocked her head and her brow knit. "What questions?"

"Would we be good together? What would it be like? Will he be gentle or rough, fast or slow? And then there is the kicker, if you don't will you live to regret it?"

The tip of her pink tongue peeked out to run the width of her lower lip. Witnessing that tiny action sent a lightning bolt of desire streaking to his groin. He thought he'd been hard before, but now he pulsed for her with each heartbeat. He felt the hunger and thirst for her in his gut as the need beating through him with his blood, hot, burning hot and so strong that his shoulders ached as he held himself back. He wanted her to come to him. No, he needed her to come.

He leaned toward her. "You can still run away in the morning, but at least you'll have your answers."

Her eyes gleamed. Her mouth glistened and her head inclined in a barely perceptible nod.

He blew out a breath at the mingling of relief and desire. He'd have her in his bed tonight. Now all he needed was a way to keep her there. But how could he? She was right. She was going or he was going.

But they still had tonight.

He lifted one hand over his head and grasped his cotton T-shirt at the spot just between his shoulder blades, dragged it off and tossed the shirt aside. The gauntlet had been dropped. Her gaze dipped, raking his chest. He felt his skin pucker and tighten. She reached with both hands as her eyes flashed hungry as a tigress. He opened his arms wide.

Chapter 12

Johnny lowered his mouth to Sonia's in a hard, demanding kiss. He dragged his fingers through the thick satin of her hair and then gripped her, controlling her head as his tongue glided against hers. Her yielding mouth and hot tongue drove him crazy. He needed to get her to that bed, needed a moment to regroup. The fragrance of her skin and the softness of her body pressed to his, filled his mind with crazy thoughts, Sonia on the counter, legs splayed. He planned to go slow, but she was rubbing against him and he wanted her so badly.

It was Sonia who broke the kiss, but not to reconsider. No, judging from what her nimble fingers were doing to his zipper, she wanted him naked. He worked the buttons free on her blouse and offered a prayer of thanks at the sight of the black lace bra that cupped her breasts in a way that made him jealous.

He drew her in, needing to feel her soft skin pressed to his. He kissed her neck and the shell of her ear, taking the lobe into his mouth to suck the sweet morsel. She gasped and clung, lifting a leg and locking a heel behind his back. Sweet mercy, they'd never make it to his big empty bed.

"Bedroom?" he whispered.

She shook her head against him. "I can't wait. Here."

He reached behind her back and unfastened her bra, then pushed off the blouse. She rounded her shoulders and the lacy scrap of fabric fell away. He stopped to stare at the wonder of Sonia topless in his kitchen. He'd seen her in her cammies, a bathing suit and in that red dress. He'd imagined her this way, and now she stood still for his appraisal. Her breasts were larger than he'd realized. Everything she wore until this evening downplayed her lovely cleavage. Sports bras and cammies all flattened her glorious curves. Her nipples where budded tight and a dusty rose color. He reached. Her head dropped back and her eyes shut instantly before he touched her. She leaned forward, eager for him. He splayed his hands over her plump flesh and a moan rumbled deep and feral in her throat. He kissed and licked his way from one plump breast to the next as she arched against him. Johnny moved north, back along the lovely column of her neck, the enticing hollow of her throat and the secret recesses of her mouth.

He wanted to touch her everywhere. He knew that she wanted his body, but she wanted to keep him at arm's length. He wouldn't allow it. Just like all those days and weeks ago when she had tried and failed to shut him out of what really mattered, out of what made her who and what she was. Tonight he would allow no holding back. He would do whatever it took to make her open not just her body, but herself. He needed to be inside her. But he also needed to be inside her thoughts and her dreams and hopes. Sonia was the only woman he'd ever met who completely captivated him.

He lifted her up onto the breakfast bar. She gasped as her bottom hit the hard marble surface and her eyes popped open. They shared a wicked smile. Then she reached and dragged his trousers and boxers along his thighs. She glanced down, measuring him first with her eyes and then reaching, taking him in her hands, stroking the underside of his erection. He set his teeth together and inhaled through his nose, clenching his jaw to fight the need to take her, giving her a chance to explore his body as he explored hers.

She lifted one hand to her mouth and licked her palm, then used that moist surface to stroke him again. Slick fingers wrapped him tightly and he gasped and groaned at the pounding beat of desire. When the fire burned too hot he drew her hands away and tugged at the waistband of her blue jeans.

"Take them off," he ordered and she did.

A moment later she sat there on his breakfast counter like a bounty, creamy mocha flesh light against the black marble. He memorized the sight of her, treasuring the gift she gave him and vowing to be certain she never regretted one single minute of this night. Regret. It made that small still-functioning portion of his brain reengage. Something he needed.

He groaned. The condoms were all the way in his bedside table. They might as well be on the moon. She kissed his neck now, her hands traveling down his back and over his hips, then she used her nails to graze his skin on the return trip. He closed his eyes and groaned in pleasure and frustration.

"Bed," he said and scooped her up against him. She clasped her arms around his neck and her legs around his waist, riding high on his hips as he carried her deeper into the house. The fragrance of her filled him like nectar. He breathed deep, drunk with the scent of her skin and the scent of her arousal. As he moved she pressed tight to his torso, giving him the unbelievably arousing pressure of her breasts hot, soft and heavy against his needy flesh. The light from the hall spilled across the floor of his bedroom in a bright rectangle. Johnny cradled her against him and he reached the bed and lowered her to his coverlet. She stretched out before him like a lithe cat. Reclining now, waiting. He took a good long look at Sonia naked and aroused. He found the sight the strongest of aphrodisiacs. And he hadn't even tasted her yet. But he could smell her need and see the slick pink flesh as she lifted her knees and splayed her legs.

He dropped to the carpet before her as her gaze wandered over him, pausing at his chest, his stomach and finally his engorged sex. A sensual smile broke across her face and he returned it. He'd been afraid to break the mood. But that was nonsense. The look in her eyes said she wanted this, longed for it, just like him. This ache great like a monsoon. Neither of them could turn back now.

He eased himself onto his outstretched arms and then lowered himself to kiss her sweet mouth. She arched to press her chest to his and he made his way south, taking his time, exploring every nook and hollow, every succulent bud of flesh and each long flat plain. At last he reached her core, savoring how she stilled when he took her in his mouth. Loving the soft panting and tiny quavering cries she made when his tongue dipped inside her. As he sucked and licked and petted her, she arched, pressing to his mouth. He slipped his hands to her bottom, splaying his fingers and he lifted her, rocked her, drove her mad.

She gasped and bucked, rubbing against the friction he lavished. Sonia seemed to stop breathing as he continued to kiss and suck and taste. She was the sweetest thing that had ever come into his life and he wanted so badly for this to be perfect for her. He wanted—no needed to give her this release. He would do anything for her. Did she know that?

Sonia's breathing told him she was close. She came in a rushing sound, a long extended moan that went on and on as her release rolled and her fingers curled into fists in his hair. Then, by slow degrees her fingers slackened and fell away as her body went limp in his hands. She stretched as she made a humming sound of female satisfaction. He rubbed his slick mouth on her thighs and then moved back up her body, dropping a hundred tiny kisses along the way. When he neared her head, she lifted an arm, moving with a clumsy lethargy he knew well, as she stroked her fingers through the tangle of his hair.

"I've never felt anything like this, oh, Johnny, it was so delicious."

"More where that came from." And he knew he wanted her coming back for more, needed her to come back. No more one-nighters with a stranger for her, he vowed, no, never again.

She groaned and closed her eyes. "So tired."

He kissed her neck and her ear. Slowly she rose to his gentle stroking. Reluctant, playful and then aggressive, reaching for what she wanted. Well, he was happy to give it to her. This time, when she came he planned to be looking at her lovely face.

He let her fondle him, even though he was approaching the point where need grew too raw, too mindless to be controlled. Then she slipped from his embrace and lowered her mouth to take him. It was too much. The pressure of her hand as it gripped him and her tongue moving over his wanting flesh drove him wild. He pulled her back to his arms and she smiled up at him with swollen pink lips, slick with moisture. And he could see it all with just the light from the hall. Bless his werewolf sight, he thought, wondering if she could see him at all.

"You're driving me crazy," he whispered.

She chuckled and straddled his hips. He stilled her by grasping her at the waist. She lifted her brows in a silent question. A moment later he had the silver foil packet out of the drawer. She plucked it from him and tore into the foil. Then she unrolled the sheath over his aroused flesh.

"I've imagined doing that," she said, smiling down in satisfaction. She rocked her hips over him, sliding her slick folds along the length of him.

He held her hips and pulled her down beneath him in a quick take down that would have made his high school wrestling coach proud. She smiled up at him, with her eyes hooded and her pupils large and black.

He rocked against her once and then drew back, slipping into position. She spread her legs, lifting her heels to his hips to encourage this last joining. He stared down into her eyes and dropped until their hips locked, sheathing himself within her body. He watched her as he began to move. The sight of her flushed face and parted lips made his stomach twitch. He wanted to bring her pleasure again, wanted them both to fall into that madness together. But she was so hot and so wet and it had been so long. He growled as the need gripped him, rocking harder, deeper into her body.

Sonia cried out in pitiful little moans that grew louder and more frenzied. She raked his back with her nails and tossed her head from side to side.

Go ahead, he wanted to say. *Go ahead. I'll follow.* But he could not say anything because he was so close. He gritted his teeth and held back, closing his eyes for a moment to try to retain the control that slipped away like water in his hands.

She arched and howled, crying out his name as the contractions beat inside her. He felt them grip him and cast him into mindlessness. He came in a mad rush of heat and power, the pleasure pulsing out from his core and burning along his nerves like fire.

Sonia went slack and her eyes dropped closed. Johnny fell to his hands, holding his weight off her before collapsing down at her side. He had just enough strength in his trembling arms to drag her against him. She nestled, one leg sprawling over him like a boneless cat.

"That…was…wonderful," she sighed.

He brushed the hair from her face, kissed her mouth and wondered what he had ever done to deserve a night with Sonia Touma.

When her skin grew chilled, he dragged the comforter over them before drifting to sleep. He woke as the moonlight stole across their bed, leaving her to walk to the window and stare up at the silver orb ringed in a yellow haze. When he returned it was to find her half awake and reaching for him again. They made love more slowly this time as he explored her body from toe to fingertip, becoming familiar with each curve and the arousing cocktail of her body spray mixed with her desire. Late in the night, long after the moon had set, she woke him again, pressing the third condom into his palm.

The woman was trying to kill him. But as they say, what a way to die. Werewolves had great stamina. He just never knew that included sexual stamina.

He dozed with Sonia tucked close to his side and dreamed of running in the woods after vampires. The scent of them was heavy in his nostrils. He growled and felt Sonia stir beside him.

"Johnny!"

The panic in her voice brought him instantly awake. One deep breath told him there were no vampires here. But she was shaking him and calling his name.

"Johnny!"

Why was she so little? He reached out to stroke her face and ask her what was wrong. But his voice failed him. He froze at the sight of his own hand covered with black hair and tipped with thick curling claws. He startled and fell out of bed then scrambled to his feet, staring down at himself. It was morning and he was once again a werewolf.

She was crying now, her voice bereft and full of pain. "Was it because of what we did? Strong emotions, they said. Johnny, did I do this to you?"

* * *

Sonia's heart thudded painfully against her ribs as she scrambled out of bed, taking the bedsheet along with her. She clutched it to her body as she stared at Johnny who was now covered in black fur and his face had distended into the elongated shape that was neither man nor wolf.

"What happened?" she cried, the tears already welling so his image swam before her. Guilt lashed through her stomach, tearing her apart inside. *Oh, God, was this my fault?*

His feet slapped the floor as he staggered back against the wall and patted his own hairy chest as his mouth gaped showing long, dangerous teeth. The strangled sound he made left no doubt that he attempted speech, but that ability was gone with his handsome face and form. He stared at her, his brow wrinkled in confusion. Then he started signing.

Don't know. Why didn't I feel it?

"Maybe you're learning to change. Maybe you just don't have control over it yet." But in her heart, she knew something was very wrong. This wasn't supposed to happen. The change had to be called. That was what the captain said. Deep inside herself the panic began creeping up into her body, clouding her mind. It threaded through her like the roots of some invasive plant. She had not felt this panic since her childhood, but she recognized the darkness growing stronger. Johnny stood before her, his nostrils flaring as he waited. For his sake, she reined herself in. He needed her. She couldn't fall apart. But she wanted to scream, "What is happening?"

I dreamed of vampires, he signed. *Could that cause the change?*

"I don't know. Maybe." Sonia reached for the phone. "I have to call the captain."

He lifted a hand and waved it.

Give me a minute.

Johnny sank to the bed and cradled his forehead in his hands. Sonia wound the sheet tight about her and rolled the top as she would with a bath towel and then she sat beside him. She wrapped one arm around his waist and rested her head on his shaggy side and whispered into his pointed ear.

"They'll figure it out."

He lifted his head slowly as if it were suddenly too heavy to bear. His yellow eyes were bloodshot and red rimmed. He moved his hands and she read his words.

Step back. Let me try to change.

She moved away and watched him as he closed his eyes but nothing happened. He glanced up at her and then cradled his head in his long, clawed hands. Finally his arms dropped to his sides and he looked up at her. The defeat was clear in the hunched shoulders and woeful expression.

I can't.

Sonia grabbed the phone and made the call. Thirty minutes later she was dressed and they were back in the underground medical facility. Doctor Zharov looked grim and the captain's bright pink complexion showed he was clearly livid.

Sonia listened carefully to the doctor speak to Johnny, who sat still and silent on the examining table.

"This happened with a small portion of the test subjects. Involuntary change."

Johnny signed his question. *It was a full moon last night. Does that matter?*

Sonia translated and the doctor answered. "No, the moon has no effect on your condition. Superstitious nonsense. Possibly people were more likely to see were-wolves in the moonlight. But it doesn't bring a change."

Sonia asked the next question. "Johnny and I were together last night."

Zharov's brows shot up as he looked from one to the other.

"You said strong emotions can trigger change. Was it because...because..." Words failed her.

Zharov rubbed his chin and considered. "I'm not sure, but I doubt it. I have some tests to run. Then I'll know better how to answer your question."

Johnny was signing now. Sonia waited and then turned to the doctor. "He says there was no warning."

"No. Had you been awake there would have been. Dilation of the capillaries just prior to the change would make you feel flushed, perhaps light-headed."

Johnny signed again and Sonia spoke. "Why can't I change back?"

The silence in the room was deafening. Sonia felt brittle as glass as she looked from the doctor to the captain and her hope died. Zharov clasped his hands behind his back and rocked from heel to toe. The captain scrubbed his bristly jaw with his knuckles and winced.

"Answer his question," she said, her voice a feral growl. The news was bad, obviously, but he was entitled to hear it instead of being kept in the dark. She inched closer to Johnny's side.

The captain glanced at the door as if he wanted to be anywhere but here. Then he gestured with his head and Zharov backed away and out that same door. Sonia's chest felt tight as it did when her mother left them alone in the apartment to go out. The air seemed thinner as she tried to breathe.

"You better go," he said.

She shook her head. She was staying. The captain nodded his acceptance of her decision.

The captain's mouth went flat and grim. Johnny braced, gripping the edge of the table as he waited for his captain to speak.

"It's my fault. I wanted you human again, so I told him to go ahead and give you the injection. Zharov said he couldn't guarantee it. He's working to make it right. But it looks like you are one of the fifteen percent that doesn't hold his shape. That means you can't change back without another injection."

Sonia's blood flashed hot. "Don't you think you should have told him this was a possibility before you gave him the treatment, instead of making the decision without him, sir." She spat that last word, turning it into an insult.

Johnny motioned for the captain to bring him another shot. Sonia's ears began to buzz as she recalled his reaction to the first one.

"No," she said and grasped Johnny's hand. "We have to wait until they get this right. Until they can be sure that you'll stay human."

"That might be a while," said the captain.

"We'll wait," she said, making the decision for both of them, as if she had any right.

Johnny shook his head. She met his yellow eyes and read his thoughts before he even signed to her. He was going through with this.

His fingers moved and his hands swooped. *Not waiting. Bring the shot.*

She repeated his order to her commanding officer.

"It isn't that simple," said MacConnelly. "Diminishing returns, they call it. You were human for four days. The next time will be less."

Johnny straightened and began signing.

"How much less?" she said, repeating his question but finding her voice a strangled thing.

"We aren't sure."

Johnny was signing again.

Sonia cleared her throat but her voice still cracked. She was coming apart inside stitch by stitch. "He asks, 'Is there anything that will make me stay human?'"

The comrades exchanged a long look. Finally the captain said, "I'll arrange another shot but that's all I can do. But first they are going to need to run some tests on your blood the way it is now."

Johnny started signing and Sonia's eyes went wide. She felt her ears heat as the words poured out of him.

"Slow down," she said.

"What is he saying?" asked her captain.

"He's angry. I don't think—"

"Tell me what he said. You're his translator. Not his damned editor. So translate."

Johnny now had his arms folded over his chest and was glaring at MacConnelly.

"He said that you need him like this to defend Brianna. You don't want him human. That you're just like…" She glanced at Johnny and he spelled the name for her again. "Just like Colonel Lewis?"

The captain's face went red and his hands curled to fists. Sonia blinked as she noted that his blue eyes were changing color. The captain was fighting off the transformation. She knew it and instinctively stepped closer to Johnny. His arm went about her waist for a moment and then slid away as he began signing again.

"He says he's not your dog anymore and if he has to die to be human than he'll die. At least his mother can bury him in a casket instead of dumping him at the vets." Sonia clasped her arms across her chest as she waited for the captain to speak but he didn't. Instead he just spun in a half circle and marched out of the room.

She looked at Johnny. "Do you really believe that he would do that to you?"

Johnny didn't hesitate before shaking his head. He began to sign. *He wouldn't. But I can't stay like this anymore, Sonia. I can't be a monster.*

Sonia felt her throat burning and knew she was about to cry. She threw herself against him and he gathered her in his arms.

"You're not a monster. Just wait. I'll wait with you. I'll be able to stay now. We can be together. I'll live with you. You can cook for me and…we can go home." Tears choked her as she realized what they'd both lost and threw herself into his arms. He held her for a little while and then set her aside so she could see him sign.

It's not our home.

"Please, Johnny."

I want the shot.

Sonia began to cry.

Chapter 13

Burne Farrell waited for his chaser to return. Chasers were those whose job it was to track and capture their females as soon as they became sexually mature. Most females tried to run. But up until Brianna Vittori, none had succeeded for long. It was a sore spot with him and with his best chaser.

Burne didn't like Hawaii. Since his arrival, the stars and the moon were too bright and the lack of cloud cover meant it never grew truly dark. The cities here were small and lacked the amenities to which he was accustomed. A creature who moved only in darkness needed a place with 24-hour services and plenty of people venturing out at night. New Orleans, now there was a city that understood the pleasures of the night. He hoped Hagan had finished his sweep of this wretched little volcanic disgorgement so they could continue to the next godforsaken upheaval of rock.

Burne stood on the balcony of the Palm Breeze Hotel inhaling the scent of roasting pig. It seemed they were always roasting something and banging those infernal drums. He saw Hagan Dowling race across the pool deck below, moving at a speed too fast for a human to perceive anything more than a slight breeze. But Burne could see him clearly. His legs pumping and his cadaver-like white arms flashing at his sides. A moment later Hagan knocked on the door of his eighth-floor suite. Farrell had to rent the room wearing the stretchy elastic beige face covering worn by burn victims, a tactic he disliked but was sometimes forced to employ in public.

"Enter," he commanded and his chaser let himself in, lifting his sensitive nose and then following it to his superior on the balcony.

Hagan's ghostly composition already showed the telltale road map of blue veins on his arms and face, the pulsing blood vessels engorgement indicating that his chaser had stopped for a meal.

Irritated, Burne scowled.

"Good evening, sir," said Hagan. "I have heard from Richard Gould. He reports strong signals of a female on the island of Molokai and also the presence of two male werewolves."

"It's her!" Burne could not resist pumping his fist in triumph.

"I agree, the signs are good. But he withdrew without visual confirmation, as you requested."

"Thank God one of my chasers follows orders." He paced the balcony as his mind raced. "We go in force. Every available man. How long until they are assembled?"

"I can have six chasers here within twenty-four hours. If you are willing to wait forty-eight, I can call in our men in Europe and the Middle East."

Farrell rubbed one palm over the other. His greed for her urged him to hurry. And the more vampires that knew of her the more he would have to battle for her custody. Still she had evaded six before with the help of her two shaggy protectors. "Call them all. We go when we have a dozen. Two werewolves, even U.S. Marine–trained fighters, cannot possibly handle so many."

"True. But Gould says they have defenses. I suggest tunneling. The volcanic rock is riddled with existing channels. We could expand them to gain entry well past their perimeters."

"Fine."

"I will notify you when we are assembled. Would you like me to make a visual confirmation? I have seen her and would recognize her appearance."

"No. I don't want them tipped off. They would move her and we'll lose her again." Were all his men so reckless?

Hagan's mouth went thin and tight. Suspicion stirred in Farrell, rising like filth in a cesspool and he inhaled, finding the scent of a male who was sexually ready. Ready at just the mere mention of her. Was Hagan planning to steal her before he could assemble his team?

Farrell stared and Hagan swallowed. Did his chaser recognize that his master read him so easily? Hagan had best take care that his master didn't decide to open one of his chaser's arteries.

"Would you like to relocate to Molokai, master?"

"I'm going to lead the damned raid."

Hagan lowered his head and nodded. But not before

Farrell saw the narrowing of his eyes and the threat burning in their depths. So he had another rival for Brianna. He wondered if he should kill Hagan now or wait until after the capture.

"We will be honored to have you lead this chase, sir," said Hagan.

And I'll be honored to water my peonies with your blood, thought Farrell. He glanced at his chaser with speculation. It seemed doubtful that Hagan would live long enough to see his skin turn the color of a ripe plum.

In a fight, one should always put his money on the old dog.

Despite Johnny's insistence, Zharov refused to give him the shot until after all tests were completed on Johnny's wolf blood and the doctor had a chance to study the results. The following morning the tests were in.

Johnny and Sonia waited in silence in the medical facility for news of what was happening. Johnny knew Sonia didn't want him to take the shot and she'd done all she could to convince him. But damned if he'd stay like this. He only agreed to wait to could see if his blood work would reveal anything that could help maintain his human form.

It seemed hours before Dr. Zharov arrived in the examining room carrying a thick file folder. He was trailed by Mac, Brianna and Major Scofield. Johnny's skin prickled at the assemblage.

Brianna moved to the far corner of the room. Johnny knew with one glance at Brianna's face that the news was bad. Mac, more controlled, still showed a definite tell that Johnny recognized. Whenever he ground his jaw like that, Johnny knew he wouldn't like what came next.

"Well, it's not good," said the doctor without preamble. "Your body's immune system recognized the invading protein quickly and mounted an attack killing the agent you need to remain in human form."

Johnny signed a question and Sonia repeated it.

"He wants to know if he can have another dose."

Mac and Zharov exchanged looks. Brianna folded her hands and studied her white knuckles.

The major stepped forward and lay a fatherly hand on Johnny's hairy shoulder. "You can, son. But the result will likely be the same and faster this time, as your body has this particular protein on its hit list. It's a search and destroy with a known target. You understand?"

Johnny nodded and signed to Sonia. He tried not to notice the silver tear stains on her cheeks but they hit him in the gut like the butt end of a rifle.

"He says he still wants the shot."

Zharov looked to the major who nodded.

"Give it to him."

Sonia grabbed Johnny's forearm. "But he almost died the last time."

"Unlikely now. His body adapts quickly, too damned quickly, to new types of assaults."

Johnny patted her hand and peeled her away. Sonia shook her head, silently pleading with him not to go through with it. Didn't she understand, he'd do anything, anything, just to spend ten more minutes as a man. And to spend those minutes with her, it was all he wanted and he'd pay whatever price he must and when the shots no longer worked, well there was always the pistol.

"Do you have anything else, any other studies or something that won't do this to him?"

Zharov shook his head, fiddling with the tubing of his stethoscope. "I'm working on something but…" He glanced at Mac and Johnny saw the captain give a single shake of his head. What were they hiding? The doctor cleared his throat and continued. "We don't know why this protein is absent in Lam or how to encourage his body to produce it. We don't know why he's rejecting it when it is so prevalent in Captain MacConnelly's blood. In time we might…."

Johnny pounded his fists on the exam table, denting the metal. The doctor's words fell off. Johnny panto-mimed a shot to his gums.

Zharov nodded and turned toward the door. Twenty minutes later Johnny lay stretched on a surgical table, Sonia standing beside him. Her skin was pale and her eyes round as a doll's.

"How long will he have this time?" she asked.

Zharov shrugged. "Less than the last time. Two days? I'm not sure."

Johnny opened his mouth and the serum was in-jected. Sonia gasped when his eyes fluttered. Zharov watched the machinery but Johnny did not lose con-sciousness this time. His heart raced and he felt a rush of electric energy shuttering through him, as if he'd touched a live wire. He watched the hair cascading from his hands and gave a little shake, sending more falling. His claws retracted and he saw his trimmed nails and neat, pink cuticles. The pain hit him then and he stiff-ened like an electroshock patient as his vision blurred. He could hear them, but his sight was gone. The rip-ping agony became the center of his existence as every muscle seized, then convulsed. The straps broke away and he tumbled to the tile floor. On hands and knees he panted and then retched, finally collapsing to his side.

This was better than the last time? Johnny was suddenly glad he'd passed out during the first shot. Gradually the pain ebbed and his muscles responded to his tentative efforts to control them. He sat up and Sonia draped a sheet around his shoulders, then helped him rise.

"Am I human?" he said, grinning at the sound of his own voice.

"Back on the gurney, Lam. We have to get you to a room. I want to examine you. Find the location of the initial attack," said Zharov.

"No offense, Doc, but I'm not spending my time in this stinking hospital playing doctor with you." He grasped Sonia's hand and headed for the door.

He met Mac just outside and for one minute worried he might order him back. But he didn't. Instead, he extended his hand and they shook.

"Thanks for the blood," said Johnny.

"Thanks for not dying on me." He released Johnny's hand. "John? I have some information about the night we were attacked in Afghanistan. I had them pull your medical records. Reports from the field hospital show your blood had traces of an agent used to cause memory loss. That's why you can't remember."

"Why would they do that?" he asked.

"Don't know. But we'll find out. We have to find the physician who treated us. Some of your files were destroyed. I'm looking into that, too."

A corporal appeared carrying a freshly pressed set of cammies and Johnny slipped into them. They left the captain and he and Sonia headed up the hill on foot to the home they might share for a day or perhaps two.

They stopped at the falls before Johnny's swimming pool watching the pulse of water cascading to the rocks before settling into the slow and gentle journey through the deep natural pond. Sonia gripped his hand.

"Maybe you should have stayed. Let the doctor check you. Maybe…"

"Sonia, please. I want to be with you."

"Do you think they might be wrong?" she asked.

"That I only have a day or two? No, Sonia. I think that's all we have. Maybe all we'll ever have."

Her lower lip trembled and she caught it between strong white teeth as she struggled with her erratic breathing. When she spoke, her voice was strained. "I wasted all those days."

"We were searching for a vampire most of it." He used his knuckles to lift her chin until their eyes met. "You didn't know."

"But they did. That's why they were concerned when you couldn't change. But they didn't tell us. Why didn't they tell us?"

Johnny gave her a sad smile. "I don't know."

"They're hiding something else. I feel it."

"Sonia, I've never met anyone like you. And if I only have two days I can't think of anyone else I'd rather spend them with."

She threw herself into his arms and he wrapped her up in a strong embrace. The sweetness of his body pressed to hers was punctuated by the knowledge that this would not last. She would not have him next week or next month. He'd be there, but beyond her reach.

"I should have been here. I just…I was afraid." She

met his gaze, no longer hiding, no longer running. "Now I'm terrified."

He dipped his chin and she raised hers so that their mouths met with a sweet blending of texture and taste. But the need burned too hot in them both. Soon his kisses turned fierce. His tongue delved, mingling with hers in a dance of urgency. He caressed her throat, moving down to release each button of her shirt before casting the garment aside. She tugged his shirttails from his trousers and they separated for the time it took for him to pull his shirt over his head and for her to strip out of her bra. She fumbled with his zipper, the desperation making her clumsy. He dragged her to the soft grass and they tugged and pulled until their clothing lay strewn all about them.

Johnny gave her a wicked smile that heated her body more thoroughly than the humid jungle air. She stroked his cheek and then threaded her fingers in his hair and tugged. He kissed her lips and then moved steadily downward, each kiss bringing her a dart of pleasure. At last his arousing mouth covered her breasts. His tongue grazed across her nipple fanning the steady pulse of need into a blazing fire. The aching want beat low and deep inside her. She pressed against him and he laid her back upon the sweet, fragrant grass. The damp smell of earth mingled with the scent of this man. She breathed deep, hoping to remember each moment, each detail. How long did they have this time?

His knee pushed between her parting legs and she rose to rub against him, sending a shock of pleasure ripping through her body.

Her fingers delved into his hair. Frantic, she tried to touch him everywhere at once, exploring his back and arms, stroking her palms over his skin as she rubbed her cleft against his erection.

His fingers slipped into her hair, tangling in the long waves that fell about her and across the damp earth. His hips lowered to hers, pinning her to the ground. She felt his hard shaft against her trembling body, gliding against the moist folds of her genitalia but it was no longer enough. She needed to feel the thrust and grind of him inside her body.

He extended his arms, staring down as his dark hair fell about his face. Intent dark eyes stared and the moisture of her kisses still clung to his lips. She tried to memorize every line and plane of his face. This was how she wanted to remember him, young and naked and desperate for what she would give him.

How long until fate stole him once again? How long until his body finished destroying the protein that made him human and she lost him once more?

"Oh, Johnny," she whispered as the grief seized her again.

"Don't think about that now," he said. "Think about us and what I'm going to do to you. Give me this day to remember."

"I wish it were more."

"It's enough."

But it wasn't enough. It would never be enough.

He smiled and then lowered his chest to hers as he kissed her neck and ear and finally back down over her throat to find one plump breast and hard nipple.

There was only now.

This time when their mouths met there was none of the playful exploration or lustful heat of their earlier meetings. Now, he sensed a wildness, a frenzy that approached panic. Each second that ticked by was a second lost. Johnny gripped her tight and she wrapped her legs about his hips, her body slick and ready. He hesitated.

"I don't have protection."

"I do," she whispered. She drew a foil packet from the front pocket of her discarded clothing and tore it open before rolling the condom over the long length of him.

Another moment and he had slipped inside her in one long, delicious slide. She dug her heels against his thighs, driving still deeper as her tongue delved in frantic, greedy thrusts. They fell into that magic complimentary rhythm, the perfect blending of friction and slick liquid heat. Each moved in opposition and each thrust, each withdrawal brought them closer to madness.

This time the pleasure was so sweet, so piercing that her eyes rolled back in her head as the tension built and built.

She threw back her head and arched against him as she came, her rippling contractions gripping him and casting him over the edge with her. Her eyes opened wide to see him staring back at her with the same ecstatic amazement. Could anything ever be that perfect again?

Johnny felt the shattering orgasm go on and on as he forgot how to breathe. In that moment of supreme surrender, he knew that it was worth any price to have Sonia in his arms. He lay her back on the sweet-smelling grass falling beside her, rolling to his back. He stared up at the blue sky, there in little flashes through the green canopy. White and yellow butterflies flew in crazy patterns from one cascading group of flowers to the next. He pulled Sonia close. She nestled against his side, her hand resting familiar on his chest.

If only he could stay with her like this forever. How long did they have? A day? A night? He didn't know.

They stretched out on a soft cushion of moss in the warm humid air and her breathing changed as she dozed. He turned to watch her sleeping, memorizing the shape of her face.

He felt it coming this time. His skin tingled and then burned. His joints ached like the worst fever he'd ever had. Then his muscles pulled as if they were about to tear. He lifted a hand and saw the hair sprouting and his nails turning yellow, then black as they grew in a moment to claws. He glanced to Sonia, but she lay languid and still, with eyes still closed.

He called her name but the sound strangled in his throat.

"Johnny! Oh, no, Johnny, no."

He saw the horror in her eyes as the change gripped him. *No,* his mind screamed. It was too soon. He rolled in agony as if his skin were on fire.

The change back lasted only a few moments. He was a werewolf again and it had been less than half a day.

Sonia scrambled into her clothing. He stopped her when she had her shirt and pants on by grasping both shoulders in his big, thick hands. She kept her head down and he made a sound in his throat, a huffing sound. The sound of an animal.

She lifted her chin and met his gaze. Tears cascaded from her eyes and raced in silver ribbons down her cheeks.

"Oh, Johnny. It was too quick. What are we going to do?" She fell against him and he gathered her up in his arms.

He didn't know but together they headed back to the medical facility.

The next shot changed him back, but he knew it was the last time. He had time to kiss Sonia and tell her he was sorry. Then he changed back. Johnny tore the exam room to pieces. Even Mac in werewolf form couldn't stop him. But Sonia did by telling him that he was scaring her. He finally came to rest to see the metal table shredded like aluminum foil and the machinery shattered into a million tiny pieces. He slumped against the wall and Sonia fell into his arms, curling against him with her head on his shaggy chest.

"They'll find a way. And I'll stay with you. You won't be alone this time."

Johnny hung his head and covered his eyes with his gnarled hand. He couldn't have her. She deserved better than an animal for her guy. He realized one terrible truth. He did not want to live as a werewolf, even if Sonia was willing to stay with him.

Johnny just wanted to crawl under a rock, but there was blood to draw and tests to run and results to consider. He spent the night in the facility. Sonia refused to leave him so they brought in another bed. The next morning Scofield, Zharov and MacConnelly came with the news that Johnny already knew. The shots would no longer work.

But they did have another option. Johnny pushed himself up and stared from one grim face to the next. Whatever it was, not one of them liked it.

Sonia must have sensed doom, as well, for she inched

closer to his side and curled her cold hands around his furry bicep.

It was his captain who broke the silence.

"Zharov has been working on an avenue that shows some promise. This is entirely different than what you had. It's not a treatment. More like a weapon. Instead of enabling you to change forms, it changes you back to human. All the way back. You'll lose your special vision, enhanced sense of smell and you'll lose your strength, too. We didn't want that for you. We were hoping to keep you as a shifter, like me."

So he could fight vampire assassins overseas?

The major took over here, seamlessly picking up where the captain left off and confirming her suspicions.

"This formula is being developed for enemy combatant werewolves to give our men a chance."

A chance that her captain and Johnny never had, Sonia realized.

The captain went on. "It works—100 percent in lab tests. It changes the dogs back to canine form."

Johnny's sign was obvious as he thumped his chest. The captain shook his head.

"Zharov has gone as far as he can with animal tests. We were hoping to field test it on an enemy werewolf before offering it to you. That opportunity has not been forthcoming."

Johnny signed his answer and listened as Sonia spoke his words.

"We're hard to catch."

Mac's smile seemed forced. "Yeah, we sure the hell are."

Sonia watched Johnny's words and then shook her

head. He motioned to Mac. Sonia gritted her teeth as she spoke. "He says he'll be the first human subject."

Zharov stepped forward, hands clasped behind his back, seeming at ease, but Johnny smelled the stress pheromones pouring from him like mist from a lake.

"There is a seventy percent mortality rate, Lam. It's consistent and I haven't been able to increase the survival rate."

Johnny reached for the doctor gripping the front of his pristine white lab coat. Sonia saw murder in his eyes. The captain started towards Johnny, but Sonia was closer and she grabbed his thick wrist with both hands and tugged. She wasn't strong enough to stop him, but she was strong enough to distract him.

"Senior officer," she said, appealing to his training.

Johnny's eyes flicked to her and then back to the doctor. He leaned in and growled, showing his powerful canines. Then he let go. Zharov staggered back, holding his chest.

Johnny started signing.

"He says he should have been given the choice."

"It was decided that the best option was to keep you safe and…"

His words fell off and now Sonia was angry. They wanted Johnny to remain a werewolf. Sonia lunged at the doctor and Johnny swept her off her feet, holding her for the few seconds it took for her brain to reengage. She'd gotten into more trouble on impulse than anyone she knew.

"Thanks," she whispered.

He released her and patted her shoulder.

He signed his answer and Sonia threw up her hands

angry at Johnny now. He didn't care. This was his life and his decision.

"What did he say?" asked Mac.

"He said better odds than he got on his last mission." She turned back to him.

Mac took over here. "This wasn't even an option until recently. This treatment, wasn't intended for your situation. This is a weapon developed to neutralize the enemy. They plan to use it to kill werewolves. It's lethal."

Johnny signed that they said they'd modified it so it wasn't as lethal.

Sonia spoke quickly, her voice sharp. "Not as lethal? Are you crazy? Didn't you hear them? Seventy percent, they said. I'm not going to stand here and watch you die."

Well, he wasn't staying like this and he told her so.

"Why not? Why do you have to do this stupid dangerous thing instead of being patient for a little while longer? Wait until they catch a wolf and try it on someone other than you."

He signed and she translated.

"Do you have anything else in the works?" Her eyes pleaded with the doctor, but Zharov shook his head.

"This is our best option to date. We are predicting that if he survives, he would be human and all traces of the werewolf protein would be eliminated. He would not be able to shift again."

Johnny looked to Mac as he signed. Sonia spoke in cadence with his signs.

He says, "What about Bri?"

Mac met Johnny's stare in silence for a moment. "Not your objective, soldier. You're relieved of duty."

Johnny turned to Zharov.

Do it, he signed.

She didn't translate. Instead she turned on him and clasped his hand in both of hers. "Johnny, don't. I'll wait if you will."

No.

She didn't give up. Just changed tactics like any good marine. "You have a family that needs you. Without you, they will lose their home. Remember? You're mom doesn't make enough to support them. Your sister won't go to college. Don't do this."

If I live, I can support them.

She rested a hand on her hip. "What if you don't?"

He drew a deep breath and met her angry eyes. *Death benefit.*

Sonia punched him hard in the chest with the backs of both her fists. He barely felt it.

If I do this, then I can have you.

"You have me. Johnny, you already have me, if you'll only wait."

Mac stepped to the opposite side of the bed. "I think she's right," he said. "It's too dangerous."

Johnny shook his head and began to sign. This time Sonia translated.

"He is asking you to look after his family, Captain." She pursed her lips and glared fire at him. "Don't you do it."

The captain flicked his gaze back to Johnny and nodded. "I'll see to them."

Johnny lay his head back on the examining table and closed his eyes, releasing his breath. *Just like dying,* he thought.

Sonia fell across his chest, warm and small and fragrant as summer flowers. "Johnny, I'll wait for as long as it takes. Do you hear me? I love you. I'll wait."

She stared up at him and he knew it was true. She did love him. He knew she had never said those words to anyone and never felt that way about anyone. Now she said it to him and he couldn't say it back because he was a goddamned werewolf again. No longer fit for her, no longer able to offer himself to her.

Johnny felt the sweet ache of longing for what he wanted most while knowing that he might never have it. He had her love. But it wasn't enough to keep him from trying for the brass ring. Because he loved her, too. But he wasn't going to sign those words. He was going to whisper them in her ear as they made love or he was going to die trying to be human.

She must have seen something in his expression because the hope drained from her eyes with the color from her face. He could not stand to see her hurting so he stroked her hair and held her until she pulled away.

"Look at me," she demanded, her words lashing angry and quick.

He did. She was flushed and her eyes flashed fire.

"You're still going through with this?" Her words were crisp, staccato, like gunfire.

Johnny released a breath, suddenly weary with all this. He met her troubled stare and nodded, knowing it was not what she wanted to hear.

"I love you, John Lam. Doesn't that mean anything to you?"

His heart twisted and throbbed in his chest because it meant everything to him. But her confession only made him more determined to go through with it.

She must have known she was losing the battle for

she added a threat. "I won't stay to watch you die." Then her voice went liquid with promise. She whispered to him. "Be patient. It can be like before. We can go home together."

It could never be like that again. Maybe she believed they could go back to being roommates. He knew better. They had moved far past that. Sonia looked away. So she knew it, as well, but she was desperate enough to say anything to stop him. But he couldn't wait. Not if there was a chance for them. But he couldn't say all that to her. Couldn't say anything at all. So, instead he signed just one word.

Goodbye.

She stiffened and shrank back, huddling beside his bed.

"Johnny?"

He was a brave man, but not brave enough to see the grief on her face and the anguish glimmering in her tear-filled eyes. So he looked away.

Sonia turned and fled the room.

Chapter 14

Sonia waited for the captain outside Johnny's room. When he appeared he looked tired and unhappy. His gaze flicked to her and his jaw bunched as he returned her salute.

"Dismissed, Touma." He tried to stride past her but she took up beside him, matching his pace.

"I want a transfer."

The captain stopped walking. "You really going to run?"

"I'm not running." She flapped her arms like a flight-less bird. "Can't you see what's happening here? It's the gun in the medicine cabinet all over again. That treatment is the bullet only this time I can't stop him."

"You could stay with him."

"No, Captain. All due respect, sir, I can't." She cupped her hands over her eyes. "All right. Yes. I'm running. I'm not strong enough to see this through."

"Yes, you are."

Sonia swallowed back a sob. She'd seen her mother's self-destruction. But she wasn't riding along for Johnny's.

Her throat burned like fire, but she held it in refusing to fall to pieces, not until she got clear of the last security point.

"He gets to choose, Touma. His choice. Not ours."

She dropped her hands from her eyes and glared up at him. "But what choice is he making? Is he trying to be human again or is he just giving up?"

"Maybe he'd rather die than live like that." There was a haunted quality in the captain's tone, the truth that comes only from experience. "Who are you to judge him?"

Sonia stared in horror. The captain was giving up, too.

"Are you trying to bury him? Say a few prayers and move on? Better than having to look at him everyday and know what you did."

"You're out of line, Touma," growled the captain, his eyes changing color on their way from blue to icy blue, husky blue—wolf blue.

She didn't care. He was going to listen to her.

"Well, I don't want him to die. Especially when I know why he's so eager to be human again." She beat a hand on her chest in rapid succession. "Me. That's why. He's thinking crazy."

"He's a big boy. He knows what he wants."

"Yeah," Sonia said. "And either way he gets it. He's either human or he's dead." Her arms went slack as all the fight drained from her. "So do I get my transfer?"

He fixed her with wolf-blue eyes. "The sooner the better." He snorted his disapproval. "I knew you'd quit."

She leaned in, refusing to back down. "You told me to distract him, keep him occupied and you didn't care how. I did my job."

"Now I'm doing mine. You'll ship out tomorrow. Get packed. Dismissed, Touma."

She made it to the elevator on a hot rush of anger that erupted into tears before she reached the barracks. She was moving again. Running again. At least she wasn't going back to jail. She'd gotten what she wanted, hadn't she? She was still free.

It didn't take long to pack a footlocker.

Sonia headed up the hill in the late afternoon to retrieve the few personal items she had left in Johnny's place. She tried not to think too hard, tried not to look about the empty house or to recall how happy she had been here with him. Tried not to remember that for the first time in her life she had felt at home. It was all gone, vanished with her silly dreams of tomorrows. All anyone ever had was now. Johnny understood it. It was why he took that second shot.

But it was done and she had to move again because she knew very well how this would all end. She had held out her heart to him, had offered to wait and he had cast her aside. The pain of his rejection was so great that she just felt numb as if her spine wasn't really connected to her body. Just sort of moving through the motions as her mind was hidden safely away behind a hard armored shell.

Why had she ever let him get past that armor? She'd just never thought that a werewolf could possibly be someone she'd be attracted to and he had sneaked up on her. She'd made a mistake and now it was going to cost her.

Funny. This time it wasn't just her closing doors; he'd shut her out, too.

Sonia's throat was raw from crying and her eyes were puffy. She allowed herself one more look out the porch but instead of seeing the glorious vista of the Pacific Ocean, her eyes were drawn to the path that led to the natural grotto where Johnny had made love to her that last time. Sonia glanced to the path and then back to the stairs, feeling pulled in two directions. She didn't know if staying was right or leaving was right. She only knew that Johnny didn't love her enough to stay alive.

She wasn't enough. Had never been enough. Not for her mom and not for Sergeant John Loc Lam. Johnny was going to do this. Either way he would be going someplace she could not follow. She pressed the pads of her fingers to her chest over her heart and rubbed as if the pressure could ease the ache that went to her very core. Not good enough. Not good enough to keep, not good enough for him to stay. For just a moment in time she thought that Johnny shared her feelings. But just like every man, beginning with the father she never knew, he was leaving her behind.

Sonia spun away and marched double-time out the front door. She tossed the plastic bag of her belongings into the passenger side of the Jeep and headed down the mountain. When she neared Brianna's home, she found herself turning into the drive. She needed to say goodbye.

Brianna greeted her with a warm smile that flickered and died at the first look at her. "What happened?"

Sonia opened her mouth and the tears started again.

Brianna ushered her in and then brought her some water before sitting across from her on the far side of the dining room table.

Through tears and some choking, Sonia managed to get it all out. Brianna shook her head.

"Men and their codes of honor. Of course Travis wouldn't see that accepting the duty of looking after his family would make it possible for Johnny to do this. Wait until I get a hold of him."

Sonia didn't want to cause trouble between newlyweds. "I told Johnny I loved him and he said goodbye. I want to make a home with him but..."

"Sonia," Brianna's tone sounded chiding. "No matter where Travis is he is with me. My home is in his heart and his home is in mine."

Sonia squinted at the cryptic comment. What did that even mean?

Brianna gave her a gentle smile and said, "If you love Johnny than nothing can separate you. Certainly not this."

Sonia squinted as she shook her head thinking of all the things that separated them. His condition separated them physically. And even if that wasn't the case, Johnny wanted a combat assignment and Sonia wanted to serve out her term of service in some safe little backwater. Johnny wanted to travel. She wanted a backyard. And there was that little problem of her transfer and the bigger problem of the rule prohibiting fraternizing. Brianna and her husband might not ever be apart, but she and Johnny most certainly would be. Often. Always.

"You don't understand, he's already said he doesn't want me."

"I don't believe that. I've seen you two together.

Maybe Johnny just can't stand that you'd be stuck with him the way he is."

"I don't care," said Sonia, her voice rising.

"But he cares. The man has his pride, Sonia. We don't always understand it, but we have to acknowledge it."

"I've been reassigned."

"I see. Then you'll have to go, won't you?"

Sonia noted Brianna's enigmatic smile. Why did Brianna make it sound as if Sonia had some choice, as if she were missing something? Brianna almost sounded ironic. As Sonia puzzled at her true meaning Brianna's expression went blank. Her hostess was on her feet an instant later and with such haste she sent the chair, upon which she sat, tumbling to the floor. Sonia stood, suddenly on alert.

"Do you smell that?" she whispered, glancing furtively about the empty room.

Sonia inhaled and found nothing but the sweet tropical air laced with the hint of jasmine. "What?"

Brianna's body began to vibrate and then, right before her very eyes, Brianna vanished.

Sonia stumbled back and nearly fell. Someone bounded up the porch stairs with a heavy footfall and Sonia turned to see something zip to the screen door in the kitchen at the same instant the front door crashed open. It was a man dressed all in black. Who wore a turtleneck in this heat? she wondered as he charged right for her. There was something wrong with his head. It was misshapen, as if he had some terrible allergic reaction or a dreadful skin condition. Purple welts covered the lumpy mass of his face. But it was the glowing white eyes that triggered understanding. The man opened his mouth and she saw the glint of his long white fangs and Sonia cried out.

How had they gotten past the perimeter?

She threw the chair at him and retreated, only to find herself captured by the one coming through the screen.

"That's not her," said the first.

Sonia struggled against the unbreakable grip, her skin chilling at the strange cool touch of her attacker.

The first one slapped her. The blow sent an explosion of pain blasting through her jaw and made her so dizzy she nearly threw up. The creature leaned forward and inhaled.

"Human," it said. "Kill her."

Instantly a hand gripped her forehead forcing her chin up, exposing her neck. The sweet, cloying scent of gardenias surrounded her, so strong she thought she might be ill. His mouth descended and she became unnaturally aware of the pounding of her heart and the thrum of blood in the great vessels at her throat. This thing was going to kill her right there in the captain's living room. She turned her head farther to the side and then dropped, as she had been taught in basic training, performing a quick half turn and elbowing him in the groin. Sonia had the satisfaction of hearing the wind leave his lungs before she dove away. But she didn't get far.

The other one moved with a speed that made him only a blur and she found herself in his arms, staring up at his hideous mottled face, slitted nose and the bone-white fangs pressing deep against his thick, liver-colored lips. She shrank back in horror and he smiled, showing the three-inch fangs all the way to his crimson gums. *Hideous,* she thought, trembling.

This one smelled like blood. Her skin dimpled as the chill took her. Sonia tried for his thumbs, intending to break them in her bid for freedom, but he struck her so fast she went dizzy. He had her in the crook of his arm, squeezing her like a boa constrictor. She fought fiercely at first but, as the dizziness increased, her movements became clumsy. He was suffocating her.

"Give her back to me," said the lavender one, his image blurring before her watering eyes.

This would be the last thing she ever saw.

"Johnny," she choked.

The second vampire released her and pushed her into the arms of the first. The fangs grazed her neck. Sonia inhaled, trying to clear the fog from her brain and mount another defense.

"No!" The voice was female.

Brianna appeared before her and threw a punch at the one who had already cut into Sonia's neck with his razor-sharp teeth.

"Get her," howled the mottled vampire and Sonia was discarded like an old banana peel as the two vampires shot after Brianna who had disappeared. She could barely see the males. But Brianna had vanished once more. The males chased her out the front door. Sonia reached for her phone and flipped it open hitting the favorites button as she staggered out into the yard. She had to help Brianna.

Before she could press the captain's number, Brianna appeared. "Get in the Jeep. Hurry!"

Brianna grabbed her arm and hustled her along. They were ten steps from the vehicle when the vampires reappeared, one, two, three…nine. Brianna's hands slipped from Sonia's arm.

"Let her go," Brianna ordered. "She's nothing to you."

Several of the males eyed Sonia and licked their lips.

"Take them both. Don't kill the human—yet," said the one with the purple bruises on his face.

Sonia took one step before they grasped her but she still managed to hit the captain's number as the phone fell from her hand. A glance told her that they'd captured Brianna, as well. The vampires used thick plastic zip ties to secure Sonia's wrists and ankles and she remembered they hated metal, iron especially. What did she have that was metal? Her brass belt buckle. That was all.

Two of the males lifted Sonia carrying her so quickly that the landscape about her blurred. She shut her eyes to contain the dizziness. From then on, she felt the jarring gate of their run and the uneven ground over which they charged at superhuman speeds. Now and again she looked about and saw they were taking her over the opposite side of the volcanic peak, through dense cover and then open, rocky terrain.

Had the captain gotten her call?

Johnny waited, mouth open as the IV was inserted into an artery beneath his gums. It hurt of course, but there was no helping it since they couldn't get a needle through his skin. They'd placed a block between his teeth to keep him from moving and disrupting the IV. Also, he supposed, in case he went into seizures.

But if he didn't die, if he were human again, he could go after Sonia and explain, apologize and ask her to stay. If he didn't survive she was better off gone.

This treatment also involved a shot of some other

damned poison that killed something in his blood. He didn't understand it, but he didn't have to. His job was to survive it. He thought he'd already survived worse.

Dr. Zharov put his hand on the white plastic switch on the IV line, his thumb poised to introduce the new treatment. "Here goes. You'll feel uncomfortable. Try to lie still."

This weapon was being developed in a gaseous form to spray any werewolves they found. But it would kill them. Turn them human and then stop their breathing. Now the chemicals were in liquid form. The good doctor aimed to avoid burning his lungs beyond repair. Some of the test animals had survived. A few pigs, half the dogs, zero rabbits, zero chimps. He was a Lam. Had they tested any lambs? He blinked his eyes. The sedative made his thinking fuzzy.

Mac stepped into view.

"You okay?"

Johnny lifted a thumb. He wished Sonia were here. Instead of staring at him with anxious eyes, she'd hold his hand.

He knew the instant the stuff hit his bloodstream. Uncomfortable? Was that what the doctor said? His body tensed and he could not keep from arching, his back rising from the table as the treatment burned like molten lead. He wheezed as the pain took the air from his lungs. His vision blurred.

"Johnny? You still with us?" Mac's voice, he knew, but he couldn't respond as he curled his fingers into the padding on the table, feeling the stuffing wad beneath his claws. "Doc, what's happening?"

"Attacking his red blood cells. I told you it would be rough," Zharov said.

"Do they all do this?" asked Mac.

"Yes."

The poison scalded down his arms and an instant later the muscles of his chest burned. A second after that his diaphragm stopped working. It was just like having the wind knocked from him. He could not breathe in or out. He stared up at Mac and saw the fear in his captain's eyes. Johnny's chest ached so badly he lifted a hand to press down on the spot and felt his heart go still. His fingers went numb. The pain ebbed. His vision darkened and his body went slack.

He felt the cold metal paddles on his chest and heard Zharov shout, "Clear."

The electricity jolted his body into involuntary movement. But he didn't feel it. In fact, he had a whole different view. Instead of looking up at the doctor and Mac, he was looking down on them from above. They were all leaning over something, hairy and black. He recognized himself but felt no attachment to that pain-wracked body. It was so much nicer here, above all the sorrow and pain.

He wanted to drift away like a cloud. The doctor shoved something that looked like a hard piece of white plastic down Johnny's throat. He watched himself and realized his old body was slack and still. A moment later a breathing tube was inserted. Monitors screamed and Johnny saw Mac cover his eyes with a forearm as he gripped Johnny's slack hand.

"No," Mac whispered. "Not Johnny, too."

Johnny felt sorry for his friend, but not sorry enough to come back. Maybe he would go to Sonia.

Sonia.

Johnny looked down at his body on the table and saw

he was now human. It worked. He was human again, but he was also dead—or dying. He wasn't sure.

Zharov inserted an IV into his slack arm and red blood began to flow from the sack on the stand.

He thought about his mother and sister. Then he thought of losing Sonia forever. No. He wouldn't. He loved her and he wanted to be with her. In that instant, he dropped back into his body like a stone heaved into a lake. The reconnection jarred him and the pain seared his insides. Surely he wouldn't survive this much pain.

The monitor's stopped screaming. They beeped and blipped in an erratic rhythm, a cacophony chorus. Was that his heart beating? Johnny drew air into his oxygen-starved lungs.

"He's back," said Zharov. "Get an IV into his other arm."

Johnny smiled. He was human again.

"Mac," he whispered, still too tired to open his eyes.

"Here I am, buddy. You gave us a scare." His captain leaned close as Johnny whispered to him.

"Sonia. Don't let her leave."

"You got it. Just rest. She's not going anywhere."

Johnny came to in the recovery room and then drifted out again. He asked for Sonia and Mac and Sonia again. Mac was there, but where was Sonia? They fed him juice and Jello. He marveled at his hands, bare and smooth.

He inhaled and could not scent who was in the room when Mac sat right beside his bed.

"I can't smell you," he whispered.

"You're human, Johnny. No more super sight. No more super hearing. No more super strength."

That was right. He'd never been like Mac, changing at will, keeping his powers in human form. Now he was just human.

"You know what that means?" asked Mac.

"Less time trying to wear shredded clothing," Johnny said and grinned. His gums ached.

"It means I can kick your ass again."

Johnny's eyes drifted closed. "You wish."

When he came to again, he was in a private room with the television playing a ball game. Playoffs. Angels were winning. Mac was speaking to Dr. Zharov.

"What time is it?" asked Johnny.

Mac startled and moved to flank the bed as Zharov took the opposite side. He was surrounded.

"Welcome back," said Zharov.

"It's sixteen hundred. How are you feeling? Hungry?"

"As a wolf."

Mac finally smiled. Then he reached for the buzzer corded around the bed rail. A woman's voice came through the speaker behind him.

"Yes, Sergeant Lam?"

"Bring some food, please," said Mac.

"Yes, sir."

Mac smiled down at Johnny. "Forgot how ugly you are."

"You're just jealous."

Mac's smile faltered a moment. "A little. But if I were human, I couldn't be near Brianna."

Johnny knew the truth of that. And now Johnny couldn't be around her any more. That realization made him sad. What else had he lost by losing his wolf half?

As if on queue, the doctor began speaking. "You're

body's reaction to the treatment was worse than expected. We lost you for several minutes. Do you understand what I'm saying, Sergeant?"

"Yes. I died."

"Just so. But we brought you back."

"I remember leaving my body." He turned to Mac. "You said, 'Not Johnny, too.'"

The color left Mac's face at that and he glanced to the doctor who shrugged one shoulder. "Sometimes you can still hear when you're heart has stopped. It's been known to happen."

"I saw you. I was up on the ceiling."

That made the doctor give him a long hard stare. "Regardless of where you went, you're back now and I have to say that it is well you survived because you would never survive such a treatment again."

"How do you know?" asked Johnny.

"We've tried with test subjects. Turned some of the successful transitions back to their were-form. Zero survival rates on any of the initial survivors when attempts were made to return them to their natural forms. Congratulations, Lam. You're human and you'll be staying human so don't forget your flak jacket, because you're not bulletproof any longer."

If it meant he could hold Sonia, he didn't care.

"How long until I can get out of here?" he asked.

"I'm keeping you overnight. No arguments. MacConnelly said you don't remember the initial attack."

Johnny nodded.

"Still there should be evidence."

Johnny had bigger concerns. He turned to Mac. "What about Sonia. Is she still here?"

"Until tomorrow."

"Does she know I made it?"

"Not yet. I'll call her shortly."

"Why not now?"

"Because, even though you didn't die, you look like you did. You'd scare the shit out of her. I'll have her report here tomorrow. See if you two can patch things up."

"She doesn't want me to take a combat assignment."

"That's between the two of you."

"But you'll cancel the transfer?"

Mac sighed. "Looks like you got it bad."

"It's not bad."

Zharov patted Johnny on the shoulder. "I'll check in with you this evening."

"Thanks for everything, Doc."

Zharov gave a rare and brief smile, and strode from the room saluting as Major Scofield marched in.

"There's my boy," he said, smiling at Johnny. "You gave us all a scare, Lam. But I knew you'd make it. You've got the heart of a warrior."

The major shook his hand and then folded his hands behind his back glancing from John to Mac and back again.

"I've got some news. If you're well enough, Lam, I'd like to tell you what we turned up about your initial attack in Afghanistan."

Mac blanched but remained on his feet, his body tense as if he expected the major to punch him in the face. Johnny gripped the bed rail.

"Yes, sir," he said, still getting accustomed to the sound of his own voice.

"I'll cut to the chase. I got ahold of the missing video footage." He met Mac's gaze as he continued. "The ones from the helmets of your rifleman, Robert Towsen, and your grenadier, John Lam. We didn't get much from Towsen. But you sure could see what attacked him."

Johnny glanced to Mac noticing he looked positively ill. Was he recalling Bobby being swept off his feet by something they couldn't even see? All this time he'd carried the guilt of attacking his own man, of turning him into a monster. Now he was going to hear what really happened. Johnny knew it would be the truth because the major was a straight shooter. His grip on the bed rail tightened.

"Captain, Lam's camera footage is very clear. You can see it for yourself, though I'd understand if you preferred not to. The camera captured you knocking Lam out of harm's way and the werewolf attacking you then leaving you for dead."

"But that doesn't make any sense," said Mac.

"I had Zharov check Johnny over. He doesn't have a scar anywhere on his body. No bite, Captain."

Johnny knew it was true. He and Mac stared at each other. Mac reached up to rub his shoulder. Beneath his shirt, Johnny knew there was a massive scar that covered his shoulder, back and chest from the jaws of their attacker. Still his friend couldn't understand what the major was telling him. He clung to his guilt like some lost child with his stuffed bear, afraid to set it aside and walk away.

Johnny lifted his hand from the bed rail and clasped Mac's forearm as the major explained.

"You didn't bite him, Captain. You saved him. And he saved you. Carried you out, called for medevac." The major turned to Johnny. "A fine job on your first time under fire, son. You make an old Devil Dog proud."

Mac looked to Johnny who nodded. His captain, his

first sergeant and the man who had lead him into combat covered his face with his hands and wept. Johnny dragged him into a fast embrace, dropping a kiss on his head.

"Is it true?" whispered Mac.

"You didn't do it," said Johnny.

Mac drew back and stared at him in confusion then turned to Major Scofield.

"So how did he end up a werewolf?"

The major made a face. "Records have been destroyed. But I know he was human when you left that building and a werewolf when he left the field hospital. Zharov thinks Colonel Lewis used your blood, Mac, to inject Johnny. Not sure if he did it or if he ordered someone else to do it. But you bet your ass, I'm going to find out."

Mac shook his head as if he had an earache.

"Might be that not being bitten was why you couldn't change. Zharov is looking at that possibility now. Back to his research. He really doesn't like treating patients. Prefers white rats, I think." The major chuckled and gave them each a final look. "Well, I have reports to file and asses to kick." He left the room muttering. "I'm going to cause holy hell over this. They'll wish their mommas never met their poppas when I'm through with them. Gonna be some court-martials."

The captain's phone rang and he drew it out. "It's Touma." He sounded surprised as he frowned down at the screen, jabbing the connect button and lifting the phone to his ear. "Touma?"

His frown deepened. Johnny pushed himself up as the first wisp of worry curled inside him like tobacco smoke. "What's wrong?"

Mac stared at the phone and then lifted it back to his ear. "Touma?" His eyes flicked to Johnny. "Dropped. We're three floors deep here. Spotty service." He disconnected and headed to the wall phone. A moment later he was calling her. "No answer."

"Where is she?"

"Barracks, I suppose. Maybe calling to check on you." They stared at each other. Both had seen enough action not to ignore that trickle of uncertainty.

"You'll check on her?" asked Johnny.

"Done," said Mac, lifting his phone again as he strode from the room.

Johnny ate his meal in record time and removed his IVs under the nurse's protests, then he wouldn't let her put them back in. Mac came back and ordered the nurses out. He'd had the grounds swept for Corporal Touma and did not find her. She'd checked out a Jeep but had not left the base. Johnny got dressed and switched off the ball game.

"She might be at your place," said the captain. "She have things there?"

"Yes. She also might be at yours."

They both thought of the phone call, the open line with no one on the other end. Realization brought the captain to stillness.

"I have to go."

"I'm coming, too."

"No, you're not. You can barely walk."

The captain headed out the door with Johnny on his heels. The captain didn't protest further. "Do you think it's them?"

Johnny didn't have to ask who he meant.

Vampires.

Chapter 15

Somehow Johnny kept up with Mac as they leaped into the Jeep. He was faster now than Johnny remembered, but that was the werewolf in him. Johnny glanced down at his watch and noticed the numbers were a bit blurred and suddenly he recalled the glasses he used for reading and now obviously needed again, though his distance sight had been twenty-twenty.

"Brianna's not answering," said Mac gunning the engine.

The radio on his hip clicked on as he accelerated up the road leading to their two homes. The voice on the other end sounded tinny.

"No perimeter alarms, sir. Your wife is not visible on any outdoor cameras, but everything looks quiet."

Mac lifted the radio. "Check the last twenty minutes. Use the super slow-mo."

"Roger. Out."

"She might just be indoors concentrating on her work," said Johnny.

"No, she would have answered. Doesn't feel right. Touma's not answering her phone, either."

Johnny set his teeth together as worry ate away at the lining of his stomach. A few endless moments later they roared into the driveway. Mac threw the Jeep in Park and leaped out.

"Bri!" he shouted and charged toward the open front door.

Johnny stepped to the drive and saw something hot pink on the ground. He stooped and lifted Sonia's mobile phone, neatly cased in the brightly colored rubber sheath. His fingers curled around the phone and he knew something terrible had happened. He searched the ground for blood.

Mac charged out of the house. "Not here. Can you smell them? The vampires are everywhere."

Johnny lifted his nose but the air smelled as it used to, giving him no useful information.

"Sonia?" he asked.

"Some of her blood is inside," said Mac.

Johnny charged past him, finding a small red puddle on the tile in the living room. Not much, just enough to stop his heart. He spun to face Mac. "They took them?"

Mac nodded. "Both. And headed up the mountain. I'm going after them."

"I'm coming, too."

Mac shook his head. "You can't keep up. Even if you could you can't beat a vampire anymore. Johnny, you're food to them now."

He stared at Mac as the truth of his words tore

through him. He'd lost his tough skin and his claws and everything else that might keep Sonia alive.

"I'll change back."

"You can't. You heard Zharov. You barely survived the transition. He told you to your face you'd never survive it again."

Johnny didn't care. He had to save Sonia.

"You could bite me."

"Are you crazy? No! Get back to base. Tell them what happened and bring help."

Johnny hesitated under the direct order. "Why did they take Sonia?"

Mac didn't answer because they both knew. They were going to drain her blood and leave her behind as a warning to not follow. Johnny swayed.

"Take the Jeep and bring a squad with full body armor. Seal off all ports and close down the airfields. The bastards can't swim and they are not getting off this island."

"How'd they break perimeter without us knowing?"

He shook his head in bafflement.

"How many do you detect?" asked Johnny.

Mac lowered his head. "Nine." They both knew the captain would never best that many. Not alone, he wouldn't.

"They'll kill you," said Johnny.

"They have my wife."

Mac tossed Johnny his radio and phone. The captain lay his personal sidearm on the hood of the Jeep before dragging off his shirt, boots and trousers. His transformation was so fast Johnny barely had time to retrieve his weapon and climb back into the Jeep before Mac was charging up the mountain after the scent of the vampires. Johnny barked orders into the radio, closing the ports and grounding all aircraft. He also ordered Zharov to the medical facility, issuing orders that Mac had never given him. He didn't care.

Without him, Mac was dead, Sonia was dead and Brianna was worse than dead. He knew what they'd do to Mac's wife. She'd be a living breeder for the next decade, bearing as many vampires as possible in that time. All the while the indoctrination would take place. A year, a decade, it didn't matter so long as they turned her into a puppet and all the time her soul-killing powers would be growing until just one night in her arms would mean death to any human unfortunate enough to be her target. The perfect assassin.

Johnny floored it. Was Sonia still alive? He knew that the moment they recognized Mac was on their trail, they'd kill Sonia. Johnny skidded to a halt before the medical facility and raced inside to find Dr. Zharov in his lab.

Zharov was none too pleased that Johnny had checked himself out of the hospital and was now issuing orders.

"Mac ordered that you release one vile of his blood to me."

Zharov's eyes narrowed.

"Direct order. He needs it to fight the vampires," said Johnny, but he could see his lie didn't work.

"His blood won't do him any good. It's not toxic unless injected…." His words trickled to a halt as he stiffened. "No. He can't ask you to do that."

"He didn't ask."

"Lam, are you crazy? I explained it to you. You do this and you never come back."

"Give me the shot, Doc."

"I will not."

"They took Sonia."

The doctor remained where he was. Johnny knew where he kept the blood and made for the refrigerator. Zharov tried to stop him. Johnny disengaged himself as gently as he could. Still, he thought the doctor would have one hell of a shiner. He retrieved Mac's blood, neatly labeled, and found a syringe. He'd been around this place long enough to know how to fill one and how to get the air bubbles out.

Zharov rose from the floor, rubbing the place where his head had cracked the wall.

"Lam. Don't. There has to be another way."

"There isn't."

Sonia's capture had made everything so clear. Johnny didn't hesitate. He had to rescue Sonia even if it meant he'd be a werewolf forever because he couldn't live knowing he might have saved her and didn't. She was his family, too. Not the kind you were born into but the kind you choose. He pushed the plunger into his arm. Mac's blood mingled with his. Either way, he'd have no regrets because he was doing all he could do to save her life.

The rush of power flooded his nervous system. He threw his head back and roared as his body shifted, stretched and transformed into his wolf form. His senses buzzed to life. He headed out the back, charging up the mountain, following the scent trail that was now as clear as an open highway.

Nine vampires and two were familiar to him. He

recognized their odor. These were the ones who had escaped the first attack, back in California. This time, none of the vampires would escape because he planned to kill every last one.

I'm coming, Sonia. Please don't die.

Johnny tore over the open ground, leaping like a lion over the rocky pinnacles and dangerous chasms. How did those vampires beat their perimeter alarms?

Sonia's image floated before him, urging him on. He knew he would catch the vampires and he knew he would kill them. But he did not know if he would be in time to rescue Sonia and help Mac or if he would be there only to exact revenge.

The promise of her recovery and the pain caused by the possibility of her impending death stabbed at his heart, peaks and valleys of hope and despair. He loved her. That truth he could no longer deny. He would rescue her if he could or he would die in the attempt.

The scent of the vampires grew stronger with each powerful stride. He followed Mac's trail, straight at those purple-faced monsters. He could find Brianna's sweet fragrance there, as well. He scented Mac's fear and Sonia's terror. He knew Mac's upset came from the same place as his own. He did not fear death, except the death of the one he loved.

Close. He was close now. As he tore into the cover of the jungle he heard the helicopters thumping blades as they sought a visual on the escaping vampires. But Johnny knew, even burdened with two women, the vampires moved too fast for even a werewolf to see. It was one of many advantages to the bloodsuckers. They were fast and they could only be killed by opening a vein and keeping it open until they bled out. Impossible for a human to accomplish because the vampires healed so damned fast. But they couldn't heal a wound inflicted by a werewolf. Advantage, werewolf.

Vampires had teeth strong enough to puncture a werewolf's hide and, once open, they could inject their deadly poison. They used a little to stun their prey, but they could inject enough even to stop the heart of a werewolf, if they got a good hold. Advantage, vampire.

He pictured Mac facing nine of them. Seeing them only when they slowed to take a bite. Brianna could see them, too. She could also move as fast as they could. But only if she were free.

He heard Mac's roar an instant before he broke from cover and took in the scene. Two vampires were down, bleeding out, one decapitated and the other torn nearly in half. Four surrounded Mac, circling like hyenas as another two held Brianna and Sonia. He didn't think. Just acted on instinct, leaping at the closest vamp and using his front claws to puncture its lungs as he tore a bite out of the side of its neck. He dropped the dying carcass and bounded toward Sonia's captor who released her, pushing her at him like a weapon as he ran. In an eye's blink he had vanished.

Johnny changed direction and swiped at Brianna's captor, tearing away the side of his face. Screaming, the vampire released her instantly, baring his teeth and lunging. His movements were lightning fast. Johnny could not see them, but he blocked and got in a lucky blow, sending the bloodsucker reeling. It took only one more slashing cut of all four of his claws to tear through flesh until he contacted the thing's spine. It writhed and screeched, not recognizing it was already dead. Even its ability to heal would not save it because the blood poured in a river from the artery that supplied the lower half of its body.

"Look out," shouted Sonia.

Johnny ducked and rolled, coming to his feet as another vampire sailed past him in a vain attempt to land on Johnny's back. He saw Brianna chew at her bonds and Sonia grab a rough bit of volcanic slag to saw through the bonds at her legs. Then she stood and removed her belt.

Johnny turned to help Mac, seeing he had killed another and now faced two more. One disappeared. A moment later Brianna screamed. The thing had her and was vibrating as he prepared to vanish with her. Sonia stood only a foot away. She had wound her belt around her hand, the buckle on top like brass knuckles. She smashed her fist into the creature's cheek. Flesh seared as it screamed and released Brianna who vanished instantly. The vampire reached for Sonia who had time for one backward stride before it had her.

Johnny leaped and got hold of its leg cutting the calf muscles to the bone. The vampire screamed and crumbled to the earth. That would teach him to touch Sonia. *Let's see it run with no Achilles tendon,* Johnny thought. He used his claws like a mountain climber's crampons to climb the bloodsucker's downed body as if it were K2. When he reached the thick thigh, he twisted its leg to expose its inner thigh and he sliced with his right and his left, opening deep gashes, shredding the femoral artery that spouted in a red fountain like a dying sperm whale. The thing made a last lunge at Johnny's throat and Johnny cuffed him with an open hand. He died in a pool of his own warm blood.

The remaining vampire rushed Mac and got so close to biting him, Johnny saw the poison squirting from his distended fangs. Johnny flipped, grabbing his enemy's head and twisting until he heard a snap. He knew that wouldn't kill him, but it gave Mac time to bite its neck, tearing away a massive amount of muscle and bone. Mac then dropped the body to step onto the center of his enemy's lower back gaining better leverage. He twisted until he severed the head, tossing it away. It came to rest in a tree, the eyes still blinking and its lips still moving.

Johnny looked to Mac who held up two fingers. Johnny scanned the ground finding seven bodies. Mac had told him he scented nine. Johnny had scented nine, as well. He knew the scent of the vampire he remembered calling the shots in California. None of these scents matched.

One had run. One had been long gone when Johnny arrived.

Now they faced a dilemma. Track the two remaining vampires or get Brianna and Sonia to safety.

Chapter 16

"Brianna?" Johnny heard Sonia call for her friend.

The female vampire reappeared before her husband who was still a blood-covered gray werewolf and threw herself sobbing into his arms.

Johnny gathered Sonia up in an embrace. She held tight, clutching the fur at his chest, the bloody belt dangling from her trembling fingers. He wanted to tell her how brave she had been, but that could wait. There were still two vampires loose and if they didn't kill them, they'd be back.

He stroked her head and relished the feel of her tucked close to him. He'd done it: he'd gotten to her in time and she was alive. That was all he wanted in the world.

Johnny lifted his head to see Mac and Brianna locked in a similar embrace. The two marines caught each other's gazes and Johnny motioned in the direction the retreating vampire had taken with a slight gesture of his head and then lifted his brows. Mac shook his head, glanced at his wife and then back toward the base. Johnny understood. He wanted to take them to safety. He drew back and Sonia met his gaze. He started to sign.

Sonia watched him, speaking as he gestured. "He says, 'We need to go after them now or they'll come back with more.'"

Mac could not sign but he shook his head. He was taking Brianna to safety. Johnny started signing again.

Sonia shook her head, not liking his idea but she translated word for word. "He says, 'They can't fly. Get the women to the helicopter and then we can track the bloodsuckers.'"

Mac nodded and started off in the direction of open ground. The journey seemed to take forever with Mac and Johnny scenting the air and listening for signs of attack. He knew he wouldn't see them. They moved too fast. Brianna could, however, and she kept her head swiveling as if she were center court at Wimbledon. Once on the rocky ground above the cover of the jungle it didn't take long for one of the pilots to spot them. Johnny loaded Sonia onto the helo and Brianna kissed Mac's furry cheek.

Once they were away, Mac and Johnny communicated wordlessly. They found the trail of the vampires and pursued. Both were determined to finish this and them. Surprisingly, the two vampires did not separate, which would have been a better tactical move. Perhaps the vamps didn't feel pursuit was likely because they had the advantage of speed. True, they were faster than werewolves for short stretches but they lacked the endurance of the wolf.

Mac and Johnny followed their scent trail over ground and through a short mostly natural volcanic tunnel that undermined the fence system and broke ground beyond the reach of cameras and sensors. The trail lead overland from there and continued all the way to the docks, ending at a sixty-eight-foot yacht.

Mac and Johnny surveyed the vessel. Close quarters gave them a large advantage because their quarry could not outrun them here. But the vamps had speed and knew the layout of the vessel. Both Mac and Johnny recognized that the vampires might have set an ambush. One quick attack, one bite and the vampires won. But if Johnny and Mac could get a hold of them, they would finish them.

It was hard for a nine-foot werewolf to go unnoticed and as they had feared, the vampires had human sentries who sounded the alarm with a cry and gunfire before Mac got on deck and threw the shooter overboard. Johnny took out the other two humans, heaving one into the water after his comrade. He could sense the vampires stirring below decks and Johnny and Mac separated, blocking the two exits.

The first ran right into Johnny's arms. He tried for Johnny's neck as Johnny opened his and left him to bleed out on the steps. He met Mac before the main cabin. One vampire left and he was behind that door.

"I know you're out there," said a male voice. "I also know my associate is dead. I have a deal to propose."

Mac made a snorting sound, dismissing any deal. Johnny kicked down the door.

The vampire stood with his back to the window,

his white eyes seeming sightless and his mottled skin a mask of scarlet and purple blotches. God, he'd seen snapping turtles who were better looking.

"Others of my kind know our position. If you kill me, more will come."

Mac pulled up extending his hand to Johnny.

The vampire spoke very fast now. "I have to report in. If I don't, they'll know. But I could lead them away from here. Keep her safe while you escape." He let his words die.

Mac looked to Johnny who drew a finger across his throat. He didn't trust this vampire. Better to kill him than leave him knowing their position.

Mac stepped back behind Johnny and transformed. Johnny kept his eyes on the vampire, waiting for an opportunity to kill him.

"Why should I trust you?" asked Mac.

"Because you are a marine. We work much the same as you. What would happen if a squad did not check in?"

Johnny and Mac exchanged looks.

"What are you offering for your miserable life?" asked Mac.

"I will depart for our next location. I won't report any trouble until I am in, let's say Japan. That gives you time to move to one of the locations we have searched, Europe, Africa, North America. We haven't finished the Middle East or South America. They are all looking for her there, too."

Johnny knew why the vampires would go to such trouble for one of their own. Mac had told him how rare Brianna was.

"This female we hunt is special, you know," said the vamp. "First generation. Her mother was an actual Leanan Sidhe, a true fairy muse. So this halfling can bear children from vampire or humans. But I don't know if she can bear your young. To my knowledge there has never been such a liaison between natural enemies."

"Maybe if you didn't keep your women captive, they'd be more likely to stick around."

The vampire laughed. "Look at me, Captain. What woman would willingly choose this?" He motioned to his deformed face. "The rest of me is just as pretty. My kind does what it must to survive."

"What's your name?" asked Mac.

"Burne Farrell. We met briefly in California."

When he and Mac had killed all but two of his men, Johnny thought.

The vampire glanced at Johnny. "Your friend was in werewolf form then, too. Brianna said that this one can't change back. Is it true?"

Johnny growled. Why would Brianna tell them this?

"Why should you care?" asked Mac.

"Just curiosity. We've never seen that before. Did you know that you cannot sire werewolves? Unlike Vampires, werewolves are made, not born."

Johnny saw Mac's shoulders sag with relief before he stiffened again. His captain had never mentioned children to him. Now he knew why. Mac didn't want to pass his wolf trait to his babies. Johnny realized it was a problem he had not even anticipated, Sonia having his children, the children being werewolves. He narrowed his eyes on Farrell, feeling a renewed sense of hate. The vamp might have killed her.

"Why should I believe you?" asked Mac.

"I have no interest in helping you create more werewolves. Why would I lie?" He flicked his gaze back to Mac. "So, do we have a deal?"

"You might just as easily call in more men."

"I might. Or I might value my life more than you do."

"All right." Mac extended his hand.

Burne drew his closer to his chest and stared at the offered hand then glanced at Mac. He was wise to be cautious. Mac could kill him just as easily while in human form. Finally Burne accepted. Mac clasped his hand and pulled him in so that their noses nearly touched.

"She's my wife, Burne. If you visit us again nothing will stop me from killing you."

Burne cowered and Mac released him.

"Understood."

"You've got ten minutes to be off this island," said Mac. "We'll be tracking you. If you turn back, I'll have your ship blown out of the water."

"As you wish. Until we meet again, Captain," said Farrell.

"We better not."

"Oh, I don't know. We often work with your government agencies. Our paths might cross after they let you off your leash."

"Ten minutes," said Mac and left the vampire and his dead comrade on their floating morgue.

Sonia sat next to Brianna as their helo circled far above the island. The view would have been incredible if she was not sick with worry over Johnny and the captain. Finally the pilot received the call that the marines were both safely back at base. She was so relieved that Johnny had not gone through with the treatment. That, even more than their rescue from the vampires, filled her with hope and joy that lifted her like a bubble in sparkling wine.

When they touched down, Major Scofield waited and hustled them into a secure facility. The major seemed more harried than usual to Sonia, though still thoroughly in command.

"Lam and MacConnelly are waiting inside."

The marines guarding each entrance snapped to attention at their passing.

Scofield continued speaking as he returned their salutes without breaking stride. "You gave us a scare, Brianna. I thought you could outrun them. That was the only reason I gave you permission to live off base."

Brianna glanced away.

"It was my fault, sir," Sonia said. "She came back for me and they caught her. She saved my life."

The major stopped and turned to look from one to the other. "That was very brave, Brianna. But if it ever happens again, you run. Touma is a marine. She knows how to fight."

"I hate to contradict, Major, but no human can best a vampire unless the vampire is lying on a bed of iron and even then I'd advise extreme caution." She looked at Sonia and her eyes twinkled. "Though Corporal Touma did manage to use her belt buckle to burn the face of the one holding me. Kept him from making off with me and gave Mac and Johnny an important edge."

The major stared at Sonia and smiled. "I'm not surprised. She's a Devil Dog, after all."

Sonia felt a painful bubble in her chest. It took a moment to recognize the unfamiliar emotion as pride.

She smiled at the major and he returned it with one of his own. Then he motioned for them to precede him.

"Let's get you two secured. Lam and Mac are waiting. Lam, however, is in some very deep shit." The major followed them into a bunker of a room, located two floors down and surrounded by volcanic rock. "Oh, apologies for the language."

Why was Lam in trouble, Sonia wondered. Before she could ask, the major left them. Brianna drew a chair from the conference table and dragged it to the far corner of the room. Sonia sat at the opposite side, restlessly jiggling her leg as they waited.

A few minutes later Mac entered the room, tall and handsome in a uniform that showed fold marks on the trousers. Brianna rushed to meet him, kissing her husband with an enthusiasm and vigor that made Sonia's cheeks go hot. Johnny was not right behind him and Sonia grew worried. The major stepped into the room and cleared his throat. Mac pulled away from his wife, seeming to only just notice them.

"Where's Johnny?" Sonia asked.

"I ordered him to the medical unit," said the major, "So they can check him out. Damn stupid thing, he did. Brave, though. Very brave."

Sonia's skin tingled in dread as she wondered what Johnny had done. She was happy Brianna intervened because she found her voice had suddenly abandoned her.

"What did he do?"

Mac stared from Sonia to his wife and then back again. He left his wife and came to stand beside Sonia.

"Sit down, Touma."

She sank to a chair, her heart now racing in her chest.

She waited tense and still, one hand cupped around the other which was bunched in a tight fist.

"He took the treatment," said her superior without preamble.

"But it didn't work?"

Mac shook his head. "It worked. Johnny was human again. Then we got your call and we searched and found you both gone. I knew from the scent what had happened and I took off after you both. Johnny saw your blood, Sonia. I ordered him to the base to get help, which he did. But then he disobeyed orders. He…" The captain cupped his hands over his eyes.

Brianna came to stand beside him, resting a hand on his shoulder. Her eyes were wide and glimmering with the tears that already filled her lower lids to near flood stage.

Sonia's back went rigid as her jaw clenched. "No. He didn't take the treatment. He's still a wolf."

Her captain dragged his hand down his face and cast the major a beseeching look and Scofield took over the tale.

"Johnny survived the transition to human and when he discovered your abduction, he came back here and, long story short, he injected Mac's blood into his vein without permission. He did it to help Mac and to save the both of you."

"I was losing when he showed up. There were too many," said Mac.

Sonia, bewildered glanced from one man to the next. "What does this mean?"

The major lowered his head. Sonia thought he looked as if he stood beside an open grave.

"Zharov warned him that he'd never survive the

treatment again. None of the test subjects have. He barely made it the first time. He didn't, actually. He died and Zharov managed to revive him. But he was dead for several minutes. Despite that, he injected himself with werewolf blood. He's a werewolf, Touma, and he's not changing back ever again."

Sonia was on her feet. "I need to see him."

Johnny heard them coming. He heard everything again, private conversations from the nurses' station twenty yards away. The ding of the elevator past the double doors and the familiar footfall of Private Sonia Touma.

She didn't stop at the door but rushed at him and threw herself across his chest, weeping. He supposed she knew the truth now. She was alive and she was leaving. It was hard, but he pushed her gently away and looked to Mac who stared back with that screwed-up face that he'd seen only once before, after they lost all three fire teams in the Sandbox.

He signed to Sonia to stop crying, but she didn't. Even though she couldn't seem to speak, she managed to sign.

They told me. Oh, Johnny, why?

To save you, he thought. But he signed back that Mac needed him.

Sonia signed, *That's not true. You did it to save me.*

Mac is my captain. Couldn't leave him to fight alone.

He could see from her expression that she wasn't buying it. It was the truth, but only part of the truth. He might have done it anyway, but it was the image of Sonia in trouble that made it easy to push that plunger.

"Maybe in time they'll think of something they can

do to change you back," she said, her words raw as her anguish.

He shrugged. *No going back.*

She grasped his hand in a fierce grip and sat at his bedside. "It doesn't matter, Johnny. I love you and I'll wait. I'll wait forever if I have to. I just want to stay with you."

No, she wouldn't because he was not letting her throw her life away on a man who would never be a man. She was going to serve her time and get out, like she planned. She was going to get herself that house she always wanted, the one with the rope swing and a yard. And she was going to fill it up with children. Sonia was going to be a mother, and have a family who loved her because she deserved that.

You have transfer orders, he reminded her.

Her grip faltered. "But I'll ask to stay. I don't want to transfer. I want to stay here with you." Sonia looked to her captain. "He needs a translator again."

Johnny met Mac's eyes and shook his head. Mac understood. He wanted her out of here.

"We'll talk about it at another time," said Mac.

Sonia turned back to Johnny. "This is because of you. You tell them the truth, John Lam. You tell them that you love me and that I love you. We were meant to be together."

He made the sign for *finish,* shaking both hands. The signal was clear. It was over between them. Only this time she did not look devastated. She looked pissed.

"You're hurting. I understand that, but I'm staying. It will be all right."

Mac took Sonia's arm and tried to bring her to her feet. "Come on, Touma. Another time. He needs rest."

"No." She jerked her arm free and fell back across him, clinging now. "You fought for me. Now I'm fighting for you. You love me. Tell them, Johnny. Tell them you love me, too."

She was breaking his heart. Johnny looked away to gather his nerve. In a moment she'd be sorry she ever taught him to sign. He turned to face her and formed his words with care.

Love you? You are the reason I am a wolf again. If not for you, B-R-I-A-N-N-A could have escaped and I wouldn't have had to come after you both. This is your fault. I want you gone.

Sonia gasped, releasing him as she staggered back from his bedside as his words slashed like a straight razor across her heart.

"Johnny?" she gasped.

"What did he say?" asked Brianna.

Johnny pointed to the door.

"He said it's my fault. The whole thing," Sonia whispered. "And he's right."

Johnny watched in relief as Sonia darted toward the door. Brianna reached to stop Sonia and then let her pass.

Zharov entered the room studying a chart and then belatedly noticed the crowd circling his patient's bed. He saluted the major. "He's as he was. Same exactly, except he has less of the human proteins than he had before this second injection." He looked at Johnny. "It was too much. The count was half your levels after Afghanistan."

Johnny shrugged. What did it matter? He knew the price. He would pay it. But what he wouldn't do was let Sonia throw away her future waiting around for his shaggy ass. He didn't have much left but his pride and that was still dear to him.

Brianna stepped to the end of the bed. "I had a talk with one of the chasers. A vampire named Hagan Dowling. He told me that werewolves are made, not born."

Johnny knew that very well because Burne Farrell has said the same thing to Mac.

"He also told me that all werewolves can change form at will."

"Clearly not," said Zharov, pointing at Johnny.

"Why were you speaking to them about this or anything else?" asked Mac.

She smiled at her husband. "Because they thought carrying Sonia was slowing them down and they wanted to kill her. My questions kept them from doing that."

Johnny's stomach dropped as he recognized how close he'd been to losing Sonia forever.

"Hagan also said that werewolves are made only by a bite and only in the very rare circumstance when the inflicted wounds are not fatal. Most werewolves attack to kill," said Brianna. She stroked her husband's chest and Johnny knew that was the place that Mac bore the scars of his attack. Somehow he had survived, but he was the only one. "I don't think you were bitten, Johnny."

He had arrived at the same conclusion.

Zharov interjected here. "I've searched his body and found no scars. All evidence points to the same conclusion to which you have arrived, Mrs. MacConnelly. Johnny was made intentionally by the U.S. Marine Corp."

"No, sir," said Mac. "He was made by an embar-

rassment to the uniform, former Colonel Lewis, may
he rot in hell."

The major chimed in. "He will, son. No doubt about
that."

Zharov pressed the tip of his pen to his lower lip.
"I've already opened this avenue. I've been using in-
fected rats to bite normal rats. The delivery method is
more effective and all rats can transform."

Johnny had a moment's flare of hope. Could that
work—a bite?

"I'll be exploring this method on rabbits, canines
and monkeys over the next three months."

The hope winked out and he groaned.

Zharov ignored him and continued. "But for now, everyone out. Lam needs rest. It's very late and we have
more tests tomorrow."

Tests and tests and tests, thought Johnny. He was
tired of waiting and of Zharov's methodical, tedious
research.

The major motioned to the door and Brianna swept
out, followed by his doctor. Mac tried to follow but
Johnny made a sound in his throat and motioned him
back. Mac told his wife he'd be right along. Brianna
hesitated and then nodded and withdrew.

"Be careful," she said.

Johnny stared at Mac wondering if he'd do it.

"You want me to bite you, don't you?" asked Mac.

Johnny nodded.

"Damn if this doesn't work we are both fucked."

Johnny waited as Mac disrobed down to his boxers.

"Where?" asked Mac.

Johnny threw back the sheets and pointed to the thick
musculature of his thigh.

"You sure about this?"

He nodded. Johnny didn't have to remind him that he'd just saved his ass and helped rescue Mac's wife. Mac knew he owed him. He was ready to pay up.

"You believe that I never bit you?" asked Mac, his voice a tight whisper.

Johnny knew the burden the captain has born, thinking all this time that he'd attacked his own man.

Johnny nodded. Then he bared his teeth and made a pantomime of a vicious bite.

"Okay, deep. I get it. Grab the call button and press it before I bite you."

Johnny nodded, lifted the button and pressed down.

Chapter 17

Sonia got almost to the door when she realized she had done it again. She had let Johnny decide whether she came or went. She'd allowed him to sever the ties between them. Running again, she realized.

Sonia stopped and lowered her head as a certainty filled her. She didn't want to wait out her service with the easiest, least challenging assignment possible and she certainly didn't want a home if Johnny wasn't in it. Suddenly she understood the meaning of what Brianna had said back there before the vampires attacked. Her cryptic words rolled through Sonia like a perfect breath of fresh air.

No matter where Travis is he is with me. My home is in his heart and his home is in mine. If you love Johnny than nothing can separate you. Certainly not this.

Now Sonia understood. Brianna was right. Johnny wasn't tossing her aside. He was trying to protect her.

But she wasn't going, because now she knew exactly what was missing from her life. It wasn't a house and a yard. Not a wall she could paint or a garden to plant. It wasn't a place at all. All this time what she wanted had been right here. She had been searching for Johnny. What was missing was the one person who made a place a home. That's why she was so comfortable in Johnny's bungalow. Not because of the view or the flowers, but because Johnny was there. *He* was her home.

And she *wasn't* getting evicted because he was trying to protect her from living with the big bad wolf.

She spun in place and marched back the way she had come, her determination growing with each stride. The buzz of activity in the corridor outside Johnny's room slowed her progress and brought a leaden lump of dread to her throat. She stared at a cart covered with blood soaked pads and bandages. Now her heart pounded in her throat as she saw Zharov exiting Johnny's room, his head down as he removed the bloody blue rubber gloves and tossed them in the red biohazard container in the hall.

He lifted his gaze and spotted her. She did not recall setting in motion but she was suddenly there before him unable even to form the question.

"He's a crazy man. You know that? They both are," Zharov said. "Who else but a crazy man would do something so reckless. I could have MacConnelly arrested for attacking him and that's just a start."

"What? What happened?"

But Zharov merely thumbed over his shoulder and continued on his way muttering, "Should get disciplinary action at the very least. They have to follow orders with the rest of us."

Sonia glanced toward the door, feeling her feet heavy as she crossed the threshold. She saw Mac buttoning his shirt as he glanced at her. Was that blood on his mouth?

"What's happening?" she said, surprised to hear her voice coming from such a long way away.

Mac stepped aside giving her a view of Johnny's hospital bed, which was empty save for the bare mattress and rumpled, bloody sheets. Her gaze flashed about and came to rest on the man standing just beyond. All the air whooshed from her lungs and she swayed, grasping the bed rail for support. She recognized him, even though his head was still sheathed inside a fresh white T-shirt. She'd know that abdomen anywhere. His muscles flexed and knotted under his healthy copper skin as he drew on the undershirt, covering his taut stomach. His head emerged a moment later from the neck hole, leaving his long hair mussed. She rounded the bed and hesitated as her gaze dropped to the bandage visible beneath his boxers. The thick gauze covered him from hip to knee and he carried all his weight on his uninjured leg.

Johnny was human again. He spotted her now and his eyes sparkled. "You're here! I thought I'd have to run after you."

She stood blinking at him in astonishment. "But they said... They said."

Johnny waved a hand. "Doctors. They think they know everything."

The confusion and relief battered Sonia like a stick to a piñata and she felt her bottom lip begin to tremble. Johnny limped over to her, gathering her up in his arms.

"I'm not leaving, Johnny. Don't ask me to."

"I won't. Not ever again. I'm sorry for what I put

you through." He held her tight, his strong arms making everything seem all right. *Home,* she thought. *I'm finally home.*

Johnny shifted and did a funny hop, recalling his bandaged leg to her mind. She pulled back and looked at the enormous wrapping. "What happened?"

"Werewolf bite." He grinned, seemingly delighted. "First time."

Sonia gasped and her gaze flashed to Mac. Johnny drew Sonia under his arm and leaned heavily upon her as he held her tight to his side. "Seems you need a bite to be able to change shape."

Her fingers gently grazed the bandage. "Does it hurt?"

"Like a son of a bitch, but I've never been happier. Besides, I'm a fast healer."

"Might leave a scar," said Mac. "Mine did." He rubbed his shoulder.

"Small price," said Johnny. "See you around."

"Not sure you can go yet."

Johnny and Mac shared a silent exchange.

"Dismissed then," said Mac. "I know where to find you. Call if you need anything."

"Driver," said Johnny.

Mac made the call and Del met them out front. A few minutes later, Del had Johnny settled in his own bedroom.

Sonia walked Del out and then returned to Johnny.

Johnny sat on his bed and she stood in the gap between his legs, careful not to touch his bandage.

"I saw the blood at the hospital. Your blood," she said. "Scared me to death."

Johnny smiled. "It bled. Mac got the femoral artery. We had to be sure his spit got into my blood."

Sonia scowled up at him. "You might have bled to death."

Johnny shrugged. "Doc stitched it up. I'll be healed by morning."

"It's already morning," she said.

He wrapped his arms low behind her back and dragged her slowly forward. "So it is."

"Johnny, I understand if you need time to recover. But I don't want a transfer. I want to be with you."

"Well that's very good news because I'm in love with you."

Her heart gave a funny little shudder and her eyes closed for just a moment as she felt the joy of those words rising like mist from a deep lake. Then she opened one eye and narrowed it at him.

"You said you *didn't* love me," her tone was accusatory.

"Tactics to encourage a retreat."

She lowered her chin and gave him a smug smile. "Backfired, didn't it?"

"Should have known."

"Why's that?"

"Because you are a marine. Marines run into trouble, not away from it."

"Well this marine is done running. From now on I stay put. So what does that do to your tactics, Sergeant?"

"Ground conditions have changed. I have a new objective."

"And what might that be?" She trailed a finger down

his cheek and the strong column of his throat, becoming familiar again with his smooth skin.

"Getting you to spend the rest of your life with me."

She tapped a finger to her lower lip as if thinking. "I might be willing to sign up for that tour of duty. Is there a signing bonus?"

He lifted his brow in speculation. "Might be."

"Super. You know there are regulations against this."

"And did you know I can get you honorably discharged?"

"What!"

"If you want to be discharged."

She shook her head in bewilderment.

He tugged her closer and then stroked her cheek. "You don't mind that I'm still half monster."

She smiled. "No more monster than most men, less than some. And I like your wolf side."

His shoulders sagged with relief. "And your home? You'd be willing to wait until I finish my tour of duty? It might be six years or more."

Sonia used her hands to speak to him. *I love you. So I'll follow you if I can and I'll wait for you if I must because you are my home.*

Johnny threaded his fingers in her hair and his mouth descended to brush hers. She relaxed into his kiss, feeling the rush of sweet desire and the rising ache of need. He eased her down beside him on the bed, kissing her in a hot rush of passion, taking and giving. He stroked her, as he trailed kisses over her most sensitive places. Sonia stretched back and let him touch her with greedy hands and a hungry mouth until her emotions blended with pulsing sensation. He knew her, this man who was part wolf; his instincts were as perfect as his timing.

Her need quickly grew impossible to bear and he finished her with a bright burst of bliss that drove through her like a conquering army. This marine certainly knew how to capture and hold territory, she mused as her thoughts reengaged.

"That was wonderful," she whispered, her body settling languid and replete.

He tucked her close beside him, her body half sprawled over his. Johnny flicked the sheet over their glistening bodies and she shut her eyes.

"When you first arrived," he said. "I tried everything I could think of to get you to quit."

"I almost did," she murmured.

"Now, each day for the rest of my life I'm going to do everything I can think of to make you stay."

"Everything?"

He nodded, his face suddenly serious. She stilled at his solemn expression losing her playful grin.

"What is it, John?"

"I love you. And I want to wake up beside you every damn day."

She managed a smile as her eyes welled up. "I want that, too."

John drew her down for another long, languid kiss. When she came up for air, his eyes were blazing with heat and her body hummed with need. She draped a leg over his waist and then straddled him.

Thirty minutes later she lay panting at his side and he lay motionless with one hand draped over his eyes. "I didn't know you could ride like that," he whispered.

"Save a horse, ride a marine," she muttered, her words slurring as she drifted toward slumber.

"We need to get you a ring."

"We need to get me some sleep."

Johnny chuckled and closed his eyes.

Johnny did, indeed, heal quickly. The following day, Mac and Sonia watched as the bandages were changed. Sonia saw the wound had already closed and the scar tissue was raised and pink. The ghastly horseshoe shaped marks marred the otherwise perfect skin of his thigh on both the front and back of his leg.

"Does it hurt?" she asked.

Johnny grinned and she couldn't help smiling back, he seemed so happy.

"Never felt better."

Sonia left him so she could shower. When she returned it was to find he had shifted into his wolf form. Her initial panic was quickly allayed by his hurried signs. He'd changed intentionally, his first time and after reassuring her, he lifted her off the ground to spin her in a circle.

Mac insisted she leave the room while he shifted back which she did with reluctance. Ten minutes later she was readmitted to find John sweating and pale, but still in high spirits.

"You did it!" she said, elated.

Sonia rushed to his side arms open wide. She didn't know who was more pleased that he now had control of his transformation, her, her captain or Johnny.

"He'll get better at it," said Captain MacConnelly, the relief evident on his tired face. "Just takes practice."

She flanked Johnny's bed and he scooped her up beside him for a celebratory kiss. The captain cleared his throat and Sonia tried to scramble off the bed, but Johnny refused to let her go.

"Touma, my office in thirty to discuss your reassignment."

She went cold and then hot as she recalled her transfer orders. Suddenly the room did not seem to have enough air. Was he shipping her back to the mainland? Johnny lifted her chin so she looked back at him instead of at her captain's retreating back.

He was signing, reassuring her. Still she wouldn't be at ease until she heard what the captain had to say.

He told her that Johnny needed a translator once more and he needed to learn sign so that the two of them could better communicate in the field. The discovery by the vampires made it imperative that he quickly get his wife out of the Pacific. He and Johnny were shipping out to Germany in just one day and her orders were to accompany them.

The captain and Johnny would train for combat assignments while she acted as translator and taught them sign. When they were in the field she would accompany them as far as possible and in some circumstances she would watch by remote camera, translating their words to headquarters.

Sonia liked the assignment. The work was important. She would be near Johnny and she would be useful. The only concern she had was teaching Captain Travis MacConnelly because he still made her nervous.

What didn't make her nervous was leaving the country and all that was familiar to her. She didn't care where she was as long as Johnny was there, too. There would be separations, of course, but she would bear them because it was important to Johnny to "get back in the game" as he called it. She no longer wanted to serve out her time in a quiet backwater. She wanted to be with John Loc Lam.

The rest of the day was a hectic frenzy of preparations for departure. Her second ever flight was much more relaxing than her first as she no longer feared her future. Instead she anticipated it. She began speaking to the captain both verbally and with sign, just as she had done with Johnny.

Her quarters in Panzer Kaserne unfortunately looked nearly identical to her old ones. And Johnny no longer had his pretty little cottage on the mountain. He didn't need one. But they both missed the privacy. Johnny missed it so much that he proposed after only a week in Germany. Sonia accepted both the proposal and the lovely white-gold engagement ring set with a single half-carat diamond.

Three months later, Johnny and Mac, as she now called him, had finished their training and received orders to return to the Sandbox. Sonia would be joining them as far as Kabul, Afghanistan. But before deployment there was one final bit of business to finish. And to accomplish it, Sonia left her uniform behind in favor of a lovely mermaid style lace wedding gown. Paperwork had been signed, exemptions made and approval received in triplicate. Sonia was cleared to marry Sergeant John Loc Lam.

Johnny stood beside her in his dress blues looking so handsome he took her breath away. She was even getting used to his new haircut, though she did miss all that thick long hair. Johnny had promised to grow it back when he was discharged. Sonia suspected she would have a long wait.

Behind them, their guests filled the first three rows of the nondenominational chapel on Marine base as the chaplin, Father Tejada preformed the ceremony. Beside him, a female translator kept up with his words. To John's left, Captain MacConnelly stood, ramrod stiff, clutching their two rings in his fist as if their protection was vital to national security. Marianna, Sonia's sister stood to Sonia's left. As maid of honor, she held both bouquets in a gentle hand, rendering her momentarily speechless. Her sister shifted her attention between the translator and the chaplin, reading the signs and his lips as she waited for the moment when she would return her sister's cascading arrangement of white orchids and rosebuds. Beside Marianna stood Johnny's sister, Joon, as her only bridesmaid.

The chaplin called for the rings. Her captain dropped them from his hand onto the open bible as one might release dice and stepped back, his duty done. The rings came to rest and where exchanged.

Sonia stared down at the twinkling diamonds that studded the white-gold band and felt herself well up. It was real and really happening. Johnny's mom and sister had flown all the way from San Francisco to Germany to see them wed. And somewhere back a few rows, as far from the others as possible was Brianna, Mac's wife, intentionally leaving space between her and the humans she so affected.

Father Tejada raised a hand to God as he spoke about the power vested in him and gave his permission for John to kiss his bride. Johnny turned to her and lifted the short, modest veil.

Sonia beamed up at her new husband who looked proud enough to bust a polished brass button. He held her lightly by each shoulder and leaned forward from the waist to kiss her lips, sealing his promise. The cheers reached her and Johnny drew back to present his bride to the assemblage, raising their joined hands as if they had just completed a race.

Sonia looked out at the happy faces, some cheering, some whistling and others dabbing their eyes. Marianna kissed her sister and returned her bouquet. Johnny drew Sonia's hand into the warm crook of his arm and covered it with his opposite hand. Then they marched in unison down the aisle and toward the new life they would make together.

In that moment she felt the promise of a future bright with love and hope. He said she had given him a reason to live again but he'd given her much more than that. Johnny had made her a part of his family, his brotherhood and his life. He had given her his love and her first real home, right there in his heart.

* * * * *

MILLS & BOON®

Why not subscribe?
Never miss a title and save money too!

Here's what's available to you if you join the exclusive **Mills & Boon Book Club** today:

✦ *Titles up to a month ahead of the shops*
✦ *Amazing discounts*
✦ *Free P&P*
✦ *Earn Bonus Book points that can be redeemed against other titles and gifts*
✦ *Choose from monthly or pre-paid plans*

Still want more?
Well, if you join today we'll even give you
50% OFF your first parcel!

So visit **www.millsandboon.co.uk/subs**
or call **Customer Relations on 020 8288 2888**
to be a part of this exclusive Book Club!

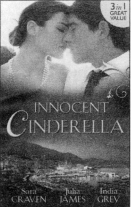

1214_ST_5